God Is a Bedlamite:
Channeling Elisabeth Nietzsche

God Is a Bedlamite:
Channeling Elisabeth Nietzsche

Katie F. Salvo

Creators Publishing
Hermosa Beach, CA

God Is a Bedlamite:
Channeling Elisabeth Nietzsche
Copyright © 2016 Katie F. Salvo

Cover art by Peter Kaminski

FIRST EDITION
Creators Publishing
Hermosa Beach, California 90254
310-337-7003

ISBN 978-1-945630-25-5
Library of Congress Control Number: 2016961556

CREATORS PUBLISHING

∞

To my husband, Jorge, whose infinite love for me, and unwavering belief in my success, gave me the confidence to embark on this project, and take up writing as a full-time career. I love and adore you so.

∞

Contents

o o o

Author's Note

One of the greatest things about literary fiction is the outlet it provides a writer to take certain liberties with history, as previously presented, by imagining the little details that nonfictional narratives of recorded fact limit biographers from postulating.

The following manuscript, while it generally follows the timeline of events in Elisabeth Nietzsche's life, is a fictional account of the life she built around her brother, Friedrich. For this reimagining of events I studied a number of nonfiction sources. The few direct quotes in my story are limited to those spoken or written by either Elisabeth or Friedrich Nietzsche. For those who may wish to conduct further exploration into the life of either or both Nietzsches, I have provided a bibliography of the works that I studied in preparation for this project at the closing of the book.

∞

∞

All that we do, and all that we are, pivots on the dictate of man, proffered in the name of God. What, then, is God? It is the eternal question that tortures my heart's blood as he agonizes in mute confinement, shrouded beneath the mask of madness. Truth is divined from the lifeless, yet lustful, orbs staring back at me from a bed of transience, taunting with hovering spirit. Hovering and hovering, endlessly haunting, a sacrilegious, tempestuous dance of seduction in mock damnation of my mortal soul. Revealing, defining, and burying, at once, the anguish of our love.

Naumburg, Prussia

1850

The stench of death, first his father's, followed by his baby brother's in rapid secession, infiltrated his nostrils as master Friedrich Nietzsche lay awake listening to the cries of distress piercing the silence of darkness. Elisabeth. Sweet, innocent, adorable Elisabeth. Fatherless, left with a mother as frigid as the grave within which the youngest Nietzsche had just been laid to rest, his four-year-old sister was alone in this world, save for himself, barely two years her senior. Shaken, as he always was, by this realization, Friedrich kicked away his covers and jolted from his bed, making haste to his sister's side in the cramped lodgings of Grandma Nietzsche's home, to whence the family removed upon the passing of their patriarch. This was not the first night, nor would it be the last, that Friedrich would spend soothing his sister back to sleep, for she was and always would be . . . *his.*

∞

CHAPTER I

∞

In His Afterlife, even as his madness shrieked its desire for "a woman, any woman," he would deduce upon reflection that an ignorant and awful female would have served him a more suitable partner.

∞

Summer 1863

It was hard not to smile, Friedrich begrudgingly realized, as he watched his two oldest friends dash around like puppies vying for the master's praise. Elisabeth almost always had that effect on the young men of her acquaintance. Wilhelm Pinder and Gustav Krug were no exceptions. What spectacles they made of themselves pretending to be outrun and outfoxed by a slip of a girl, weighted down as she was by a wide-hooped confection of white muslin, trimmed in green. Acutely aware of her brother's scrutiny, Elisabeth led the besotted and the damned on a merry chase around and about, in and out of, every shaded and sunlit hollow, sculpted from blue-violet hued Alpine aster and gentian, offset by pink Alpine roses, and entwined with the sun-kissed yellows of arnica and auricula. Indeed, he was surprised to find, as he took in the panorama of Grandma Oehler's garden, very little had changed since his last summer at Pobles: the grounds immaculate, the setting warm, his mother frigid in her distance, and Lizzie ever coquettish.

"So which poor sot would you lay your money on?" Unwilling or unable to wrest his eyes from the scene playing out before him, only a slight incline of Friedrich's chin indicated to Paul Deussen that his question had even been heard. Paul had avoided this visit for years, turning down one invitation after another to accompany Friedrich home for a holiday from The Royal Boarding School at Pforta. There was always a hint of derision in Friedrich's tone when he spoke of his family. Imagined, no doubt, but off-putting all the same.

This invitation was different, however. The two would be off to the University at Bonn next year, and so Friedrich insisted that his family have the opportunity to get to know his soon-to-be college roommate. The Nietzsches were tight on money and worried often about Friedrich's comfort away from home, convincing Paul that they would rest easier if they could but put a face to the friend that would accompany him along the journey. Paul expelled a breath on an ironic smile.

Two students starving together were, apparently, less of a worry than one who might suffer the pains of hunger alone.

"Gustav Krug, hands down." Paul broke from his reverie at Friedrich's response, having forgotten his query. "He's wealthy, he's landed, he's devilish handsome – almost as pretty as a girl," quipped – *or snipped?* – Friedrich as something akin to menace crept in to shadow his face.

Paul barked out a laugh as he slapped Friedrich on the back. "That's deuced conceited of you, old man! Devilish handsome may be too generous a description for one who was made in your image, wouldn't you say? *Pretty as a girl* . . . I can accept that," he teased on as he reached out to flip up a straight, nearly shoulder-length lock of Friedrich's light, golden-brown hair. Krug was slighter than Friedrich and had a somewhat hazel tint to his eyes, where Friedrich's seemed to reflect a range between light and dark brown in accordance with his mood. Aside from that, it was true that his boyhood friend could easily be his twin.

"You have to admit the resemblance is amazing," Paul observed absentmindedly.

Unable to tolerate his sister's antics any longer, Friedrich pushed past Paul and dashed into the fray, swinging his Lizzie up by the waist and spinning her round and round until they were both dizzy and drunk with laughter. Nearly tumbling to the ground, Friedrich righted himself, holding tight to Lizzie as he slowly slid her back to solid ground, halting briefly to nuzzle her neck with his nose in affectionate playfulness, clearly oblivious to the indignant stances of Pinder and Krug as they looked on in jealous astonishment.

Paul briefly considered why he was not equally astonished by this display, but only very briefly. Incongruent with his expressed distaste for his family, Friedrich had always spoken very protectively of his sister, and was clearly immune to the fact that she was no longer a child. Moving forward to put an end to the uncomfortable scene, Paul approached Miss Elisabeth Nietzsche, bowed his handsome head of brown hair over her hand, and then raised his brown eyes to hers, expertly proffering a mischievous wink.

"Friedrich," chided Elisabeth, "why have you not introduced me to your charming friend? What poor form of you to leave him to make his own introduction!"

"And it's poor form of you, madam," teased Friedrich as he tweaked her nose, "to forget yourself in front of a guest." He turned to Paul. "Did I overlook her curtsey, or have you just been slighted, old man?"

With a sharp intake of breath, Elisabeth immediately dipped with practiced perfection. "Forgive me, Mr. − um, I'm sorry, I don't . . ."

"Deussen. I'm Friedrich's Pforta class and cell mate," he teased, in reference to the regimental nature of their boarding school. "May I hope that you will call me Paul?"

"Hope all you want, Deussen," cut in Friedrich with an affable grin, "but as the head of her household, I'm the one from whom you'll need to seek permission for the honor of sharing familiar address with my sister. The answer is no. Now, shall we?" Friedrich gestured toward the back entrance to his grandmother's kitchen. "I believe we are expected to dine soon."

As the others made for the house, Elisabeth rounded on Friedrich, yanking him by the arm. "What is the matter with you?" she demanded with a stamp of her foot. "You ruined my lovely time with Gustav and Wilhelm, and any chance I might have had of impressing Paul."

"*Mr. Deussen*, Miss Nietzsche. You will call him Mr. Deussen."

With an aggravated harrumph, Elisabeth cut her eyes at her brother. "How authoritative you sound for one who is rarely around! Head of the household indeed!" Lizzie threw her arms up in exasperation. "It's been months since you've visited me, and so I came to you, as I'm sure your headmaster must have mentioned, for his wife took an immediate disliking to me. The audacity of that woman! She's practically a servant—no better than she should be, anyway. Can you conceive that she was impudent enough to lecture me about proper manners and the loose reputations of ladies who roam about the countryside unattended? I was not. Unattended, that is. Grandma Oehler had no objection to Gustav, who is practically a member of the family, accompanying me. So I can't imagine what right the Grand Dragon of Pforta has to express an opinion on the matter. Besides," Elisabeth said, playfully batting her brother's arm, "what do you think took us there but to inform you that Gustav has decided to pay court to me?"

Friedrich's head snapped up with alacrity at this bit of news. "Decided? *Decided* to pay court to you? I'll have Krug's head! He took advantage of our grandmother's good-natured trust in him to, to . . ." At a loss, Friedrich waved his hand about aimlessly. "I don't know what! What I do know is that I'll snap his neck, and Deussen's, too. God's teeth! You are but sixteen and —"

"Friedrich, please!" Elisabeth swiftly raised two gentle fingers to silence his lips, a tactic that never failed to assuage his anger. "I'll be seventeen in less than a fortnight. Mother was only sixteen when she married Papa, and, well, what is it that Aunt Rosalie always says?"

"Lizzie." Friedrich attempted to murmur a protest against the stubborn, feminine fingers that held him silent.

"Admit it, darling! Girls are not raised to *be* somebody. They're raised to *marry* somebody." Lizzie yelped, snatching her hand away from the teeth that were but a hair's breadth away from clamping down on her middle finger. She had forgotten that she held his lips still. "Gustav is as good as any other," she went on crossly. "Isn't he just beautiful? But, then, so is Paul." She lightly punched Friedrich's arm in exasperation. "Why did you have to bring him here now?" she demanded. "Now I shall have to rethink my arrangement with Gustav."

Friedrich had had enough mindless banter for the day. He scooped Elisabeth up, plopped her over his shoulder, and took long, determined strides towards the house with her hanging limply over his backside. As if she were still a child, she thought angrily as she attempted to squirm loose of his hold.

"We will go in for dinner, dear girl, and revisit what marriage prospects I have for you at a later date."

The truth was she had not lied in the letters she sent to Pforta; she was beginning to exhibit that particular refinement required of all young ladies ready to make a debut into society. While Friedrich was lost in this rumination, Elisabeth struggled to pull herself upright, just enough to ensure that he could see the tongue she was sticking out at him. Her brother tried to suppress a smile. Perhaps she was still a child yet, he surmised with a gratified grin.

Elisabeth set her teeth at her brother's obvious mirth. "You are not quite two years my senior! Why do you have to act like such an old man?" Of course, she didn't expect a riposte to a question she knew Friedrich could not answer for himself.

∘ ∘ ∘

For there to be so many seated at the table, dinner was a quiet—perhaps even tense—affair, Paul thought, as he studied those seated about him. There was Nietzsche's mother, Franziska, from whom Elisabeth clearly inherited her looks: determined, dark eyes set off by a straight-bridged yet soft-tipped nose, so characteristic of the Prussian race. Though mother and daughter both had brown hair, it was clear that Elisabeth would never be able to tame her curls into the severe bun that her mother now sported. Paul's gaze traveled on to the tawny-headed Aunt Rosalie, and further still to the unfortunate carrot-topped Wilhelm Pinder, who, with his prominent under-bite and sickly appearance, would never win Elisabeth's attention. His gaze finally settled on Gustav Krug, a strapping aristocratic Adonis in the flesh, upon whom, Paul observed, Friedrich's discontented gaze was also fixed.

8

To everyone's relief, Mrs. Nietzsche finally broke the discomforting silence. "Friedrich, tell us of your latest literary contribution," she urged, nodding to Krug and then Pinder in turn.

The three friends had formed what they dubbed the *Germania Literary Society* during their gymnasium days. The requirement of a monthly submission from each was the primary factor for the endurance of their friendship after Friedrich's move to Pforta. Nodding approval in his mother's direction, Friedrich regaled the group with his increasing interest in philology, a study that was progressively distancing him from his intended vocation in theology. In particular, he had taken to intensive scrutiny of the philosophy of Arthur Schopenhauer.

Pinder nearly choked on a bite. "Surely, this cannot be! Where is the 'Little Parson' who is to take orders in the near future?"

Friedrich blanched at the use of his loathsome childhood nickname. It was true that, as a lad, he had gadded about with childishly pedantic pride in his father's vocation, but must he be reminded at every turn of the provincial ass he had been? Rudely, and uncharacteristically, Friedrich rose before the meal was concluded, threw his napkin on the table, and excused himself, claiming to be under the influence of yet another of the chronic migraines that had plagued him of late.

"He wouldn't have those migraines if he weren't so serious all of the time," quipped Gustav.

Elisabeth and her mother exchanged worried glances. Years before his passing, the Reverend Nietzsche began to suffer a similar ailment. So great was the toll of the pain, his eyesight suffered, causing him to miss a step on the stairway and tumble to his death. Or so it was said. A postmortem examination resulted in the discovery of head trauma that several doctors attributed to an aneurysm and epilepsy—likely sources for the cause of his fall. A dissenting opinion was formed with the conclusion that the head trauma came as a result of the fall. Though she had heard her mother publicly repeat the former over the years, Elisabeth preferred the latter explanation, for it would not do for anyone to believe her father had suffered "weakness of the brain."

o o o

"That was poorly done of you," chided Elisabeth later that evening, as she climbed into bed beside Friedrich and rested her head on his chest. Out of old habit, Friedrich curled his left arm around her shoulders, tucked her head under his chin, and gently ran his fingers through the tangled mass of hair she had never been able to successfully brush out before bed. Lizzie sighed contentedly. "It makes me so angry that I can never *stay* angry with you," she pouted out.

Friedrich chuckled. "If you want to be angry with me, my darling, you need only will it." His hand paused briefly and then resumed its soothing task as he completed his thought. "The problem is we have no control over what we will."

"Is this what your Schopenhauer teaches you? That there is no such thing as the free will granted by God?"

Friedrich craned about to position his face within her peripheral view so that she might see his eyebrows raised in challenge. He released her from his embrace and turned her to face him. "Ah, but did God grant you this will? If so, then it is not free, but instead comes with an arbitrary price." He turned his palms upward, simultaneously raising one while lowering the other in demonstration of the chaotic motion of an indeterminate scale, weighing out justice by the chance measure of man. "What is good and what is evil?" he prodded with a raised brow that dared her to choose a hand. "Choose carefully," he warned in a low tone. "For if you are wrong, the fires of Hell await with a vengeance!" he finished, with a flick of his fingers so unexpected and so close to her face that she jumped back in startled surprise.

"No, my dear sister, you are smarter than this," he patronized with a pat atop her head. "You may have been the only person at the dinner table tonight, save Deussen, who could divine the freedom and peace of mind unleashed by rational thought. Society clings to its god now, but what will become of this Maker of Man and his gifted will, when his subjects decree a definition of justice?"

Elisabeth hastily scrambled to her knees before him and placed a single finger against his lips, her visage clouded with what could only be described as terror. "Friedrich, you blaspheme! Quick! Say a prayer for your immortal soul!" Friedrich stared into her eyes studiously. What did he find there? She hoped it was God.

As if just coming to himself, Friedrich kissed the tip of her finger, then cupped both his hands behind her neck and pulled her forward, planting a soft kiss to her forehead. "Eli," he murmured against her skin.

○ ○ ○

CHAPTER II

∞

Is Chaos as superficial as Fortune? We perversely cling to one while paying pretense to the other. What of a woman whose vanity cannot be quieted? Or is it her womb that wails so? No matter, he says. Nations and constellations cannot be contained without both.

∞

January 1864

Though the family's quarters at Weingarten 18 in Naumburg were by no means substantial, the kaffeeklatsches she hosted in her mother's small parlor on Wednesday afternoons were a source of great pride for Elisabeth. Coffee and chatter with good friends presented her with the prime opportunity to remind one and all of her brother's brilliance and good fortune in not only being admitted to Pforta to begin with but also his being promoted recently to the *Oberprima*, the school's top class. Oh, yes . . . and did they know that the Nietzsches were distantly related to the rising composer Richard Wagner? Friedrich, himself, was a composer, weren't they aware? But of course they were! Who, but an unrefined recluse, had not yet heard that several years back he had written a Christmas composition, *Phantasie*, just for "his Lizzie"? It was by no means his first musical composition, though she was sure that it was his most heartfelt.

The young ladies in attendance always took her boasting in stride, for they feared if they did not, they would no longer receive the invitations that promised to afford them a glimpse of the man himself. To hear their hostess talk, her brother was a nonpareil, both in looks and intelligence—an assessment that most assuredly must be taken with a grain of salt. So rarely was he seen, that his existence was, mayhap, a thing of mythology. A celebrated legend to all. All, that is, with the exception of Elisabeth's closest friend, Hadassah Dahlberg, who had met Friedrich on a number of occasions. Hadassah sat quietly by, smiling as Elisabeth praised her brother's every breath to the Huffstetler twins, Louisa and Lenora. For herself, Hadassah never considered Friedrich handsome, at least not in a masculine sense. It was only that he exuded a certain presence of self that eclipsed beauty, striking many dumb upon introduction.

"Hadassah, pay attention!" Elisabeth chided with two light slaps to her friend's knee, recalling her to the conversation at hand. "Tell them, darling. Tell them how you would not be sitting among us if it were not for the influence of Friedrich's good name."

Hadassah looked about uncertainly. What was she to say to this? True, Friedrich Nietzsche was known to be somewhat of a contrarian, publicly interrogating those held to be authorities on The Jewish Question. Of particular popular recount in Naumburg was the legend of an eleven-year-old Nietzsche, traipsing to the library to attend a lecture on the history of Jews in Prussia. Clad in a tweed suit, with cap in hand, he looked more like a little professor than a "little pastor." He sat stoically as the speaker lauded the Prussian Empire's unique place in history as a State of tolerance within which Jews enjoyed a certain amount of equality. And that is when Friedrich did the unthinkable: he raised his hand and interrupted the speaker.

"It is true, sir," he had piped up without acknowledgement, "that the Prussian Constitutions of 1848 and 1850 granted full equality to the Jews, but what of the enforcement of this guarantee? Not five years since, there are anarchists and revolutionaries on the streets barring the entrance to shops, eateries and all manner of public domains. Case in point, on my way here today, I passed the park, lined, as always, with signs forbidding dogs and Jews from the grass. I thought to test the force of that dictate myself by standing on the green to see if I might, like so much dog dung, find myself exuding the stench of hypocrisy from the sole of a Prussian shoe. For as children of Abraham, are not we all Jews?" A roar of laughter went up in the crowd, rendering the lecturer speechless. Dog dung, indeed!

With the remembrance of this tale, Hadassah could not but laugh aloud and admit that there might be some merit to Elisabeth's assertion, though she hoped she was at Elisabeth's side by virtue of her own merit.

∘ ∘ ∘

The annual winter festival presented every feminine heart in Naumburg with the long-awaited glimpse of Elisabeth's idol. Friedrich and several of his comrades sauntered into the dance hall, turned out in their smart Pforta evening wear of stark black trousers, long-tailed coats over gray waistcoats, and high-collared shirts of white linen, complemented by staunch black cravats, top hats and shiny leather boots. Among them were Paul Deussen and Heinrich Köselitz, who now went by the name Peter Gast, as if a name change could wash away the stain of his birth. The swooning sounds, followed by an awe-inspired hush among the attendees, might lead one to believe a platoon of dashing Prussian officers had besieged the hall, so dumb-stricken was the crowd.

Hadassah clapped her hand over her mouth to stifle an involuntary snicker, and then quickly sobered up at the sight of one particularly gallant figure that rounded up the entourage. He was more handsome than any man had a right to be with his patrician nose, piercing blue eyes and firm lips. The *en vogue* devil-may-care, boyish coiffures sported by his friends looked utterly ridiculous in comparison to his carefully combed, red-tinted raven hair that spoke of maturity and self-confidence. She was not the only one drawn to him, she noticed as she observed a flutter of lilac silk cascade across the floor to settle at Friedrich's side. There stood Elisabeth, niggling for an introduction, Gustav Krug forgotten and muted by her abrupt abandonment mid-reel.

The newcomer was Karl von Gersdorff, son of a baron, heir to a title. Landed and wealthy though he was, Gustav knew he had just been out-ranked. The future politician in him demanded that he hold his temper, and let the embarrassment of the moment pass. He, like everyone else, watched as Gersdorff bowed over Elisabeth's hand, and then elegantly raised it high in the air to lead her out for a waltz.

Friedrich winced as he watched his sister enact the false pretense she had labored to perfect for years. It was not so much that she was sought after as it was that she put herself in the path of those who would not have otherwise noticed her. The oft-practiced maneuver was so effortlessly executed that everyone present believed her to be of singular importance. *They were not alone.* Hadassah, however, was. Friedrich pushed off the wall he was carelessly leaning against and strode over to this humble wellspring of information.

"Why, dear girl, are you not dancing?"

Hadassah started at Friedrich's unexpected approach, and then relaxed when she realized it was he. "Have you not checked my pedigree, Mr. Nietzsche? I was born under the stars."

The corner of his mouth quirked of its own accord in admiration of the Jewess's straightforward manner. She would never change her name. "Ah, that you were," he susurrated. He considered his next words carefully. "Perhaps you could tell me what you see in the constellation before us?"

Hadassah shot him a knowing side-glance. "I see Mr. Krug lying to waste at Mr. Gersdorff's fine boots. Or are they yours?" she asked with astounding impertinence; it was astonishingly refreshing. What must it be like to have no choice but to be one's self?

He looked out on the madness of the crowd, just as the final waltz ended.

∘ ∘ ∘

The wee hours of the morning found brother and sister lying side by side across Friedrich's bed. Elisabeth had been too eager to recap the events of the evening to take the time to change. She had barged into his room and plopped down backwards atop the coverlet, completely unconcerned about the state of her finest evening gown of lilac taffeta, or his state of undress, bared as he was down to his waist. Even in this intimate position so familiar from their childhood—both staring at the ceiling, fingers intertwined in affectionate caress—he felt disconcertingly disconnected from her, somehow. "You were quite in demand tonight," he muttered.

"Not so much so that you couldn't have asked me to take a single turn," she responded pointedly, and a little petulantly.

At that, he leapt from the bed and beckoned her with an upturned hand, extended in invitation for a dance. Every word Elisabeth uttered came as a challenge to him. Without hesitation she ensconced herself in his arms, resting her head on his pale bare chest, paler now than ever. He was not well, she knew, but she would not speak of it now. They danced to Silence, a secretive confidante of long standing familiarity.

"Do you fancy Gersdorff?" Friedrich set aside the sagacious specter. Elisabeth raised her eyes, filled with pain and pity, to meet his. He damned himself for a fool as she cupped his cheek with her hand. *Words.* He wanted *words.* "Why must you touch me that way?" he barked out.

Elisabeth spun away from him, her heart filled with hurt. It was always thus; it was inevitably her fault when Truth demanded an audience. "Why do you look at me so accusingly?" she demanded on an ominous whisper. "What faith have I broken with you when it is you who have subjected me to one letter after another about your new love in Berlin? Did you ask for my blessing?" Her voice swung to a near shout as her fury intensified. "You'll marry and where will that leave Mother and I? Besides, you forget that I am all but promised to Gustav. Do I regret that I formed an understanding with him before you, with your Deussen and your Gersdorff, came home? Of course I do!" She pointed a rage-filled, shaking finger in his direction. "But what choice had I? Your schooling cost Mother a fortune, and now there is university to attend. Gustav can afford to keep us until . . ." she trailed off, raising her now quieting, yet hesitant, finger to smooth away the tautness in his jaw, but then thought better of it. "Until you have a chance to establish yourself."

Establish himself at what, she could not say. She only knew that he would succeed in having his way.

Friedrich raked a hand through his hair out of frustrated habit and expelled a defeated breath as he moved to the window and leaned heavily on the sill to better gaze out into the night. "You're right. Gustav may be just what you need.

He has a political career ahead of him, a vocation that will soon serve us, each and every one, well. *Kleindeutschland*," he mumbled, his breath creating an ominous fog on the glass pane, beyond which his gaze was fixed on something that only he could see. "Prussia will not long suffer her pride. She hungers for a legitimacy that only war can satisfy. The leviathan that is Nationalism will make monsters of us yet. Chaos will rail against all except those who have the will to political power to keep it at bay."

He pushed away from the windowpane to find his sister standing just behind him, completely mesmerized. He took her chin between his forefinger and thumb and gave it a little tug. And just like that, their squabble was forgotten.

o o o

CHAPTER III

∞

I once thought to "be somebody" in spite of it all. But then I remembered myself and the plight of Woman — aut liberi aut libri (either children or books).

∞

Fall 1865

With the onset of autumn came Friedrich's graduation from Pforta, and Elizabeth's entry into finishing school in Dresden for a six-month stay. Her brother was not quite satisfied with the choice, preferring Hannover instead, as he believed it to be more grandiose and, therefore, a worthy placement for his Lizzie. Brother and sister, however, had strongly opposing opinions on what constitutes a state of grandiosity, one preferring edification of mind, the other elevation of social station. If her letters were any proof, he mused, she had achieved her goal: *You will not recognize me! Your once awkward Lizzie now moves with the confidence born of grace and ease that only the Countess Ross could instill in her pupils.*

He could never fail to recognize her, he assured her by return mail, no matter how transformed she may be. *How could he not recognize the innocence that filled his dreams?* Indeed, he needed no reminder of her physiognomy. In spirit, she plagued him night and day, trailing like a phantom from Pforta to Bonn, suspended somewhere within the rooms he and Paul had taken at Bongasse 518. Whether she was there at his behest or Paul's he could not determine, though he suspected and feared.

∘ ∘ ∘

There was to be a school dance at the conclusion of Elisabeth's term in Dresden to include family and friends — part celebration, part exhibition. Franziska Nietzsche had high hopes for this event that would surely see her daughter married off to Cousin Rudolf, who had quietly paid court to Elisabeth since her sixteenth year, though Elisabeth had done very little to encourage his suit. Surely, the girl could be made to see reason. A quick marriage upon her come-out would secure the family's future and allow for her son to complete his studies at ease.

Though Elisabeth thwarted her mother's aspirations at every turn, it came as a blow to both when Rudolf announced his engagement to another less than a week before the dance.

To the relief of mother and daughter, Gustav Krug stepped forward to claim his place at Elisabeth's side, a slot he had every intention of securing beyond question.

° ° °

As she twirled around the dance floor in Gustav's arms, Elisabeth felt a deep sense of foreboding that she couldn't quite shake. She took in her partner's handsome visage and aristocratic bearing. Why could she not love him? He was like a brother to her—beautiful, intelligent, gentle—and, yet, she could feel nothing but his despair. Her feet stopped beneath her, halted by the weight of her thoughts. Gustav mistook her hesitant step as the invitation he had long awaited. "Darling, it seems you are in need of fresh air." He took her by the hand and steered her to a set of French doors opened wide in invitation to the dark recesses of an elaborate garden. What was surely touched by God's hand during the light of day stood in pale illumination now, visible only by the dim lighting of Japanese lanterns that breathed like fading dragons.

Elisabeth realized Gustav's intentions with plenty of time to prevent the moment, but could do nothing more than watch herself see it through. The walk into the garden seemed interminable, her thoughts at war with the echo of her mother's admonishment: *If you spurn the seed, you will be left with the chaff.* Elisabeth's response of *or perhaps with nobody* had been cavalier on the surface, but the possible reality of her words consumed her with despair. She would burn in Hell for this betrayal of self, mother, brother, and God. She shook her thoughts away and steeled her spine, for she was loved after all.

She knew in later years she would look back on Young Lizzie in this moment and assure her she had done all that was required of her.

Gustav Krug would look back on the still form of Elisabeth Nietzsche and wonder where her spirit had gone on that evening, in that moment, that she should express no discomfort.

∘ ∘ ∘

The new day dawned black, accompanied by a turbulent tempest of self-loathing. Sleep, having proved to be an elusive companion, left Elisabeth no choice but to give up chase and face the reality of morning. She sat up in bed and willed her eyes to affix on that which she knew she would find on the floor. Her best gown, pressed of its wrinkles for last night's entertainment, now lay in tattered lilac ruins on the floor. From those ruins she was determined to arise anew. A comforting voice echoed in her head: *You must be ready to burn yourself in your own flame; how could you rise anew if you have not first become ashes?* He was constant, her brother. But her role as little sister was resolute in its end.

Decision made, Elisabeth rose, scampered across the room to her writing desk, and lifted the lid on what she, heretofore, had fondly referred to as her "treasure box." She sifted through the carefully tied bundles within, separating Friedrich's letters from his unfinished works, which she had rescued from the waste bin — efforts demolished and despised. Would she be so discarded? She closed her eyes tight in an attempt to banish the doubts she so detested to the deepest recess of her being, if she could but locate her soul in the darkness. The search was quickly abandoned. Elisabeth was not one to dwell on what could not be changed. She closed the lid on her treasure box, and reached down to pluck her dress from the floor. It was ruined beyond repair.

∘ ∘ ∘

CHAPTER IV

∞

There is liberty in sexuality. Whether I loved it or reviled it, I cannot say. I know only that I lived it with a masochistic self-loathing that cloaked itself in the muted wisdom of mortification. "Give it all to God," they say, and so I shall try.

∞

Spring 1865

From wisdom to witlessness, Bonn was quickly shaping up to be a portrait of two extremes. The philology department enjoyed the expertise of distinguished professors Otto Jahn and Friedrich Wilhelm Ritschl. Yet, inexplicably, Friedrich's college-mates seemed to prefer fraternity life over the profundity of existential enlightenment. He had reluctantly allowed Paul to talk him into joining the *Franconia* fraternity, with the first order of business being a visit to a bordello. If Hell exists, he thought, as he waded through the stench of squalid sex, then, most assuredly, here it resides.

Paul slapped his friend on the back. "What gives, Nietzsche? Enlightenment is gained through experience, is it not?" Paul extended his arm in introduction to a sitting room full of prostitutes and awaited his friend's long-in-coming response.

Friedrich scanned the destitution before him, his eyes reflecting the incompatibility of compassion and contempt. "Innocence lost is indeed an enlightening experience," he said over his shoulder as he walked away from Paul toward a piano in the corner, upon which he began to play *Phantasie*.

∘ ∘ ∘

As the weeks passed, Elisabeth's mood swung from enervating melancholy to impulsive rage that manifested itself in an exhibition of self-empowerment, alarming Franziska Nietzsche to no end. Gustav, too, must have been put off by it, for he had not called on his near-betrothed in over a month. For her part, Elisabeth did not seem to be overly troubled by his sudden withdrawal of attentions, choosing, instead, to redouble her efforts to draw the attentions of other prospective suitors.

Clad scandalously in red since the odd disappearance of her lilac dress, Elisabeth seemed immune to the forward reputation she was making for herself. Franziska had always believed that if one smiled in the face of embarrassment, it would be as if the offending situation never happened. And so it was that the local matrons clucked their tongues in dismay, as a flush-faced Franziska looked beyond her daughter as if she were an apparition only others could see.

It wasn't until Elisabeth took to the floor for a reel with Peter Gast that her mother was forced to acknowledge the mounting spectacle that was her daughter. He could change his name to whatever he wanted, but Peter Gast was still Heinrich Köselitz beneath his Prussian attire. Yes, he had been Friedrich's classmate, and, true, she had allowed him into her home, but that was her Christian duty, was it not? If nothing else, she wanted her children to walk among God's creation, but never had she envisioned the possibility of procreation between them. Indeed, she had hoped to pull off a match between Gast and Hadassah Dahlberg, upon whom Elisabeth had concentrated her Christian duty.

Weary of Elisabeth's diminishing marital prospects and fearing that her daughter would ruin herself beyond repair, Franziska implored her son to pay a visit home. *Friedrich, your Lizzie is in need of her brother's influence. She has, of late, been committing shameful displays, throwing herself at one young man or another. It's so very strange. At home she holds men in contempt while in public she holds herself out to be condemned. Please hurry home. She requires a man's hand.*

The Easter break upon them at Bonn, Friedrich and Paul Deussen made their way to Naumburg for a visit, during which Friedrich fervently hoped to find his mother's concerns exaggerated. He suspected that Elisabeth was simply testing the validity of an intellectual exchange they had recently had over the systematic oppression of society cloaked in Christian morals and faith. In essence, he had instructed her that she could either be a follower or a leader in life. Followers along the path of faith would certainly find peace and contentment, but they would never be disciples of Truth. One must flout social dictates in order to scratch the surface of the superficiality that is spirituality.

Much to his dismay, Friedrich had barely arrived in Naumburg before he discovered that Lizzie had managed to do more than scratch the surface of superficiality. She was, in fact, shattering it, along with his heart. The family had been invited to dine with the Huffstetlers to celebrate his arrival home, and there sat Elisabeth, flirting outrageously with every gentleman at the table, including Herr Huffstetler. Both matrons present, the Fraus Nietzsche and Huffstetler blushed in mortification. And damn Paul Deussen's eyes! He, too, blushed like a green lad in lust! Friedrich smiled benignly in the direction of those pretending not to be captivated by his sister's display. There would be words upon their return to the Nietzsche abode, for Friedrich could not countenance his witless friend's all too obvious interest in his Lizzie.

It wasn't long before Friedrich found himself pacing the parlor floor of his family home, his mother's admonitions trailing in his wake. "You must find her a suitable husband," his mother implored. "She cannot be allowed to go on gadding about with Peter Gast."

Friedrich stopped in his tracks and turned to his mother with a single angry brow raised in inquiry. "And what are your objections to Gast, Mother?"

Franziska gaped at her son incredulously. "Surely you do not expect me to stand by and allow her to abscond with a Jew, for abscond she must! Gast would be required to convert, of course, but even so, the church will never marry them. Friedrich, it is one thing for us to champion the rights of Jews and another thing entirely to join our causes in wedlock. She won't be received!"

"For God's sakes, Mother!" Friedrich chided. "She is not going to marry Gast. She is simply flouting convention at this juncture in her life. Lizzie is as headstrong as I had ever hoped she would be. Gast is forbidden and so she will have him."

"You cannot mean to allow it," his mother objected. "What of your reputation, my son?"

Friedrich startled and clapped incredulous eyes upon his mother. "If by 'reputation' you mean conforming to the expectations of the masses, then what need have I of a reputation? Furthermore, what need has Lizzie? Would you have her waste away in solitude? Would you prefer she shun her potential? There is a Truth out there, Mother, that will set us all at liberty. I would have Lizzie in search of it."

Friedrich picked up his exasperated pace about the room. Walking stick in hand, he tapped it absentmindedly against his leg, pausing every couple of steps to glance down on the bustling street where Elisabeth now strode on Paul's arm. They were standing closer than necessary, heads bent in collusion as if they shared a closely kept secret. Friedrich moved closer to the window for a better view. Were they laughing together? Did Paul's lips just graze Lizzie's ear? Oblivious to his mother's continued admonitions, Friedrich's cane fell to the floor with a clatter as he jaunted to the stairs that would afford him quick access to the street and Paul Deussen's cursed hide.

Paul groaned as he saw Friedrich stalking down the sidewalk in their direction. "Ah, here comes the storm cloud," he muttered to Elisabeth with a nod over her shoulder in her brother's direction. Elisabeth, who had heretofore been at ease, straightened her back and turned to face the onslaught of her brother's selective wrath.

Cutting mischievous eyes at her walking partner, Elisabeth came up on her tiptoes to bend Paul's ear. "How like a bear he looks with his furrowed brow and new mustache. By the by, I do so hate that mustache, though I suppose some must find it charming."

Paul chuckled at that. "It's the contrarian in him, I believe. He sports it because he knows just how repugnant he looks, though I still say it's an improvement upon his Pforta style.

His brother Franconians found him to be a bit too effeminate. Now, if we could only teach him to turn a feminine head." The jibe was purposely intended for Friedrich to hear.

"Ah, pray tell, Deussen," Friedrich drawled as he stopped short before his friend. "Why ever would I want to turn an empty head?"

Elisabeth's eyes widened at the derogatory remark that fell so easily from her brother's lips. Sensing her surprise, Paul tucked Elisabeth's hand back into the crook of his arm and strived to keep his composure. "I'm afraid your brother, Miss Nietzsche, spends his days in the company of alpha males, otherwise called 'philosophers,'" he baited. The sooner Elisabeth noted the changes in her brother — who in one moment could defend her right to intellectual pursuits and then deny it with his very next breath — the better.

Friedrich set his gaze on Elisabeth before turning his attention to Paul. "Ah, so you mean to make me look the barbarian in front of my sister." He acknowledged Paul's savvy with a mocking bow, dislodged his sister from Paul's arm, and then possessively gathered both her hands in his own, bringing one, then the other, to his lips. "You see, Elisabeth is not just any woman, Deussen," he declared, as his gazed probed deep into Elisabeth's eyes, as if he divined the future in their depths. "She is to be the mother of a new generation of Nietzsches in a Germania that will soon be beyond our recognition."

Clasping her hands more securely, Friedrich extended his arms and began to swing Elisabeth around in circles. Her laughter filled the air as her praises were sung. "She will be the mortar that holds a broken man in repair. When she has pieced him back together, she will guide him along the path to deliverance." Friedrich abruptly stopped their roundabout to address Paul with an aside. "For whoever said that woman was man's property clearly had yet to meet my Eli." He shrugged his shoulders at Paul as if to say *resign yourself to it, man*. Turning back to Elisabeth with wonderment in his eyes, a palpable silence ensued as he looked her over, committing every aspect of her to memory.

Finally, he whispered his conclusion. "Indeed, whenever I contemplate my dear sister, Cesare Borgia rises in my esteem." Another silence consumed the air between brother and sister until Friedrich entered one final argument. "So you see, Deussen, my sister has not the head of just any woman, nor is she meant for just any man. Which reminds me, your little *tête-à-tête* is at an end." With that, Friedrich took hold of Lizzie's elbow and turned on his heel to steer her home.

∘ ∘ ∘

He knew for a certainty that he had made her angry by interfering with her plans for Paul, but Friedrich had not counted on his sister failing to appear for their ritualistic recount of the day. There was something changed about her that he couldn't quite put his finger on. Outwardly, she shined with a vibrancy that masked the nearly imperceptible vacancy in her eyes, imperceptible to all but one who knew her so well as he. Perhaps he should go to her and beg her forgiveness for his rude interference. There was really no clear explanation that he could provide her to excuse his behavior. He knew only that there was an air of vulnerability about her that beckoned him to her side. As if answering her unspoken plea, Friedrich threw his bedroom door open and stepped out into the hall intent on seeking her out. He had not far to go. She was sitting in the hallway just outside his room, slouched against the wall, feet tucked beneath her gown, arms hugging her knees, as if to shelter herself from some unseen onslaught.

It reminded Friedrich of their childhood games of hide-and-seek. As a toddler, Elisabeth had not yet reached the cognitive stage of development that makes it possible for one to discern where the self ends and the external begins. When attempting to hide, little Lizzie would simply hop up in an armchair and plop herself facedown. She thought herself uncommonly canny as she pressed her face into the seat cushion so tight that stars began to dance in the blackness behind her eyelids.

Her eyes closed tight, tight and tighter still; if she could not see herself, then surely no one could see her. The truth was, even if she had managed to keep herself from his view, he still would have found her. So vibrant and full of life was she, a giggle born of anticipation inescapably betrayed her whereabouts. Nonetheless, she never failed to pop up her head in astonishment upon being tagged. "Friedrich, how did you find me?" The blood having run red to her face, she made a formidable impression with her nose screwed into a scowl of indignation. To which he always responded, "I shall always know where my soul takes shelter."

And here lay his soul, broken and battered at his feet. He bent over and gently lifted her in his arms. Let her believe she had secreted herself away; he could still plainly see her. In the moment he was settling her atop his bed, he saw a plea surface in her eyes, imploring him to absorb whatever dark burden resided in their mature depths.

∘ ∘ ∘

CHAPTER V

∞

"For It Is Written . . ." The four words that render man guiltless of every crime against humanity. The Jew will march and the Virgin will cower. I can hear his voice still: "Is it possible? Is this honest? Is it even decent?"

∞

Elisabeth looked about before resting her eyes on her brother. He was saying something, was he not? Was he speaking to her? She scanned the familiar setting of the room from the back of her mind. Yes, it must be she, for there was no one else present—none that she could see, though she felt the presence of something oppressive weighing in the air surrounding her. Her eyes searched frantically about the room in an attempt to lay siege to the phantom that tested her very existence, her gaze finally coming to rest on Friedrich's still-moving lips. Her heart dropped and she broke out into a panicked sweat with the realization that she had descended on a moment in time that had been lived before—in a previous life, perhaps?

In His Afterlife she was sure her brother would elucidate on this experience of transcendence, but as it was now, he could say nothing more, for her fingers had risen of their own volition to silence his lips. She regained lucidity as Friedrich gently and slowly removed her fingers from his mouth; a mouth that, when shaven clean of his fashionable mustache, looked exactly like Gustav's. How she hated her brother for a brief instant! What was it the Russian novelist Dostoevsky said? Ah, yes. *If God does not exist, then everything is permitted.* She leaned forward and kissed her brother's lips in fevered desperation.

When the morning light cast a wake-up call upon Elisabeth's fluttering eyelids, it took her a moment to take in her surroundings. The last she could recall, she had been in Friedrich's bedchamber, she was sure. But this was *her* bed . . . if only she could recall how she got back to her room. What had happened last night? Had she ever actually been in Friedrich's room? Had she revealed a bit of her soul to him? She searched the recesses of her memory for answers and then lurched over the bed, retching up the contents of her stomach.

Dressed in a princess-waist day gown of blue muslin, complemented by off-the-shoulder puffed sleeves that hinted of a pale innocence hidden just within, Elisabeth made her way into the dining room for breakfast. Of course, Friedrich was seated at the table. She didn't even need to look in his direction for confirmation of his presence. She instead moved with graceful resolution to the sideboard to place an assortment of cheeses, eggs, and liver sausage upon her plate. She would not, of course, actually eat, but would instead busy her fork about her plate just long enough to create the impression that she had indeed eaten her fill. The loose folds of her dress reminded her that she would have to have the waist taken in a bit more. She frowned down at her lap. At this rate she would not be able to afford the remainder of the social season.

"Deussen and I are taking our mounts out for a jaunt in the park, if you would like to join us?" Friedrich addressed her cautiously.

"I'm told you have a fine seat, Miss Nietzsche," put in Paul.

Elisabeth looked from Paul to her brother and then back again. "I thank you both for the invitation." Her response was addressed solely to Paul. "But I am already committed to Mr. Gast this morning. We are to practice his most recent pianoforte composition, a duet, I believe."

"Ah, yes. I seem to remember giving him permission to call." Friedrich stood, signaling the end of breakfast, and rounded the table to pull Elisabeth's chair out for her. "Well refine it, dear Lizzie, and perhaps we shall play it together this evening." He smoothly excused himself from the room, Paul following on his heels.

She had not even needed to affect her pretense of eating, so brief was this morning's mealtime.

Peter's composition was truly beautiful in its melancholy, thought Elisabeth as her fingers danced over the ivory keys of the pianoforte, each note crying out to her soul in profound agony. "What is it that weighs so heavy on your heart, dear Peter? What darkness is this that consumes you so?" she asked, as their fingers continued to fly in unison.

"Schleswig-Holstein," he replied without skipping a note. "Once torn asunder, Helmuth von Moltke would rip it from the seam of Denmark and piece it back together under Prussian dominance. It is the eternal plight of the sons of Abraham, welcomed in to fortify nation states from experience born of long suffering, only to be punished for our troubles, castigated as the common enemy of the very state we helped make viable." Deep in thought, his fingers levitated over the piano keys for the duration of several notes and then picked up in accord with his partner's. "And so begins the beat of the war drums, the battle cry of Nationalism to which the worn feet of the wandering Jew will once again tap."

Moved beyond words, Elisabeth halted her playing as melody continued to flow from Peter's fingers to God's ear. Despite her mother's misgivings, she believed her father would have loved this man.

An afternoon walk in the park with Peter by her side proved to Elisabeth that *she* could love this man. Contrary by nature, Elisabeth decided that if society would reject this Jew, then, by God, she would embrace him! With his dark wavy hair, his kind brown eyes, his perspicacity of mind, and a bearing that bespoke a command of self, Peter had all the attributes she had ever hoped for in a man—everything that Gustav was not, nor would ever be. She and Peter would never be permitted to marry, but she would have him all the same. Risk: was this not what made life worth living? So determined, she drew closer to him, and, to his astonishment, linked her arm with his as they passed a sign forbidding his presence upon the very ground on which they strode. Her public impudence endeared her to him even more. He believed his father could love this woman.

As if he had spoken his thoughts aloud, Elisabeth slid her hand from the crook of his elbow down to his hand and pressed her palm against his, their fingers interlocking in a pact of solidarity. "Before my brother returns to Bonn, we are to visit my grandparents' home in Pobles. Do say you will join us, Peter. What a merry group we would make!"

He suspected her mother would not agree, but Peter could not resist, so manic was the spirit that was Elisabeth Nietzsche. In one moment her eyes reflected the painful weight of a lethargic soul. In the very next, the same eyes revealed an inner essence of calculated resolve to live with reckless abandon. All else be damned!

The impeding approach of Friedrich and Paul, freshly returned from their ride, brought an end to all reverie. "Friedrich," Elisabeth called out upon her brother's approach, "you must convince Peter to join us in Pobles."

Never one to resist controversy himself, Friedrich readily agreed. "Gast, I insist that you join us," he declared with an emphatic nod in Peter's direction. It neither escaped Peter's nor Paul's notice when Friedrich came just shy of withdrawing his invitation, his eyes having fallen upon his sister's bold embrace of her companion's hand. Averting his gaze, Friedrich recovered himself quickly enough. "It would be our honor to serve as your hosts. You and Deussen here can instruct us in the ways of the Jews and Hindus. Deussen has had his head buried in the *Bhagavad Gita* of late. I await enlightenment, fearing that neither of you have heard the shovels disturbing the dirt of the grave in which the gravediggers are burying any semblance of God as we speak."

Peter grinned at his pedantic friend. "I understand you intend to join me at Leipzig in the coming academic year. I fear I have no choice but to provide you with a good defense of my faith, lest you publicly avail me of my belief system in the same adept manner with which you cast an avalanche over Christianity."

Friedrich clapped his friend on the back. "No Köselitz need fear on that score. After all, it is for a crucified Jew that the Sunday bells ring."

∘ ∘ ∘

Their brief sojourn at Pobles turned out to be one of the most redemptive of Elisabeth's life. Yes, Mother lay abed beside herself, smelling salts in hand. So disconsolate was she that Hadassah Dahlberg was invited along just to quell gossip. The desired result was achieved, there being little opportunity for a private moment with Peter. Nonetheless, a determined Elisabeth was not easily thwarted, and it did not escape Friedrich that his sister's preference for Peter or Paul was indeterminate. One moment she was on Peter's arm, another on Paul's, and then within the blink of an eye ensconced between the two. He knew she was safe in the care of either or both, but still he could not quiet his qualms. One thing was for sure: Deussen was discontent, as evidenced by the dejection written across his face. An emotion Friedrich recognized as his own. An emotion Paul had no right to covet.

Elisabeth, too, began to feel herself gravitating more and more towards Peter. She trusted him, she realized with no small amount of wonder. There was something in his manner that promised sanctuary. If she must be taken to wife as her mother insisted, and if she must reconcile herself to wifely duties as the law dictated, then it was Peter to whom she could entrust her dignity. And so, she reasoned, she may as well dispense with the formalities. So decided, she made careful arrangements to ensnare Friedrich and Paul into an outing with Hadassah, leaving Peter all to herself for their final afternoon at Pobles.

The brilliant colors of Grandma Oehler's garden called them forth as the shaded grottos beckoned with the promise of serenity. Dragging Peter by the hand at a near run, Elisabeth steered him to her favorite alcove within which they fell to the ground laughing and eager to catch their breath.

"This was our favorite spot when we were children, Friedrich and I," Elisabeth explained once she had collected herself. "We spent countless afternoons here discussing any number of Friedrich's philosophical cogitations."

Peter sat up and placed his arm beneath her shoulder to help her do the same at his side. "And what did you discuss?" he asked as he carefully tucked a fallen tendril of hair behind her ear.

"We spoke of virtue," Elisabeth declared on a light wind of laughter. "My brother views morality as an ambiguous sword wielded arbitrarily at the discernment of the dominant, intent on maintaining supremacy. The Christian decrees the Jew to the pits of Hell so that he may commandeer the heavens. Man instills fear in woman so that he may command her obedience. Therefore, a woman who fears the fires of Hell will keep her virtue intact until a righteous man deems her worthy enough to gift it to him. So you see, a woman has not virtue, but fear: fear that she will not live up to mortal morality and thereby be adjudged unvirtuous. "

Peter's gaze searched hers with intensity. "And you, Miss Nietzsche. Are you virtuous?"

Elisabeth threw her head back with a gusty laugh. "I fear nothing, Mr. Gast!" she exclaimed heavenward in the split second before Peter's mouth descended on hers. She jolted in surprise and then admonished herself, for she had known this would happen. Had she not planned it just so? Did she hate herself so much, or was it that she simply cared for him? No, she decidedly did not hate herself she realized as she fell deeper into Peter's embrace.

He was gentle in his kiss, in his touch, in his hesitancy as his soul probed hers for consent. Yes, he sought, not demanded, consent. She watched as if from an outer orbit as he rose, then lifted and removed his shirt, followed by his trousers. Perhaps she should not fear so, but still she would not look. As he knelt down and loomed just above her, Peter cast a soulful gaze upon her in search of definitive confirmation. She reached up, wrapped her arms around his neck, and nodded her assent.

She should enjoy this, she thought fleetingly. He deserved no less. No matter how hard she tried to let go and savor the moment, she despaired that she simply could not. For Elisabeth, there was no such thing as living in the moment—for, in the end, moments were only links strung together to form a lead into the future. As if the years had already gone by, she pictured an aged Lizzie watching from afar, preserving this moment for remembrance and relishing later . . . if not now. The present came back with a crash when Peter collapsed on top of her. She at once damned and congratulated herself. Damnation for having missed what ought, and congratulation for fearing naught.

The return trip to Naumburg had been quite tedious all around. An odd combination of pomp and pall had been cast over the merry party that Elisabeth had pieced together at the outset of their sojourn. Where Elisabeth exuded majesty, Friedrich was consumed by a melancholy inexplicably directed at Paul. So short and sharp were the exchanges between the friends, all conversation had ceased before the carriage pulled up to the entrance of Weingarten 18. After saying their goodbyes to Elisabeth and Peter, Friedrich and Paul returned to Bonn for their year-end examinations. Paul was certain that his friend would return to himself once Peter Gast was out of sight and, hopefully, mind. Therefore, it came as quite a shock to Paul to learn that he was the actual source of Friedrich's ire.

"You have taken up with my sister, have you not?" he demanded of Paul. "God damn it, Deussen! I warned you to keep your distance! She is in no state to be toyed with." His words of warning seethed through clenched teeth with a ferocity the likes of which Paul had never witnessed. No matter, Paul's anger rose to the occasion.

"If she is not to be toyed with, then perhaps you are the one who could use a bit of distance."

No sooner had the words escaped Paul's mouth than Friedrich's fist connected with his jaw. That which Hadassah Dahlberg could plainly state, Paul Deussen was not allowed to contemplate. Flexing his fist at his side, Paul took a deep breath, and with every ounce of his patience, refrained from responding in kind to his friend's physical assault. He had, after all, managed to insult a lady in his effort to cut his roommate. He expelled a calming breath.

"I have not toyed with Elisabeth. Yes, I will admit that I am attracted to her—who would not be? But I am sad to say, she pays me little heed. Her attentions are directed in another direction, or perhaps several. I know not." Christ, he had overstepped again.

Friedrich cursed under his breath. "Watch yourself, Deussen. You go too far. That is my sister you speak of. I'd advise you to tread carefully."

"You need not fear, Nietzsche. I am weary of your black moods and shall tread very carefully until you remove to Leipzig this summer. I never thought I would say this of you, once my closest friend, but I shall breathe a sigh of relief at your departing form. I wish you luck in mastering your passion before it masters you beneath the bridles of madness."

o o o

CHAPTER VI

∞

I fear I may be the face of Eve, a lust-driven siren placed on this earth to give birth to God's ideal. Why, then, am I not brave enough to give issue to a Jew? It is Truth — not my body — that holds the answer, so long as it exists in the mind of God.

∞

Spring 1866

Upon arrival at Leipzig, Friedrich took up private quarters at *Elisenstraße* 7, affording him the solitude he required to devote himself to preparing his written contributions to the philological society he had joined together with Gersdorff, Gast, and an old Bonn colleague, Erwin Rohde. By the spring of 1866, the four fell into a routine of weekly meetings, tremendously enjoying their often boisterous, and at times contentious, academic debates over Schopenhauer's *The World as Will and Representation*. Is anything as it seems to be, or is it simply a depiction of individual perception; a unique manifestation of the mind? Do we exist outside of the mind of God? If not—and if there is no god—do we exist at all? In short, life is a grand deception, calculating and cruel in machination.

Add to this Albert Lange's *History of Materialism* and the dialogue between the academics grew livelier still.

The ideology that followed this coterie to Naumburg for a visit in March washed up in unison with a wave of a now-familiar tremor of Elisabeth's faith in God and man. Behind the edifice that she had erected to extricate herself from the worldly pain beyond lurked the specter whose silence could not long be guaranteed. As Prussia grew restless and angry, so it was with Elisabeth.

Her time in Pobles with Peter had filled her with a joy so great that she returned to her grandparents' home for the better part of a year, the conclusion of which left her bereft of any inducement life had to offer. Had it not been for Friedrich, who secreted in on several occasions, she may very well have ended her existence. Instead, she concentrated her attentions on her brother who mourned the loss of his friendship with Paul Deussen and began to cast a wild eye on other of his friends.

During this current visit to Naumburg, she was pleased to see that the combustive embers of Friedrich's jealousy were outwardly banked. Though Deussen was lost forever, the rest of the friends seemed to be as close as she had ever hoped they could be. She was particularly thankful to Peter for his constancy in all things Nietzsche, even in the wake of his banishment. Every attempt to visit her had been thwarted at the doorstep by the ever vigilant Franziska. Who could say how many countless letters were shredded without Elisabeth's knowledge? She would let it go for the short term, but she knew for certain that there would come a day . . .

Within Elisabeth's hearing, the group's topic of conversation was largely concentrated on the percolating war with Austria. Depending on which political provocateur one chose to listen to, any number of convention treaties signed for the administration of Schleswig-Holstein had been violated by the Austrians. Influenced by Bismarck's view of war as "the politics and the art of the possible" and Von Moltke's assurance that now was the time—a time in which Prussia enjoyed economic and technological dominance over the German nation states—"to have the war that must be had," Prussian citizens largely supported mobilization for the long-awaited realization of *Kleindeutschland* (Lesser Germany), which would exclude Austria and the southern German states, paving the way for Prussian dominance over Greater Germany. Friedrich was staunch in his resolve on this matter: The Schleswig-Holstein affliction was but a pretense for war put in motion by those fools who, as Schopenhauer would say, turn to rabid patriotism to mask their own inferiority.

In this, as in most cases, Elisabeth agreed with her brother. She had much to say on the subject, but was given little opportunity to share her ideas. It broke her heart to witness her brother at times raise his voice to drown her out, as if she had spoken nary a word, and at others dismiss her thoughts out of hand. She knew she was fast falling from his grace. Resulting from her actions or his she could not yet determine. Words spoken on the morrow—words not meant for her ears—were conviction enough that the fault lay with both of them.

When on Peter's arm, there was little that could dampen Elisabeth's spirits. The two lovers, having come to understand that clandestine affairs were best carried out under the cover of the public eye, strolled along an oft used path through the park, ostensibly in search of her brother. She could not have known that she would come to regret the moment that she and Peter stumbled upon him. Propped by one hand against a marble statue of Dionysus, Friedrich was in lazy debate with Captain Gersdorff, who was certain to soon be carried to the front line on the zephyr of battle. Elisabeth expected to hear talk pertaining to combat, but to her utter dismay, was instead assaulted by words that portended war against womankind.

"Mother, daughter, sister, friend: they all serve a common purpose, Gersdorff." Friedrich paused long enough to raise a shielded flame to light the cigarette dangling from his lips. It always took Elisabeth off guard, his tendency to smoke whenever Gersdorff was about. "They are the creators and the controllers of man. No sooner does Bismarck plant his seed than he leads troops into war at the behest of his mistress's womb in collusion with his member." A wisp of smoke flowed forth as if emanating from the essence of a sorcerer. "The Iron Chancellor may have the right of it, old boy. Perhaps, possessing a woman's body is tantamount to possessing the throbbing body of humanity. For your sake, Captain, let's hope there's something to the sweet nothings whispered upon his pillow."

"And if it is indeed a woman who sends us to war," countered Gersdorff with a chuckle, "tell me, does she exist or is she a figment of Bismarck's mind?" He paused in conversation to cast the butt of his own cigarette to the gravel, grounding it out with the heel of his military boot. "Or perhaps you have conjured her up? Mayhap, she is one of the two whores you frequent religiously."

Peter gently muffled Elisabeth's audible gasp with his hand. She cast her eyes down upon that hand that held her silent and wondered that it was not her brother's.

"Don't judge too harshly," Friedrich admonished. "Those who are not whoring are whore-mongering. Or warring under the impotent battle flag of Christianity. A tethered heart takes many liberties."

Peter quietly steered Elisabeth back onto the path from whence they came. He knew what followed when Friedrich waxed philosophical in regards to the sexual nature of those who flock to Christianity. In essence, he denounced it to be a religion that provides haven for the sexually repressed. In order for it to remain a haven, sexual repression must be fomented. "Poor Elisabeth," he once confided in Peter. "I fear that she may never willingly breach the moral barrier that holds immortality within its walls." Whether he was being issued a challenge, a warning, or a test for Truth, Peter could not be certain—and would certainly not ask for fear that he might receive an answer.

○ ○ ○

If she could not be found in her bed in the middle of the night, then Friedrich knew he would find Elisabeth reading in the seldom-used study his mother had set up for him to write in on his visits home. What he had not expected was to come upon her reading aloud to Gersdorff, she in her dressing gown and robe, and the captain still in that infernal uniform that unfailingly cut him a dashing figure. She was reading the latest installment of *Crime and Punishment* originally published in *The Russian Messenger*, translated to German and reprinted in *Neue Preußische Zeitung*.

Recognizing instantly that Gersdorff's mind was on anything but the reading, Friedrich moved forward to make his presence known. Elisabeth refolded her paper and tossed it aside. "Friedrich, I would speak with you," she commanded as Gersdorff tried to suppress a grin. What secret did the captain share with his Lizzie? No gaze was piercing enough to crack that steeled armor, and so it was to Friedrich's relief that Gersdorff said his goodnights and took his leave of the room.

Friedrich turned his full attention on his sister. "Of what would you have us converse, Lizzie?"

She picked up a half full glass of brandy that rested on the table by her chair and offered it to her brother. "Prostitutes," she answered with unabashed candidness. They would discuss his low opinion of women another time; Elisabeth had her priorities. She took him in with a pointed, guileless gaze as he threw back the liqueur with one swallow.

Never one to evade even the most awkward of situations, Friedrich approached Elisabeth head on and launched into a diatribe of counsel he had repeated to himself often enough that he had every word memorized by heart. "Is it so shocking that a man should crave a woman to warm his bed, dear Lizzie?" Leaning forward to proffer a brotherly tap upon the tip of her nose, he came down on bended knee and took his sister's hands up in his own. "I find that the comforts of home are not so readily available to me elsewhere. It is perhaps my own fault, for I have not found a woman that lives up to the ideal I have cultivated in my head from a very early age. Most boys come into manhood of their own right. My rite of passage, on the other hand, was cunningly coaxed away from me in some perverse circle of Hell in which one should hope we will never reside together."

He looked upon her face to find tears streaming down her cheeks. He should wipe them away for her, but he could not will his thumbs to do the job. Placing his head in her lap with the cowardice he so despised in others, he continued his defense as she smoothed back his hair.

"Do you remember the Countess of Pforta of whom I spoke so venomously? She was an accomplished adulteress, a temptress, a Jezebel for the ages. It was she that instructed me in the ways of debauchery and depravity, stealing into my room at night to lash out in frustration. With each punishing visit, I grew as angry as her flesh, devoid of any notion that there can be beauty in sexual congress. All that remained was a helpless boy flushed with humiliation in confrontation with a siren's mocking laughter." He raised his head for another glimpse of his sister's face. "I'll not let you be judged a siren, Lizzie. You are too pure beneath your experience."

He lowered his head back onto her lap. "I decided in the wake of that episode, that I'd not be so disillusioned again. Love is a Christian lie devised to give even the lowest among us a glimmer of false hope. Prostitutes, you see, have no need of a lie. They despise my lustful needs, but still they take my coin. For they worship at the altar of Truth. And so shall we, my love. And so shall we."

Friedrich stood to offer Elisabeth his hand so that she may rise with him. Turning about he led her along as he strode out of the study. From her position behind him, she heard him mumble something that sounded very much like "Pray that your God may achieve his goal."

Truth held firm as Friedrich wished his sister goodnight upon delivering her to her bedroom door.

o o o

CHAPTER VII

∞

Does God choose victors in war, I wonder? When all is said and done, will we find him behind the thin veil of the horizon that shrouds him from enemy fire? Who's to say that there will not come a day when the horizons shoot up in flames so great that not even the Holiest On High will be able to ignore the stench of humanity's hubris?

∞

As spring came to a close, impending war hung heavy in the skies. A military man by virtue of a long history of family service, Karl von Gersdorff was one of the first of the friends to be called up to the Prussian border with Saxony, from which Von Moltke planned to march forward into Bohemia.

Under State obligation to put in a year's service for the Prussian army, Friedrich originally thought to join his friend's regiment, but was turned away due to increasingly poor health. In addition to the migraines he suffered regularly, his vision grew increasingly poorer and he developed a stomach ailment that he often referred to as a canker upon his being. As a result, he was placed on a list for future duty with a field artillery battalion, though Friedrich would never experience actual war-time service. The war that began on June 14, 1866, was over within just six weeks, owing to Prussia's speedy railway system and procurement of advanced armaments of breach loading Dreyse needle guns, capable of firing off five or more shots before reloading.

His inability to serve on the front lines was a sore point for Friedrich, particularly as he watched Gersdorff bask in Elisabeth's adoration. No matter; the two would be back at Leipzig in the fall, leaving Elisabeth far removed from the captain's charms. Gersdorff, however, was in no hurry to depart Naumburg, giving Friedrich little choice but to head on without him. For Friedrich to hang around to witness what would surely be a courtship would only lead to him making a pathetic ass of himself, particularly since Elisabeth seemed to anticipate it so.

Elisabeth was not disappointed in her expectations of the future Baron von Gersdorff. The soldier's regiment remained in Naumburg for several months, affording Elisabeth the opportunity to be presented at the Officer's Club on the handsome captain's arm. Fleetingly, she wondered where Peter had faded too. Perhaps he, too, was back at Leipzig? She would make inquiry later. For now she was the center of attention for every roving eye in a room full of soldiers. She peeked up at Gersdorff, who was smiling down at her in a seductive sort of manner. This was a man of the world; a beautiful specimen that exuded confidence, control, command, and . . . perhaps a little chaos? She felt the pull of challenge as surely as she felt the tug of his physical needs. She could love this man, could she not? *Truth.* No, there was only one man she would ever love, and he was forbidden her. Still, she must settle in with someone, and there was none so pleasing to the eye as Karl von Gersdorff with his dark hair, determined blue eyes, and aristocratic bearing.

Elisabeth could not remember when she had enjoyed an evening so much. The officers were exuberant in their victory: dancing, singing, and toasting Mother Prussia well into the wee hours of the morning. Her mother would be furious at her long absence, but she could not bring herself to care. Though her well-worn grey slippers still pinched at her feet, her new white taffeta dress, trimmed at the collar, waist, and hem in black and grey silk gave her the confidence of a swan, gliding effortlessly across glassy waters. Every eye that lit up at her appearance formed a composite of what she imagined Friedrich's gaze would reflect had he been present to see her clad in his gift.

At the conclusion of one final dance, Gersdorff led his companion to a table for a drink to close out the evening. "Your eyes have been alight with another this evening, Miss Nietzsche. I wager it's Peter Gast who occupies your thoughts, no?"

Taken off guard by Gersdorff's observation Elisabeth feared her mouth may have gaped in a manner that would have sent the Countess Ross into a fit of the vapors. "You could not be more wrong, Captain," she protested as she reached across the table to cover his hand with her own. "I have had such a lovely evening I can assure you there has been no room for thoughts of another in my head." She hoped he interpreted her ruminations to be of him. Indeed, why on earth would they not be? Surely he knew what a catch he was. There was certainly not a woman in the room with a doubt on that score.

Before further words could be spoken, a soldier to whom she had yet to be introduced pulled a chair up and sat uninvited at their table.

"Captain!" the soldier exclaimed, proffering a salute, as if it had just occurred to him that his commanding officer was in attendance this evening.

Gersdorff acknowledged the soldier with a nod. "Corporal Ziegler, is it?"

"Indeed, Captain, indeed! I could not help but come over and pay homage to one of the heralded heroes of the Battle of Gitschin."

A sycophant, then. Elisabeth took his measure.

"I assure you, Corporal. There are many others far more worthy of your admiration," Gersdorff rejoined.

"Nonsense, sir! Made the Austrians turn tail and run, you did. Now if only the scourge of the Jude could be so exterminated." The corporal shook his head, oblivious to the icy daggers of displeasure darting from Elisabeth's eyes. "They are like leeches bleeding the German as dry as Christ's veins. Eventually, we will have to heed the call of our Savior who has deemed it Prussia's role to fortify the Nordic race against the Semitic pestilence that threatens to expunge Christian warriors."

Elisabeth could bear no more. "If you'll forgive me, Captain, I believe my mother awaits my return," she brusquely stated.

Gersdorff stood abruptly, the legs of his chair scraping against the very floor he'd like to mop clean with Ziegler's face. "Of course, Miss Nietzsche. Let us be on our way." In the corporal's direction, Gersdorff shot a forbidding glance that could surely bring an entire battalion to its knees in surrender.

The night air was breezy as Elisabeth and Gersdorff strolled arm and arm towards home. "I dreamed one night that I gave birth to a Jew," Elisabeth blurted out *apropos* of nothing. She continued at the urging of her companion's raised brow. Was that amusement or aversion? Friedrich was right; here was a tough nut to crack.

"Friedrich says that dreams breathe metaphysics into the cosmos. In my own experience, during the state of slumber the soul separates from the body, obtaining certain transcendence beyond earthly horizons . . . into the heavens, I suppose. Have you ever awoken to realize that you have seen a better world?" Elisabeth brushed a lock of breeze-blown hair away from her eyes so that she may better see the reaction on Gersdorff's face to this incredibly self-revealing, and self-incriminating, disclosure to something she had never admitted even to herself. What demon was this that possessed her tongue? It would not cease its prattling. "I have seen a foreign sphere. In my subconscious, I mean." She placed two fingers over her lips.

Noting the gesture, Gersdorff could not determine if it was done in thought or an attempt to silence herself. If it were the latter, she had lost the battle.

"It's not a nightmare, nor is it exactly a dream. It's more like a frightening entity that perhaps has something wonderful to reveal to me."

"Mayhap," Gersdorff finally put in. Clearly she had imbibed too much this evening.

As if reading his thoughts, Elisabeth rushed to her own defense. "I have confounded you, I fear. Surely, you have divined that I hang on my brother's every word. For goodness' sake, I even *dream* his word!" She laughed aloud at the absurdity of it all.

Precipitating all of this was a question, I believe?" Gersdorff prodded.

"Indeed," she breathed out quietly as if making a final determination as to whether or not she was brave enough to pose such a question. "Would it be so bad? A world where Gentiles and Jews are allowed to love one another?"

Chagrin crept in on Gersdorff's mien. "I fear it would in our time. Not even your radically fair-minded brother would countenance the direction of your metaphysical pursuit. Why, think you, has Peter Gast not been one among your company since the spring?"

Elisabeth placed a hand over her chest, gasping for the breath Betrayal had just banished from her bosom. "Friedrich? Friedrich has warned off Peter?" She awaited a response from Gersdorff's silent profile before raising her voice another octave. "What right has he? How could he dare?" *I'll not let you be judged a siren, Lizzie.* She snapped her mouth closed. She was being unfair in asking her companion to provide the answer that she already knew to be true. She placed a comforting hand on his forearm, as they approached her door. "Forgive me. I am out of sorts and have made you uncomfortable with my entire discussion this evening. I wouldn't blame you if you decided never to speak to me again."

She raised her eyes to Gersdorff's as he leaned in close to her face, their lips but a fraction apart. He stood hovering just above her as if suspended in time and then placed a gentle kiss to the corner of her mouth. "And I wouldn't blame you if you decided to break whatever mysterious hold your brother has on you that he should control your every thought."

∘ ∘ ∘

Nothing could have prepared Elisabeth for the shock she received not a month after her outing with Gersdorff. The afternoon's kaffeeklatsch brought an unwelcome surprise in the form of Hadassah Dahlberg on Peter Gast's arm. Elisabeth choked on the sip of coffee she had just taken as the couple entered the room to greet her and the Huffstetler sisters in turn. Recouping her manners, she quickly placed her mug atop its saucer, a clattering sound betraying her trembling hand. She stood to place a kiss of welcome on Hadassah's cheek and then turned in Peter's direction to do the same. A long-held practice that usually came so natural failed her in this moment as her lips checked themselves midair just an inch from Peter's proffered cheek. Too late: not an eye in the room missed her hesitation, nor did the sound of a thin air kiss escape a single ear.

"Well, please sit and join us." Their hostess carried on in the unperturbed manner that always did her mother proud. As Hadassah and Peter took their seats, there was a long silence that screamed of awkwardness until Elisabeth moved forward to pour their coffee. "Where have the two of you been keeping yourselves of late?" she queried a bit too jauntily.

Peter was the first to speak. "Miss Dahlberg's family was kind enough to invite me to take in a bit of country air with them on Lake Geneva."

"I see." Elisabeth inclined her head with laudable equanimity. "And what did you find there, darling?" This posed to Hadassah.

Hadassah bit back a smile as she looked upon Peter with veneration unmasked and innocent. "Peter! I found Peter!" She beamed as an irrepressible grin surged forth.

Peter. She called him by his given name.

"And your brother, of course," Hadassah added. "We had such a lovely time, the three of us. As usual, dear Lizzie, he could do nothing but sing your praises."

"Miss Nietzsche," Peter broke in hesitantly.

Ah, she had been thrown over, then.

"I hope you will be the first to congratulate us on our engagement. Hadassah and I are to be married in the winter."

Elisabeth's mind screamed "Judas!" as her lips offered felicitations. "How wonderful for you both! I cannot think of a more suited match. Mother will be beside herself with delight," she assured before leveling a gaze devoid of emotion at her betrayer. "And how did you find my brother, Mr. Gast?"

"Unbending as ever, Miss Nietzsche. I fear your brother will forever be a provocateur by design, and a contrarian by nature."

The expression on Elisabeth's face was unreadable. "I see. Well, perhaps he will grace us with his presence now that his fall holiday is approaching."

"Will my presence be equally as welcome?" came a voice from the parlor door.

"Captain!" Elisabeth leapt from her chair with renewed enthusiasm to make her way over to the newly arrived Gersdorff, her lips readily connecting with his cheek. Here was her salvation, a god-like figure composed of promises and new horizons.

o o o

CHAPTER VIII

∞

I have heard Dante tell of nine circles of hell, and wonder to which inferno I shall be consigned. But, never mind — to live is to burn. Is this world not scourge enough for the wanderer?

∞

Fall 1866

The sting of having been betrayed at the hands of the Antichrist consumed Elisabeth in the months that followed the news of Peter's engagement, and so it was with a tangible chill that Friedrich and Peter were received in Naumburg during their break from fall classes. On their first evening home, Elisabeth had prepared an elaborate *abendbrot* of dumplings, asparagus, curried sausage, and Bavarian crème. She was quite accomplished at the age of twenty, a fact that left Franziska at a complete loss as to why her daughter had yet to marry. Particularly perplexing was the fact that Elisabeth had not yet brought Captain Gersdorff up to scratch.

Forks clicked against plates as the table's occupants sat uncomfortable with failed attempts at contrived conversation. For herself, Elisabeth dared not speak for she knew that delicately harnessed venom would escape her lips. Friedrich noted her struggle and knew well her efforts would fail her once they were alone.

"What do you hear of Gersdorff, Lizzie?" Friedrich ignored the pained expression on Peter's face, concentrating instead on Elisabeth's stilted response.

"I find him quite well, brother. He is to join us for a picnic in the park tomorrow. The leaves are at their height of color. It would be a shame to miss seeing them."

"Then we shall all be there," cut in Peter.

Elisabeth looked him over with something akin to disdain, her nose crinkling up as if assaulted by the foulest of odors. "Very well, Mr. Gast." She nodded curtly. "Will your fiancée be joining us?"

"I'm afraid other obligations demand her attention," he replied hesitantly, for they both knew Hadassah's "obligation" was to remain far from Elisabeth's sight.

"I'm sorry to hear it." More disingenuous words were never spoken, but none dared admit they discerned such. "If you gentlemen have finished your dinner," she said, changing the course of conversation rather brusquely, "Mother and I will leave you to your port."

Both men moved to stand as the women rose from their seats, only to be immobilized by the flat of Elisabeth's raised palm. "Please." A word of entreaty that only Elisabeth could make sound a command not to be brooked. "Don't trouble yourselves." With that she whisked out of the room, her skirts as dark as her mood, rustling behind her.

Peter remained at the table with Friedrich just long enough to be polite before pleading exhaustion and a desire to retire for the evening. The friends having wished each other a pleasant evening, Peter turned to exit the room only to hear Friedrich's voice calling behind him. "You'll find her in my study. Five minutes, and best leave the door open." Peter gave a sharp nod without looking back.

And, of course, she was exactly where Friedrich said she could be found, curled up in her brother's chair and reading by the fire. Was that cigarette smoke rising around her? Had America's up-and-rising Bull Durham infiltrated every household in Germania? Peter went unnoticed for a few moments as he leaned against the doorframe and looked forlornly at the woman whose heart he was forbidden to hold or even contemplate. He knew the moment that she sensed his presence, though she did not immediately show her hand. Hell and damnation! He knew better than to think she would ever acknowledge him again, but he could not let it rest like this. He moved forward into the room.

"Elisabeth, please don't let us end like this," he implored. A mistake, he knew. Here was a woman who would never tolerate weakness. She could have made him a better man.

"I'm sure I don't know what you mean, Mr. Gast," she said as she nonchalantly tapped out her cigarette and flipped through the pages of her book. "I believe our association came to an end with the first and only breath of your heir. God is merciful, is he not?"

"Please don't speak so," he implored, coming down on his knees beside her chair.

"In what way do I speak? As one lacking in virtue, perhaps?" She raised a calculating eyebrow at him. So like her brother. "You forget that I fear nothing, darling." Her tone of cool disdain left no doubt that he was anything but her "darling." Such endearments would rightfully be bestowed on Gersdorff now, and he knew that they would be well received.

"Please do get off the floor, Mr. Gast. You embarrass yourself."

Peter watched dumbly from his position on the floor as Elisabeth sighed in resignation, snapped her book closed, and rose to make her exit. "Very well, then. I shall go," she declared, leaving him to stare mutely at the door that slammed behind her.

Peace was not to be found in her bedroom, either. She dropped her forehead into the palm of her right hand when she heard her brother creak open the door and approach the bed where she sat propped up by pillows, trying once again to read. Before she could snap the book closed, her brother carefully took it up in hand and gently closed it for her.

"Do be careful, Lizzie. The books do not deserve your abuse," he chided a little too patronizingly. It grated on her nerves.

"Ah, but perhaps you do, Friedrich!" she countered as she climbed off the bed and slammed a pillow into his stomach before turning toward a window as if she just might fling it open and flee into the night sky. She took in a deep breath. "You were spying," she accused.

Friedrich approached and encircled her waist with his arms pulling her back against the wall of his chest. "It is not spying to look out for my sister's best interests," he whispered into her ear.

"And is entering your sister's bedroom at night clad only in a robe in my best interest?"

"Lizzie," he murmured. "We do nothing wrong."

"You tell yourself that, Friedrich, and whatever master you answer to! Tell him! Tell him that you consign your sister to Hell with your every deed. Your every word . . . your every breath," she finished on a sob.

Friedrich turned her about and gathered her close to him. He planted his nose in her hair and strove to regulate his breathing. "Lizzie. Lizzie, please don't be angry," he supplicated. "You deserve so much better than Gast. He is no match for your beauty, for your perspicacity, your tenacity." He rubbed his cheek against her hair. "For your vivacity." He lifted a lock and brought it to his lips before allowing the strands to slip like silk through his fingers. "You can't possibly feel for him."

Elisabeth's eyes crackled with fire as her hand came across his face. There was a moment of intense astonishment, as if she had shocked not only him but herself as well. She pulled her hand back and examined it like a foreign object before balling it into a fist and pounding it relentlessly against his chest. His hand flew up, encircling her wrist, stilling the fist that he now held to his chest like a lame chick in need of tender care. She stared mutely at the offending appendage and then drew it back from his grasp. "Why won't you let me be?" she asked through angry, clenched teeth.

"Lizzie, I cannot let be what haunts me day and night. You are my responsibility and I will see to it that you marry a man worthy of you."

"You once thought Peter worthy of me. Is this to be my penance? Is it because I love him that you would deny me happiness?"

"*Nien*, I would grant you every happiness, my love." Friedrich ran his hand through his hair as he turned away from her only to whip back around to face her again. "You cannot possibly love him." As if staving off a demon, he grasped Elisabeth by the upper arms and gave her a shake. "For God's sake, he could not even keep your brother at bay!"

"It is I who cannot keep my brother at bay," she spat back. "Clearly I do not love myself enough to be worthy of another's love."

At that Friedrich yanked her forward and kissed her as no other lover would. Tears sprung from her eyes and streamed down her cheeks, but he kissed her still. It wasn't until he wrenched his lips from hers that she realized she had been kissing him back. And then it came, the familiar feeling of fading to black just when she should be drowning in light. Or so she imagined it should be.

° ° °

CHAPTER IX

∞

Does God hold Abraham in contempt for coveting and congressing with his sister, Sarah? Is not Israel innocent of his incestuous birth? In His Afterlife, he would conjure up the Centurion and order him to battle forth unto Truth.

∞

In a state of slumberous confusion, Elisabeth shot up in her bed and looked about for the specter that alarmed her so. Skulking about in her recollection was not darkness, but a beaming flood of memories she knew she should suppress even as she perversely struggled to call them forth. One ragged breath had followed another, unbound and liberated with the loosening of the ties on her gown. The silken glide of the material as it trailed down her calves to pool at her ankles. The forbidden, yet freeing, touch of Friedrich's hands upon her bared skin.

Mother of God! She could not deny the one who possessed her body and soul. Here, too, was a dream, an illusion of inexperience that was not hers to claim. She would never bring him to heel by fueling his debauchery. Denial was what this dilemma required. If, as Friedrich proclaimed, joylessness was indeed the mother of dissipation, then she must deny him this quest for degeneracy. If left up to him, he would see them both damned.

A knock at her bedroom door broke her reverie. She had not granted permission to enter, yet her mother poked her head around the door and peered askance at her. "Elisabeth, darling, why are you still abed? Breakfast is well beyond over, and all await your presence for a walk into the park ahead of today's picnic. Captain Gersdorff, I believe, is particularly interested in taking a turn about the nature trail with you."

It never ceased to amaze Elisabeth how easily her mother could interpret another's intentions to suit her own purposes. The captain, she knew, would never express an interest of any sort. It was not for others to know where his interests lie. If he had a particular want, he would simply command its fulfillment, and would certainly not request leave to do so.

Elisabeth blew out a breath of resignation as she reluctantly peeled off her covers and rose to dress.

∘ ∘ ∘

She could see in his eyes that he hated her this day. Never mind that it was he who came to her room, and he who initiated their lovemaking; she would always be the flagellant fiend in this familial farce. Elisabeth smiled ruthlessly as she held her brother's eyes with a scrutiny that dared him to look away. She pinned him in place long enough to let him know she was dangerously in control of herself. As if on demand, Friedrich's eyes followed hers as they traveled to alight on Gersdorff. In that moment, he had no doubt she would take up the mantle of Masochism if he wished it. Aware to the split second of the instant in which her brother had arrived at this conclusion, Elisabeth turned a dying leaf over as she drifted in Gersdorff's direction.

In the wake of such a blow to his self-conscience, Friedrich could have done without Peter's sudden presence at his side. "And how does Gersdorff fare in your estimation? Is he Aryan enough for you?"

"You are unjust, Gast!" snapped out Friedrich. "You know full well your Jewish birth has nothing to do with my objections to you making a match with Elisabeth."

"Yes, yes. Christ the crucified Jew and all that . . ." Peter waved his hand about regally in a sign that could be construed as either devotion to or dismissal of Friedrich's professed commitment to all things contemptible. "Do you know what I believe — nay, what I know, Nietzsche? Elisabeth is stronger than your will." Peter inclined his head, indicating the spot where Elisabeth now stood in intimate conversation with Gersdorff. "Gersdorff's too, for that matter."

"I would take it even further," Friedrich countered, "and venture so far as to freely admit that the captain would never even consider acquiescing to me, no matter how hard I might will it."

Peter laughed aloud at what must have been a joke known only to him. "What perverse philosophy is this, old friend?" he taunted with a foe's ferocity. "Have you not sorcery enough to vanquish the bastion of Prussian pride? Just look at him." Friedrich's eyes involuntarily followed Peter's chin as it jerked in Gersdorff's direction, opening the door for Peter to press his advantage. "There stands before us a citadel of sexuality, exuding all of the vitality that Elisabeth possesses and all of that which you shall never have." His goading was merciless, as his tone lowered to an ominous jeer. "I believe you once convinced me that there is melancholy in everything completed. Yet I cannot bring myself to express sadness for that which you currently find yourself in loss of."

A silence fell between them. One watched in triumph and the other in misery as Elisabeth and her officer disappeared behind the foliage of nature untainted.

Once out of sight, Gersdorff pulled Elisabeth up short. "What game do you play with your brother, Miss Nietzsche? His eyes follow every tilt of your head, every flutter of your hands, every turn of your shoulders, every movement of your lips. Would you have me believe you are oblivious to his jealous scorn?"

Gersdorff pulled her full against his chest so that she had to incline her head even further to meet his gaze. There was an intense silence between them as he peered into her eyes as if probing her soul. "No, I think not," he finally whispered. "For he is Phthonos to your Nemesis." A silent laugh escaped him, trailing on an expelled breath of inevitability. "Poor sot."

Elisabeth swatted his chest playfully. "Do stop carrying on so, Captain. You know my brother well enough to understand that he is generally envious of everything: envious of mortality, immortality, the cosmos, the Creator, and all creation. He's trapped in a paradoxical web of his own design." She lowered her voice in mock imitation of her brother. "'Is man merely a mistake of God's? Or God merely a mistake of man's?' He has yet to find an answer, you see, and so he covets all that he cannot have, convinced that there lay the key to eternity."

Gersdorff bowed in deference to her. "So poetic, madam. I dare say you have succeeded in making me begrudge the god of jealousy his affliction." He gently cupped Elisabeth's right cheek in the palm of his hand, tracing the curve of her jaw with his thumb. "I would deny him his Hera."

Any other woman would likely have stood powerless and mute in the wake of such a mesmerizing declaration. Elisabeth, on the other hand, found courage in such circumstances. Ever ready to seize the moment, she pulled him downward for a kiss, while simultaneously rising on her toes to meet him halfway. She immediately regretted it and mentally cursed herself. A rare opportunity for genuine romance was lost to her, snatched away by her own precipitous hand. But then again, Fate was a feckless friend in want of a steadfast companion.

His kiss left her breathless and lightheaded. He did not touch her heart as Peter had, but the more time they spent in each other's company, she grew increasingly confident that he would prove to be the lover she desperately needed to set straight her world that was quickly spinning out of control.

She was fiercely weary of having matters of import forced upon her, only to be berated for actually taking them in hand. There was the matter of Friedrich's finances, which neither mother nor brother could properly manage. *Why has Elisabeth taken to managing my funds?* Friedrich had recently demanded of his mother. And then to Elisabeth herself: *I must marry you off, Lizzie. You torture me so.* Only to be contradicted later with: *You cannot possibly love him. He is not good enough for you!* Elisabeth huffed in frustration. There was no hope for it. She must take control of her own life.

"Cut line, Elisabeth. Where are your thoughts?"

She admired his forthrightness. "My thoughts," she responded hesitantly, "linger on the fine military officer who just uttered my Christian name. Indeed, my thoughts are at war. Should I rebuke you? Should I respond in kind, *Karl*? Should I presume it was an innocent slip of your tongue, or do you possess the tongue of a serpent?"

"Oh, most definitely a serpent's tongue. But it is guilty only of responding to the song of the siren," he rejoined huskily.

I'll not let you be judged a siren, Lizzie. "Then you must heed the call!" she declared with a triumphant laugh.

○ ○ ○

CHAPTER X

∞

Sand: a fool's parable. It shifts under the waves, sifts by the hour, guards the wellspring of life, and preserves the imprinted path to salvation. The Wanderer spreads it asunder on the soles of his sandal. The Lurking Lover leaves a telltale trail in the shadows that provide cover for his slippers. The Soldier's boot packs it tight for the ages as he marches along the path to war.

∞

Naumburg 1867

Elisabeth sat in stoic attendance at the wedding of Peter Gast and Hadassah Dahlberg, the observance of each ritual pushing her closer to the brink of something she could not quite name. Self-loathing? Possibly. Fury? Definitely. Betrayal? Most certainly. Hatred? She would not give them the satisfaction. She was grateful for Gersdorff's presence at her side through this unbearable ordeal, his solid poise a testament to the strength of will that begets self-empowerment, a defense mechanism that would serve her well in the years ahead.

In keeping with Jewish tradition, a chuppa had been erected under the star-studded heavens, whence Abraham winked his approval of the couple's union. The groom entered the canopy first, followed by the bride, who then circled him seven times as he prayed. Elisabeth imagined Hadassah circling Peter exactly thus during that fateful visit to Lake Geneva. Like a vulture, the Jewess had set designs on the one honorable man Elisabeth had given her heart to. And Peter had fallen like easy prey, as inconstant as any other of his sex, ruled by his virility, only to discover himself ultimately unmanned. Having once worshipped him, Elisabeth now reviled him, as one might a eunuch.

It *was* hatred, after all, that shattered her heart like the broken shards of glass that Peter ceremonially stamped beneath his foot. It was hatred that drained the remnants of warm blood from her fast chilling veins, as the bride and groom sipped tepid wine from a sacred cup. It was hatred that flooded her eyes when Peter placed the band of promise on his bride's finger. The spiteful ring flashed a spectrum of gaudy golden rays, a daring display of wealth and dominance in defiance of the darkness.

Her mother had been right. Underneath his Prussian attire, Peter Gast would never shed the blight of Heinrich Köselitz. Hadassah would absorb Peter, perpetuate the curse upon his house, and he would spare no thought for the gypsy child, lying dead in an unmarked grave to which not even its mother could provide direction.

Elisabeth shook away her dreary thoughts. The wedding had long passed and—with Friedrich's return home and her birthday just several weeks away—she had more important matters that required her attention. Friedrich's stay would be lengthy, as he had finally been called up for his year of military service, assigned to a field artillery unit stationed just within miles of their home in Naumburg, allowing him to remain in residence with his family.

Her birthday was an event she would have preferred to let pass without notice. At the age of 21, she would be considered quite on the shelf. There was no proposal forthcoming from Gersdorff, and she had to admit that she admired him for it. Indeed, she may very well have grown to despise him had he been so weak as to bend to her mother's less-than-subtle insistences. In the same vain, she would have despised him still more had he buckled under Friedrich's blustering demands that he make his intentions known or abandon court of his sister. Where her family fretted, the usually calm Aunt Rosalie among their number, Elisabeth reveled in the freedom of uncertainty. She would not push the captain because she preferred to remain ignorant of Fate's finagling. For once, she would not interfere.

Besides, what need had she of Gersdorff's hand when she possessed the entirety of his body? Could there be any stronger declaration of love? A brief image of Peter crossed her mind, followed by that of Friedrich. Both were just as quickly dismissed. And then another thought occurred to her: Did she love Gersdorff? She had given him her body, so surely she must love him. She feared that perhaps she did not, which may have been the true reason she was not interested in his intentions, for she did not know her own.

Friedrich escorted Aunt Rosalie, who had been rusticating in Pobles as of late, back to Naumburg so that she may take up company with the Nietzsches for the summer. Elisabeth was thrilled to see the woman who had been more of a mother to her than Franziska had ever attempted to be. It was Rosalie who saw the pall in Elisabeth's eyes after Gustav had doused her innocence and disillusioned her of romantic expectations; hopes she thought Peter had restored to her. But no, Gustav had been truthful in word and deed. In helping Elisabeth dispose of her lilac gown, Aunt Rosalie made no attempt to dispel the moral of Gustav's cruel tale, and her niece loved her all the more for it. Friedrich, on the other hand, seemed to be somewhat cautious of Aunt Rosalie, a stance that Elisabeth found perplexing given that she knew just how much her brother revered their aunt.

When last they saw one another, they had parted in anger, Elisabeth and Friedrich, and so it was with an anguished relief in the hearts of both when their reunion proved to be one of forgiveness and unspoken understanding. Theirs was a bond tested by time and tempests. Friedrich often likened them to souls adrift in an angry sea, upon which panicked resistance would only encourage the waves to swallow them up and drown them within their murky, sandy, depths. Elisabeth laughed mockingly at herself. Sinking, suffering and suffocating. That was to be their lot in life, for she knew neither would ever throw the other a line.

"Let me guess."

Elisabeth sat at her vanity, yanking her brush through her tangled curls as she attempted to dress for dinner. At the sound of Friedrich's voice she turned her attention to his reflection in the mirror as he approached her and laid his hands on the back of her bare shoulders. So careful was his touch, one might think he was stroking a skittish kitten. "You are wondering if Gersdorff will be among our guests at dinner tonight," he whispered close to her ear, his breath hot on her neck.

She closed her eyes, enjoying his caress, and then, remembering her state of undress, immediately pushed his hands away and rose from her perch. "I wonder no such thing, and you should not have entered my chamber without knocking." Elisabeth lifted her dinner gown from her bed and pulled it over her head. Where she was once able to step into her dresses, she found that she could no longer pull her gown over the hips that had mercifully failed her in childbirth.

Friedrich turned her around, his fingers deftly working the buttons at the back of her dress. "Had I not entered, who would have helped you with your toilette?" He lifted her heavy tresses. "And who would help you tame this unholy mass?" Elisabeth could not help but laugh as her brother snatched an ivory comb from her dresser and clipped her hair atop her head in what could only be described as a mangled mess. "Behold, the height of fashion," he teased. How could she stay aloof from the only one who knew how to disarm her so?

She patted her hair in mock appreciation. "It will have to do," she sighed as she offered her arm to her brother. Their roles reversed, she escorted him to the dining room and pulled out his chair for him, the two of them nodding solemnly as Aunt Rosalie admonished them for their antics. Duly scolded, Elisabeth's mirthful eyes caught Friedrich's. He shrugged his shoulders at her in response and the two laughed aloud.

"What has gotten into you two children?" Aunt Rosalie demanded.

"War, Aunt Rosalie. War."

Gersdorff, who had indeed taken up this invitation to dine, noticed that Elisabeth, too, had formulated a retort but was beaten to the punch by her brother's response. He dearly would like to have known what her answer would have been. There was something about the silent exchanges between brother and sister that gave the lie to war.

"And what humor, pray tell, do you find in war?" Rosalie asked chidingly.

"It is not in war that we find humor," Elisabeth rejoined. "The humor of it all, you see, is in our Friedrich being called up to cut a fine figure on a fine horse so that our countrymen may puff their chests out in patriotic pride. The joke is on Friedrich, of course! Called forth to serve as a symbol for all that he finds repugnant in our society." Elisabeth lifted her wineglass as if observing the swirl of liquid inside. Only Friedrich caught the mirthful wink of her eye, distorted by the glass through which she peered at him.

Gersdorff dropped his spoon into his now empty soup bowl and ran his napkin over his mouth in preparation to protest. Elisabeth could not help but admire his long fingers and the masculine manner in which he observed even the most basic of etiquette. Good Lord what was wrong with her? She was pining over the way the man wiped his mouth at table. Perhaps she was in love after all.

"No doubt, war is a sorry enterprise." Gersdorff's voice recalled her attention. "And, no doubt, pomp and pride can blind a nation to the dangers of misplaced confidence. But I fear if we do not cultivate unity among the nation states, pride will turn us one against another when it is France we should be weary of, not our compatriots of the German tongue." Realizing he had cast a bit of gloom over the mood of the moment, the captain lightened his tone. "So do us proud with your Prussian seat, Nietzsche!" he finished in a tone of levity, which, from the look on Friedrich's face, clearly had not been received in the same spirit. Dear God, thought Gersdorff as he eyed the empty hourglass that sat atop the wine credenza. It would be a long night.

Of course a full bottle of port had been brought to the table after dinner, and, of course, Friedrich expected the two of them to chat until the last drop had been poured.

"I will take your presence here tonight, Gersdorff, as an indication that you have come to some sort of decision about my sister." Friedrich eyed the other man in a manner that confirmed there was only one answer he would accept to this challenge.

Never one to flee a challenge, and never one to be bullied, the military veteran held his own. "I tell you what, Nietzsche, why don't you tell me what your intentions toward your sister are? And then we'll determine whether or not there is room for me in this equation."

Friedrich had all but lurched across the table before Gersdorff reached over to stay him by the shoulder. "Stand down, friend. I mean only to say that I know the two of you are very close, but you must know me well enough to understand that I will not place myself in a relationship in which a gauntlet is repeatedly thrown at my feet. I would marry her, but I will not wed you both."

Friedrich considered his port glass as he turned it about atop the table. "Already, I take issue," he smirked. "You speak of gauntlets and you assume that I will be the one casting them. How well do you know Elisabeth?"

Having just placed a cigarette in his mouth, Gersdorff lit it up and blew out a long stream of smoke before responding. "I know Elisabeth so well that I can tell you a challenge from her is always welcome. You, however, will find that our friendship will not survive repeated interferences. I don't need your permission to ask for her hand, but I would like it all the same."

Friedrich rose from the table and offered his hand in a conciliatory spirit. "Let me speak with Lizzie and I will notify you of my answer before the week is out."

The two men shook hands and, as Friedrich headed for the door, Gersdorff made his way over to the hourglass that had annoyed him all evening and turned it over. He stood mesmerized for some time thereafter, lost in consideration of The Jewish Question as he watched the sand fall through the narrow passage that demarked one point in time from the next.

○ ○ ○

It had been awhile since Elisabeth had been trapped in this scene. She had thought the episodes were a thing of the past.

Yet here she wandered, suspended in an ethereal existence that she could not speak of to anyone. Little did it matter, for it was an experience beyond description. All the world would condemn her as mad if she were to speak of it; all, that is, except Aunt Rosalie who had listened patiently each time her niece tried and failed to put into words what tormented her mind and soul.

Elisabeth could not pinpoint to where her subconscious had taken her so that it may deprive her another night's sleep. For her, there would never be peace in slumber again, only an endless, arduous slog towards something beyond her control, something that her being compulsively flocked to even as terror formed in beads on her skin. No, she would not fall prey to the menace of her memories. She would call out for help. Why wouldn't her lips move? Why would not her voice call out? Because Gustav would rob her of her will again and again. Because she would never revive Peter's promise. Her eyes flew open. Because Friedrich's lips were pressed against hers, gently shushing her as sobs she would not have recognized as her own betrayed Night's sacred trust.

When he was certain that he had succeeded in calming her, Friedrich rolled back to Elisabeth's side. Propped up on his elbow, he rested his head in hand and smiled down at her. "You have always been prone to nightmares, my love, but never one as fearsome as this. What torments you, Lizzie?" He tapped the tip of her nose with his index finger. "Tell me and I shall make it go away."

Elisabeth propped herself up to face him at eye level. "Can you match Moses' feat in parting the Red Sea? Can you command a lilac haze to disband?" She looked on in trepidation as Friedrich scanned her face, searching for some indication of a jest. He thought her mad, she knew. And perhaps she was, but she would not bear it alone any longer. She shook her head at him. His response was too long in coming. "No," she whispered an answer for him. "Innocence lost cannot be restored."

Friedrich lowered his face to the crook of her neck and nuzzled his nose against the soft skin he found there, breathing deeply of her scent. "You are all innocence, Lizzie. What transpires between us is my fault and my sin to repent. But I am mortal, am I not? Like Peter, I hear the cock crow, but remain in denial." He leaned forward and his lips lingered on hers in what may well have been a kiss for all eternity.

"Lizzie, I have a question to ask you." His usually self-assured voice was oddly reluctant after their lips parted. He took up her hand and caressed her palm with his thumb. "Do you love Gersdorff?"

Elisabeth shot to an upright position. What a strange turn in conversation for such an intimate moment! "Honestly, Friedrich! Love can be such a hateful word. Its promise is great, but its possibilities rarely see the light of day. The lover lurks at night, no?"

"Not all lovers live in shadows, darling. Gersdorff would have your hand in broad daylight, and I believe him to be worthy of you. Will you accept him?"

Elisabeth looked down at their conjoined hands and then back into her brother's eyes. "If he asks, I will answer him, not you."

It was a fair admonishment, he conceded. This was the moment in which the Lurking Lover would be banished to the shadows to await his verdict in tempo with the sands of time.

○ ○ ○

CHAPTER XI

∞

Does Battle have a vulgar baroness? Does Melancholy have a mistress? Does Prudence have passion?

∞

Elisabeth always preferred Nature in her barren state and felt quite jubilant as October ushered in a much welcome chill that foretold of a harsh winter to come. She regretted that Gersdorff's proposal came a bit too late for planning a winter wedding. Spring it would be, then, which was probably better anyway, as the delay would give her extra time to help Friedrich settle in to his service routine.

He was rather dapper in appearance as he rode off to the barracks in his Prussian uniform: blue coat with red embossed sleeve cuffs over grey trousers that tucked snugly into shiny hessians, and a black-billed white and silver-crested hat. True, he would never have Gersdorff's finesse, but he looked the grand soldier all the same.

Elisabeth breathed a sigh of something close to contentment. If nothing else, Friedrich was *her* grand soldier. Before his departure, he had sworn an oath that he would forever protect her; prevent their indiscretions from ever becoming known to another living soul. She had no idea what the Antichrist would reveal to God, but never would anyone have reason to cast aspersions on Lizzie's character. If there was one thing she knew about her brother, his word was his bond, and he could be trusted wholeheartedly.

On this day, Elisabeth would see Gersdorff off at the train station for his three-hour journey to the Prussian capital of Berlin, where members of the aristocracy were to meet with Bismarck's parliamentary liaisons. Prussian King William I of the House of Hohenzollern had just taken title to the newly created office of president of The North German Confederation. In a show of solidarity with the twenty-two independent German states that comprised the Confederation, William dissolved the Prussian parliament and called for new elections to include German representatives and the formation of the Reichstag. On its face, this legislative body seemed innocuous enough in that it took up issues of universal suffrage for men over 25, common passport and postal systems, and local military regulations. Here was the crux of this specially called meeting: Bismarck had ostensibly appointed himself chancellor of this league that prognosticated the expansion of Prussian power, rousing France's wrath.

It was all well and fine to put soldiers on parade in Naumburg. In Berlin, however, another war was looming, and Elisabeth was anxious about the safety of her affianced, particularly since his heart and mind remained behind with his father who was in failing health. "Karl, do take heart," she coaxed as she lay in his arms, tracing soothing circles across his beautifully sculpted torso. "I promise I will look in on the baron every chance I get, and you must promise to look to your own health while you're away. You will need all of your strength to prepare for our wedding upon your return," she teased.

Gersdorff rose up against his pillow and snuggled her closer to him, placing a kiss in her sweet scented hair. He smiled to himself. Only Elisabeth could fill his bed chamber with lilacs when the stench of impending war lay just beyond the door. "I imagine arranging a wedding to be something akin to battle: life hinging on the positioning of every militiaman, the execution of every maneuver, the acquisition of the spoils of war. That would be you, madam," he whispered into her ear.

Elisabeth swatted his chest playfully. "I take offense! Have you really just reduced me to plunder, Captain?"

Gersdorff chuckled. How he would miss this banter. "Reward, then. A stolen reward, but a victorious prize, nevertheless," he conceded with a tweak to her cheek.

"Stolen?" she queried with one brow raised. "In what way? If you are the victor, then are not you due your reward?"

"That's the rub, you see. We are not always freely given our due, and so I shall stealthily snatch it from the hands of God, if need be, and then place my prized possession before the altar of sacrosanctity."

Giggling, Elisabeth nipped at his neck. "If we are still speaking metaphorically of me, then I must warn you to take care that God does not strike you dead for your impudence. For there is nothing sacrosanct about me, and well He knows it."

○ ○ ○

Friedrich could hardly bear the mundane exercises that filled his days of service: grooming horses, drilling for parades, and preparing for the reserve officers examination. Where his fellow bombardiers in the Fourth Horse Artillery were puffed up with the gallantry of it all, Friedrich was awash with an indignity that rendered him demoralized. How effortlessly blind obedience was cultivated! One need only invest a dazzled citizenry with an eye for fashionable wear, an ear for trumpets tuned for triumph, a nose for the aroma of arrogance, and a two-pronged tongue that beseeches God for guidance in the same breath that it defies His written command to love one another.

He wrote to his sister, Gersdorff, and Rohde without fail every Saturday, the one day of rest afforded to the bombardiers. It was on these days that Friedrich had enough down time to resume his studies and contemplations of Schopenhauer, meditations that Gersdorff appreciated and Elisabeth abhorred. The longer he remained in the Fourth Horse Artillery, the more removed from his nation of birth Friedrich began to feel. Daily, he found himself placed on display to propagate an imperialistic cause he did not believe in for an uninformed multitude who didn't know what to believe. *Will minus intellect constitutes vulgarity*, Friedrich quoted Schopenhauer to his writing correspondents. The question is, he mused, who is more vulgar in this scenario? The oaf taken in by such an elaborate display of ceremony, paid for via levies he can ill afford? Or the extravagantly clad piper, prancing about on a Trojan horse?

Replies varied. Gersdorff shared a similar sentiment, quoting Schopenhauer in return— *Every man mistakes the limits of his own field of vision for the limits of the world.* Surely, once Europe was secured beneath Bismarck's thumb, all the world would revere Prussia as the paradigm for postwar peace.

Elisabeth chose to refrain from engaging her brother in debate, as she grew almost fearful of his ever-increasing blasphemy of God and country. He confided in her that his eyes had been opened in such a way that he was no longer blind to the human condition, a plight of suffering no amount of religious adherence could blight out. Indeed, religion was nothing more than an excuse for individuals to absolve themselves of their moral and ethical obligations to their fellow man with the claim that God would eradicate suffering in His own good time.

Friedrich, who had always loved his country, was growing disenchanted with Bismarck's propaganda campaign that practically formed a religion, portraying the chancellor as the Idol of Man, and Prussian soldiers as his horse-and-pony disciples. His gut was ridden with guilt as he performed his part for the gaping crowd, cordoned off and vying for a better view of the carefully choreographed splendor of a salvation that would never be theirs.

Her brother was disillusioned and so must Elisabeth be. She plodded about that fall season trying to make sense of Friedrich's melancholic moods. Her brother was growing dark, like Prussia herself. Her friends had taken to blaming the Jews for the demoralized tenor clouding their beloved country. The shift, from jubilation in the wake of victory over Austria to vexation over a flagging economy, lent fodder for the perpetuation of anti-Semitism. Though she denounced claims that Jewish tradesmen were secretly colluding to render Prussia a failed state, she couldn't quite eradicate from her memory the image of gold flashing against the night sky. Nonetheless, she would cast her doubts aside; Elisabeth had a wedding to plan.

o o o

The wedding plans came to a halt in December with the expected passing of the Baron von Gersdorff and the unexpected passing of Aunt Rosalie. Friedrich had been given leave to visit Aunt Rosalie on her deathbed, at which time she delivered him quite the shock. She was leaving him a moderate sum of money, accompanied by much-needed advice that she had long meant to impart, but couldn't conjure up the right words to at once bring forth and then forever banish a specter she feared would follow her to the grave.

"Fritz, dear, your heart is as foolish as it is full of love for your sister." Aunt Rosalie held up a hand to forestall her nephew's objections. "Your mother may be blind, but I am not," she continued forthrightly. "I have seen the longing looks between you, masked in love, lust and, at times, loathing. You each long for a lover that God has seen fit to deny you, and He will not be gainsaid."

"I have no god, Aunt Rosalie."

She knew he was sincere in his protest, yet there was something more emphatically cynical underneath this particular proclamation. She placed a finger beneath his chin and raised it so that she may thoroughly scrutinize his determined features. "Don't you?" she queried when satisfied that she had seen his tortured soul. "You would send me to the grave with no hope?"

Friedrich smiled sadly and lifted the back of her hand to his lips. "You would have me live with no hope? I lie awake at night, consumed by Lizzie's anger. How many times have her fingers clenched into fists that wielded enough power to poleax me? Would you have me abandon my soul as it lay prostrate in the palm of her hand, while there is yet happiness to be wrenched from her grasp? What if I am the only one she can hold so dear?"

"She will hold another dear, if you will it. You are confusing rising resentment with the labors of love. Both can be exquisite in their torment," Aunt Rosalie affirmed with a soothing whisper. "I beg of you to put your unnatural passions aside. Allow your sister to move on, and you do the same. There are things that trouble your sister that are beyond your control. For, you see, she has faced off with God in shadows that neither you nor I can navigate. She needs strong arms to hold her securely when her demons taunt her. You have chosen an excellent husband for her in the captain; he will tolerate no nonsense from either of you. Now, you must let her go, no matter what protestations she flings your way. She worships the ground you walk on and will obey your wishes."

"And if I do not wish to relinquish her?" He could not prevent the words from escaping his tongue. Aunt Rosalie was the only person, aside from Elisabeth, he had ever been able to speak honestly with, and here was his last chance to garner her counsel.

"Then may God go with you," she whispered.

○ ○ ○

CHAPTER XII

∞

A sorceress, he calls me. Bar-Jesus, it's indecent!
Set it to music, and we shall see.

∞

Propriety demanded a full year of mourning, and Elisabeth was insistent that it be properly observed. She put away her bright wardrobe and clad herself in black, while Friedrich and Gersdorff each wore black armbands over the upper left sleeves of their uniforms. The wedding had been postponed for at least another year, what with grief to be mollified and arrangements for the wedding still to be made.

Drained of spirit and exhausted of moral fortitude, Elisabeth was filled with antipathy as she endured days that lagged along while she consoled her mother and visitors, in turn. Franziska was truly adrift in a tumultuous sea without her sister-in-law. Bereaved visitors, on the other hand, merely sought appointments to the future Baroness von Gersdorff's inner consulate. Her affianced and her brother would set the world aright again, they assured her. Her Christian charity was an inspiration to them all, they assuaged her. And wouldn't she consider joining their outreach missions to convert or forever cast out the Jews, they appealed to her.

Elisabeth ached with agitation, her good sense blinded by vultures bedecked in gold.

Her distress reached its zenith when word came in March of 1868 that Friedrich was gravely injured after attempting one of the many circus-style stunts assigned by his commanding officers. He had endeavored what the bombardiers referred to as a "smart jump" into a saddle, and had the misfortune of crushing his chest against the pummel. The result was a festering wound from which bone began to protrude. Elisabeth remained by his side day and night, seeing to his every need, so relieved was she that her brother was not lost to her.

After many consultations with the surgeon, Volkmann, Friedrich was declared well enough in the summer months to return to Leipzig, though he would not be able to return to military service, and he would require constant care until he was fully recovered. Thus Elisabeth traveled with him to

Leipzig and took up residence in his quarters at *Elisenstraße 7*, serving as nursemaid and housekeeper.

Where Friedrich's body was weak, his mind was strong, as evidenced by the many ruminations he had Elisabeth pen for him, his unguarded thoughts revealing a side of him she had yet to become acquainted with. "Dear Lizzie," he said as she sat poised at the edge of his bed ready to take notes. "You are most assuredly my Homeric sorceress." Not what she expected to hear. Her head snapped up and she pinned him with questioning eyes, her writing utensil having impressed nothing more than a fine point on her paper.

From his position, lying flat on his back in bed, Friedrich blindly reached out and arrested his sister's immobile hand. Lacing his fingers with hers, he began to lightly swing their adjoined hands back and forth within the confined space that barely separated them. "Can an *ass* be tragic?" he asked. "To perish under a burden one can neither bear nor throw off?" He laughed — at himself or at her, he wasn't sure — as Elisabeth continued to stare at him as if he might be mad. He ceased the pendular motion of their arms, affixed his twinkling troubled eyes on her face, and then brought her trembling fingers to his lips. Did Eli fear being dethroned? He wondered.

"Ah, but a barebacked ass," he continued, "is an idle ass. And is it not the creed of the German that idleness is the beginning of all vices?" He rubbed his thumb gently across the backs of Elisabeth's fingers. *"Increscunt animi, virescit volnere virtus,"* he whispered.

"The spirits increase; vigor grows through a wound." Elisabeth cast her eyes to her brother's bound chest as she murmured the translation.

Friedrich pulled her forward and down toward him until her lips hovered just above his. In an action that she was powerless to stop, their lips met, drawn together by some pulling force that Friedrich seized in plundering abandon. Elisabeth whimpered as he placed a hand on each side of her face to hold her still. Perhaps he *was* mad, but he could not pull himself away. Aunt Rosalie's admonishments rang in his ears: *God has seen fit to deny you. You are confusing rising resentment with the labors of love . . . exquisite torture.* He felt Elisabeth's fingers clenching his wrists in an attempt to reject him, but still he refused to relent. *May God go with you.*

Finally, he turned his head away, his breathing erratic, his breath heated against her cheek. Just as she moved to break free of him, he blocked her progress by caressing his left cheek against hers, silently beckoning her forgiveness.

"Lizzie, Lizzie." Though barely a whisper, the sound of his voice resounded about her like a wounded animal crying out in pain. "Promise me you will stay," he begged. "As Aristotle would have it, to live alone one must be a beast or a god . . . or perhaps both. Please grant me your forgiveness, my love. I promise I'll not repeat this manner of beastly behavior."

∘ ∘ ∘

Guilt was written on Elisabeth's heart when next Gersdorff visited. He tried to mollify her in every way possible, mistaking her suffering to be hurt and anger at the long absences required by his line of duty. That was certainly not the case, she assured him. He was a man who understood his obligations and valiantly fulfilled them. For all that he was a lord, he was a captain first. Not only had she come to love him; she was profusely proud of him.

"And what is it that you and your brother have been up to during his convalescence?" her betrothed asked congenially as they walked arm and arm about the grounds of a courtyard situated on the campus of the University of Leipzig.

Elisabeth blushed from the roots of her hair down to her modest décolletage. Gersdorff noticed but made no comment. "We have taken to brandy, cigarettes, and the delights of Wagner each evening after dinner." She attempted to conceal her discomfort with a light, flirtatious laugh.

At the mention of a cigarette, Gersdorff produced a case from his pocket, offering first one to Elisabeth and then placing another between his sensuous lips. Elisabeth could not take her eyes off those lips. Her fiancé was so regal, so handsome in full uniform, his hat tucked beneath his arm. He smiled at her inspection and offered to light her cigarette. His conceited knowledge of his beauty never ceased to affirm that he was the man for her. Only a man in possession of himself could so adeptly eschew false humility.

"Friedrich particularly enjoys *Die Meistersinger*," she picked up the thread of conversation. "Do you know it? It's quite comical in its depiction of middle-class master craftsmen throwing off the shackles of society, using art as an outlet to vent their suffering."

"The work is influenced by the aesthetics of Schopenhauer, I believe," Gersdorff provided in hopes of prolonging this topic of conversation.

"Yes," Elisabeth concurred. "So Friedrich tells me."

Gersdorff bit back the curse of a retort on his tongue. *Friedrich. Always back to Friedrich.*

"What I can't understand," she continued, unaware of his discontented thoughts. "If middle-class German merchants are encouraged to break the cycle of oppression, why does not Wagner make the same argument for the Jew?"

"I take it you have not yet discovered *Das Judenthum in der Musik*? It's an article that Wagner first published in 1850. I understand a reproduction is in the works. That aside, it seems that the composer blames his early musical failures on the successes of Mendelssohn and Meyerbeer. Is that not the way of it, love? Are not our failures the fault of others? What's more, cannot rumors of a man's questionable birth be eviscerated with venomous aspersions launched, like a red herring, in the direction of those most despised?"

"Can secrets be concealed beneath clayton sands?" Elisabeth rejoined, much to her lover's bafflement.

Was Friedrich that close to death? The thought took the new baron off guard and filled him with shame. Here he had just been despising the man. Gersdorff observed Elisabeth closely hoping to confirm or disprove the direction of his thoughts. She was lost in contemplation, deeply troubled by something.

"Have you ever considered," she finally came to herself, "that perhaps there is good reason to spurn a perfidious inheritance?"

Gersdorff's feet halted of their own accord as suspicious speculation seized his thoughts. "You believe the Jews to be a duplicitous people, then?" he asked disbelievingly.

"I can't be sure." Her eyes spoke of a soul crowded with confusion. "Your father's acquaintances certainly seem to think so. They could speak of nothing else when they came to pay their respects. They talk of efforts at conversion, but the unspoken intent is clearly dispersion. They convincingly point out that, for a people so persecuted, the Jews certainly have amassed wealth that speaks of anything but oppression."

Gersdorff couldn't believe what he was hearing from the very woman who would have flung him over for a Jew in the blink of an eye, if the Hebrew would but say the word and do penance. "*Wealth* is the operative word, Elisabeth. The Jews are no different from the merchants in Wagner's comedy. They are tradesmen, making livings to feed their families. No doubt they enjoy a great deal of success, and perhaps if the elite were not so fearful that social position might fall to merit, they would consider the Jews' success to be Prussia's success. I recall that we were once a nation that prided ourselves on our progressive acceptance of Abraham's brood."

"Perhaps," she conceded. "But surely you sense it. Our nation is changing. Tensions are growing. A breaking point is coming. It's understandable that the surname Wagner is far more preferable than Geyer."

"Well, with all this talk of Wagner," he attempted to lighten the mood, "I believe you and Friedrich will be pleased with the surprise I have in store for you. During my stay in Berlin, I met a professor by the name of Hermann Brockhaus. He is an East Asian scholar, and, as it turns out, he has read drafts of your brother's writing provided to him by Paul Deussen.

Deussen, by the by, has decided to take to India for further contemplation of existence as can be derived from the Hindu experience." Gersdorff shook his head as if to clear his thoughts. "But I digress. It seems that your brother left several installments of his essay on Diogenes Laertius in Paul's keeping. Brockhaus is intent on arguing for the publication of such a masterpiece."

Masterpiece. Elisabeth grinned up at him. She knew that Gersdorff was more attuned to Truth than others might realize. But she was not fooled. Her lover despised Friedrich in some small way, though he had mastered his passions to the extent that he would never let on that such was the case. Elisabeth popped up on her toes and kissed his cheek. "You are too good to me, my lord."

"Don't be hasty, madam. For I am even better still," he teased. His teeth shone white behind his boyish smile. To him, Elisabeth's joy was an addiction that he would gladly feed for the remainder of his days.

"Well, for Heaven's sake! Do tell!" she squealed with excitement.

"Patience, my lady . . . patience."

She stamped her foot. "You are as infuriating as Friedrich," she chided in mock petulance.

Gersdorff's smile disappeared beneath his sobering visage. "Well," he finally spoke once again. "As it turns out, Brockhaus is married to Wagner's sister, Ottillie. The two of them are quite impressed with Friedrich's writing and enthusiasm for Wagner's compositions. They have invited the three of us to join them for Wagner's concert here in Leipzig next month. Do you imagine that Friedrich will be up to it? Is he so very ill?"

"I believe it would be just the thing for him!" Elisabeth declared, near bursting with excitement. "He has been able to join me on short walks, though his wound still pains him, slowing his stride. But a concert, I can't think of any reason why he should not be able to attend."

They stopped walking as Gersdorff turned to face her. "Then it is done, my love," he decreed as he dipped his head to claim a kiss. His was a kiss that gave as much as it demanded. As her lord's lips moved across hers, Elisabeth fleetingly thought of Friedrich's consuming lips. Did they give or only take? Her brother's desire was selfish, she decided. And Elisabeth thought that she might prefer it that way.

Gersdorff placed his hands on Elisabeth's shoulders and gently broke their kiss. His speculative eyes scanned her face thoroughly before he spoke. "By God, you are thinking of him!" He cursed under his breath.

"No, no!" she protested. "That's not it at all. I swear I have put Peter behind me. You must believe me," she pleaded.

"It is not Peter of whom I speak." Taking her chin between his thumb and forefinger, he forced her to raise her downcast eyes to meet his. "I'll not marry both of you. Do you understand?" He spoke like the born and bred officer that he was, and Elisabeth could not but nod her head in the affirmative.

"Of course, my lord," she answered softly. "You know that I do. It's just that Friedrich's illness has consumed so much of my time that I can't seem to put his frailties out of my head. I'm certain that the joys of hearing Wagner in person will do him quite good. Bring him back to his old self, even."

Gersdorff took up her arm and began walking back to Friedrich's quarters. "Yes, I must confess that was my intention. I will see your brother well and on his way."

He deposited Elisabeth at her front door, declining her invitation to join them for coffee.

∘ ∘ ∘

CHAPTER XIII

∞

An imposition of one's own reason, says Mikhail Bakunin, is that it compels one to "bow to the authority of special men." Anarchistic rage dictates my reason, and so I shall bow to no man.

∞

Elisabeth was mesmerized by the kaleidoscopic expressions that passed over her brother's face as overtures to *Tristan and Isolde* and *Die Meistersinger* held a packed audience enrapt, each flawlessly executed note reverberating throughout the concert hall. Wagner was as great a success here as he was in Tribschen, Switzerland: one of a number of refuges the composer had sought during his years of exile from the Germanic States, resulting from his alliances with the radical editor, August Rockel, and the anarchist, Mikhail Bakunin. It struck Elisabeth that anarchy could very well be the sustenance Friedrich thrived on, for only an anarchist would presume to lord over Lucifer. As the nation prayed for deliverance from the taint of blasphemous blood, Friedrich beseeched nothing of God.

"Are you so invincible, then?" Elisabeth had stared at the canopy over her bed all night and could wait no longer to query her brother in what she knew would be a futile attempt to settle her mind.

Friedrich rolled over on his side and propped himself up with his right elbow, his left hand reaching over, softly tracing a line just above the mounds of her breasts. "Why have you not slept, love? What torments you this morn?"

"Anarchy!" she blurted out.

Friedrich bayed out a laugh of astonishment. "And here I thought you dreamed of forsaking Marke."

Elisabeth raised an eyebrow at him. "And give the potion to my Tristan instead?" She clamped a fist around Friedrich's wrist, stilling the caress of his fingers. "You forget that the potion wears off, and Gersdorff's wishes are Reality's will. Ours is a spell that will soon be broken, and no anarchical philosophy can cast asunder that which God brings together."

Friedrich leaned in and took the lobe of his sister's ear between his teeth. "I promise to take your words under consideration, dear Lizzie. And for the record, anarchy is just another misguided form of inherency to which I shall never stoop so low. What need have I of a means to a god?"

∘ ∘ ∘

Elisabeth fumed the entire train ride back to Naumburg. It was just like her mother to "fall ill" days before an arranged meeting between Friedrich and Wagner, courtesy of Ottilie Brockhaus. Elisabeth, who was to accompany her brother, now speculated as to her mother's motives in denying her this pleasure. She suspected that word had reached home of her discarded black garments, but, honestly, what had Franziska expected? The mourning period would come to an end in just over a month, and the future Baroness von Gersdorff was certainly forgiven such conventionalities when attending a Wagner concert. At twenty-two she was unquestionably no longer a child in need of scolding. Indeed, many a meddling matrons had clucked their tongues at her advanced age and dwindling opportunities for a child of her own.

"Marry posthaste," they would admonish her in Gerdorff's presence. "Your husband's responsibility will be the future of our nation, and yours will be the propagation of it." They tittered behind their fans as if they possessed the key that would unlock the Prussian cure for all that sickened Christ's creation. If only they knew that seeds of every variation take to the earth in capricious soil compositions. Elisabeth laughed aloud at her inner thoughts. She herself was soiled by mysteries best left unsolved.

Once Elisabeth arrived home, Franziska bustled about, settling her daughter's things in a manner that bespoke her intentions for a long stay.

"Why am I here, Mother?" Elisabeth cut to the chase.

"Well, darling, as you have made clear by setting aside your mourning attire, it is time to turn our attention to your wedding preparations. I have engaged Hadassah to assist you with your trousseau." At this Elisabeth blanched. "You know," Franziska continued as if Peter had never been a part of her daughter's heart, "the dear girl has always been handy with a needle and thread."

Elisabeth cut her off. "Mother, you really have no right making such decisions without consulting me or Gersdorff."

Franziska nodded affably as she took another dress from Elisabeth's trunk and placed it on a hanger. "Well, darling, of course I consulted Gersdorff! He is to be your husband after all! You'll learn soon enough that his is to be the final say in all matters."

"Might I remind you, Mother? Until I marry, Friedrich is the head of our household. It is his money you spend on this wedding."

Her mother snapped the trunk's lid closed with a thud that made Elisabeth jump. "And I might remind you, dear, it is Gersdorff, not Friedrich, who is to be your lord and master." Franziska threw her hands up in the air as she made to exit the room. "Friedrich will just have to reconcile himself to the fact that you are no longer his responsibility."

A mutinous anger had gotten the best of Elisabeth. "I am my own responsibility!" she shouted at the door that closed behind her mother. "And any man who thinks my admiration can be acquiesced will find he, instead, stands in my abhorrence." With this parting shot, a plethora of visages took shape in Elisabeth's mind: Gustav, Peter, Friedrich, Gersdorff, and . . . Paul? What had happened with Mr. Deussen that she should think of him now? Somewhere within her there resided a rage steeped in shame.

Rage soldiered on when Hadassah appeared the next day to take Elisabeth's measurements. "Have we not already sized each other up?" Elisabeth snapped as Hadassah entered her bedchamber and began to set about her commission. "Friedrich once told me that you would never betray your people, that you would never change your name. And yet you now go by Mrs. Gast. Why not Köselitz, dear girl? Were you not able to redeem the betrayer?"

Hadassah stared directly upon Elisabeth's face for a silent moment, and then, having urged Elisabeth to stand straight atop the fitting platform, she stooped down to measure her hem. "We all have hard truths to hide, Miss Nietzsche." She spoke almost defiantly, Elisabeth noted. "Whether it be a hated history or a forbidden future," she peered up at Elisabeth pointedly, "we all must suffer society's censure the best we can."

Elisabeth's heart thundered as she recalled her fingers flying in unison with Peter's across the pianoforte, a myriad of resonant voices convening in her head. *And so begins the beat of the war drums, the battle cry of Nationalism to which the worn feet of the wandering Jew will once again tap . . . And you, Miss Nietzsche? Are you virtuous? . . . I'll not let you be judged a Siren, Lizzie . . . our association came to an end with the first and only breath of your heir . . . What game do you play with your brother, Miss Nietzsche? You are all innocence, Lizzie.*

Yes, she concurred, there were truths to be slain and still more fabrications to be birthed. What greater allegiance to anarchy could possibly be conceived?

Elisabeth could not decide who was crueler: her mother for having invited Hadassah and Peter to dinner, or the Gasts for having accepted the invitation. If her betrothed or her brother had been present, the evening would have been tolerable. Instead, she ate her dinner in a state of self-isolation, acknowledging nothing but the tablecloth from which she could not raise her eyelids, weighted as they were by the pain of solitude.

"Elisabeth, do pay attention! Hadassah and Peter have wonderful news to share." Franziska motioned for Peter to repeat his announcement.

Recognizing himself for a cad, Peter's eyes darted between Elisabeth and Franziska. It was unkind of her mother to demand his lips to again utter words that would be painful to her daughter's ears. "Miss Nietzsche," he began nervously, "Hadassah and I are expecting our first child, and would like for you and the baron to attend the bris."

"Or naming ceremony, if it's a girl," Hadassah put in gaily. "For some reason Peter is convinced the babe will be a boy."

"But, of course he is." Elisabeth reached over to pat Hadassah's hand with perfectly executed fondness. "Every man desires an heir. Does he not, Mr. Gast? Strength in male numbers, no?" Elisabeth tilted her glass in a mock toast and shot him a supercilious glare over the rim as she took a sip of her wine.

Peter flinched. It pained him to no end that she believed he had willingly given her up in favor of his heritage. He wondered if she was aware just how involved her brother was in orchestrating her destiny. No matter, she would be free of Friedrich's envious interferences soon enough. Gersdorff would not be so easily cowed, Peter knew.

Elisabeth stood from the table. "If you'll excuse me, I am tired from my journey and need to retire for the night. As for the bris, I'm told that such decisions will be made by . . . how did you say it, Mother? Ah, yes, I remember now. By my lord and master," she finished, as she turned on her heel and made her exit.

Peter sighed in sorrow as he watched her go. For now she felt herself the betrayed, but soon enough the baron and his bride would no doubt have a respectable brood beyond the reach of the Betrayer, he thought ironically as he watched a drop of wine escape his glass and pool like blood on the tablecloth. His eyes were transfixed as the red globule spread and soaked into the white linen, the sight of which mesmerized him, setting at a distance the admonishing voice of Franziska Nietzsche.

"You cannot possibly plan to raise the child as a Jew! Why, it's positively mutinous!"

° ° °

CHAPTER XIV

∞

Hunds and Judes, have you virtue? No, you say?
March off the landscape!

∞

Once introduced, Friedrich and Wagner became fast friends with shared interests in philosophy, music, and the philosophy *of* music. By January of 1869, visits to the Wagners' home on Lake Lucerne had become a bit of a routine that would soon be interrupted by Friedrich's unexpected appointment to the position of professor of Greek language and literature at Switzerland's Basel University. The appointment came as a result of the recommendation made by Friedrich's former Bonn professor, Wilhelm Ritschl—a recommendation of singular distinction, given that Friedrich had not yet earned his doctorate.

But, at present, his stays with Wagner were filled with plethoric delights. There was the music, of course. Friedrich sought only to learn a bit about Wagner's technique. It never crossed his mind that the composer would be interested in hearing the works of a novice. Nonetheless, Friedrich found himself seated at the pianoforte as a guest at Wagner's home in Tribschen, divulging his life journey in private concert.

First, he shared compositions he had written during his Schulpforta years. Among them were two rather upbeat piano scores: *Ungarischer Marsch* (*Hungarian March*) and *Zigeunertanz* (*Gypsy Dance*), the childishness of which made Wagner guffaw so uncontrollably that Friedrich himself could not help but join in the laughter. These efforts reminded him, he told Wagner, of his younger self's temerity in writing an autobiography that could only encompass fifteen years of his life at the date of its attempt. The immature efforts at music spread upon the piano before him mirrored the same cheekiness of childhood.

All laughter came to a cessation, however, when Friedrich began to play another two of his compositions, *E des titok* (*Sweet Secret*) and *Heldenklage* (*Hero's Lament*), both hauntingly mature in grace, in beauty, in melancholy.

The smile slipped from Wagner's face as he leaned forward in sober concentration, taking in every note that carried Friedrich into a state of complete and utter spiritual separation from his surroundings, invoking a sort of jealousy in the depths of the experienced composer's heart. What woman had the young Nietzsche buried himself in that he should so move the listener to join his soul in such anguish?

Friedrich's fingers slowed to a stop on the keys as he addressed his friend. "I would have you meet my sister, Elisabeth, before I away to Basel."

○ ○ ○

Friedrich had not yet told his mother and sister of his impending departure for Basel. He feared the inevitable congratulations and envious lamentations, followed by social calls of artful displays, at once obsequious and grossly ostentatious. It was unfortunate that such could not forever be avoided, thus he sat with pen in hand to write them of his news.

He would be taking up residence in Basel at *Spalentorweg* #2. With his legacy from Aunt Rosalie he could afford the spacious abode. A cottage it may be, but it was still grander than any place he had ever lived, he told them. He would require a housekeeper, and would they happen to know anyone to recommend?

It came as no surprise to him when Elisabeth turned out to be the recommendation. He thought perhaps he may have even anticipated it.

Gersdorff's was a demanding profession, a line of duty that required the baron's constant presence in Berlin, particularly as tensions ramped up between Bismarck and Napoleon III over Prussia's increasingly obvious intentions of annexing the Southern German states. The wedding was placed on delay after delay; Elisabeth's ardor was cooling to contempt. It wasn't just the endless postponements that put Elisabeth off, it was more so the highhanded commands her betrothed had been issuing as of late. He insisted that she stay in Naumburg until they could marry. More specifically, he forbade her from traipsing after Friedrich, finding no reason why she should continue to nurse her brother who, with his travels to Lucerne, had proven he was hale enough to fare on his own.

And so it was that Friedrich found her on his doorstep, bearing enough luggage for an interminable stay.

He was deeply concerned about Elisabeth when he witnessed her in the stranglehold of nightmares that had grown more volatile since last they lay together. He ran soothing fingers through tangled hair, dampened by the cold perspiration of terror. In a state of torpor, Elisabeth begged and pleaded for help only to lash out her fists in desperation when he pulled her into the security of his arms. The permanent wound that covered his heart festered. Nevertheless, he withstood her physical assaults, taking a perverse pleasure in the warranted punishment that he knew was his due.

He had done so very wrong by her, a fact evidenced by her continued presence in a bed of his making. Should he release her? No, he refused to relinquish what was his. Should he contact Gersdorff and demand the lord-captain relieve him of her? Futile, for such relief was not to be had.

As if summoned by another, Gersdorff's form came forth in the nightmare that held Elisabeth engulfed. He was relentless in the condemnation that fell from his shapeless mouth. Whore to the Jude, courtesan to the Antichrist, daughter of Lilith—Elisabeth in her demise would resemble no more than the dog-eaten flesh of the Sidonian.

Friedrich held his sister tight as she sobbed and convulsed against him. He lost himself in her tumult, certain that somewhere in the midst of this chaotic episode, he heard her curse his name. She was powerless and so very fragile. He would see his Lizzie happy.

The morning sun kissed Elisabeth's eyelids until they fluttered open to the dawning of a new day. Gersdorff. She lay in the crook of his arm, his body curved about hers in a spooning position. They must have words. Did he truly think her so vile that her soul possessed no hope for lasting peace?

Did he despise her as much as she despised Peter? As much as she despised her existence as it was?

Every time she closed her eyes she was taunted with an unidentifiable force that sought to consume her. Never had she imagined that Gersdorff might emerge from a villainous haze that had, over time, darkened from a pastel shade to something as ominous as the mourning attire so recently cast off. Perhaps that's why the baron had emerged from the vapor, had lifted the veil from her face. He would reveal her, and cast her off unto the fires that consumed many a sorceress — a merciful demise devoid of dogs.

She knew not whether it had been he who was kept in ignorance or she who had embraced obliviousness. Either way, she could not betray him upon the altar of matrimony. The Silent Specter would speak and reveal all that her brother promised to conceal.

"You know, my love. I have always known that when virtue has slept, she would awaken at peace."

Friedrich! Elisabeth scrambled, rolling over to her side in an about-face with her brother. No, she would never be a baroness. Nor would the baron be forever silent on this matter.

Letters arrived from Gersdorff, detailing events that pointed to an inevitable war with France. In the course of the past year, Queen Isabella of Spain had been deposed and consequently took refuge in Paris. The architect of the queen's deposition, revolutionary Francisco Serrano, was named regent of Spain while a search for an apposite king was underway. The House of Hohenzollern tightened the territorial noose about Napoleon's neck with the nomination of Prince Leopald Hohenzollern-Sigmaringen to the Spanish throne. Bismarck was to meet with a French envoy in an attempt to allay fears that an alliance between Prussia and Spain would pose a threat to France.

In the summarization of these events, Gersdorff waxed optimistic of the two nations reaching a pact. He refrained from expressing his private concerns about Bismarck's and Napoleon's shared hubris and a savvy knowledge of the logistical effects of warfare in bringing about a national unity that both men envisioned for their respective sovereigns.

Perhaps they should marry before war was upon them, he wrote to Elisabeth. He would not chastise her now for taking up with Friedrich in Basel, for it may even prove beneficial to their marriage plans, as the captain would be often in Switzerland on matters of defense and interference. Neutrality was well and fine so long as it sat on the sidelines in silence.

Elisabeth responded that she would, indeed, like to discuss their marriage plans, and thanked him "ever so much" in mock spirit for withholding his chastisement until he and she could face off on neutral territory to discuss her brother. Speaking of whom, Friedrich had made the decision to relinquish his Prussian citizenship so that he may stand in allegiance with his university. Eternally the provocateur, her brother was.

Gersdorff had no reason to doubt it. Friedrich had been born with a predisposition to bring agitation to what should have been the most serendipitous of life's scenarios. He was no fool. There would be no marriage, but Elisabeth would have to be the one to give voice to Truth. He would not rescue her from her distress.

o o o

CHAPTER XV

∞

Were I not destined for Hell, I would take up God's gavel, assigning him to Gan Eden and casting his mistress into Sheol. And whence would I pass this judgment? Why from Olam Ha-ba, of course!

∞

Gersdorff's lack of attentions to Elisabeth became a point of contention between Friedrich and his longtime friend. While Elisabeth seemed content enough, people began to talk — gossipmongers volunteering their personal theories as to why the baron was in no hurry to make it to the altar. Some said he kept a mistress in Berlin. Others were certain that Elisabeth's former attachment to a Jew was an embarrassment that was hindering the captain's rise in the military ranks. And still more contended that her brother's unsavory views had rendered her unfit to be a baroness. Why Nietzsche had even discussed sending his sister to school at Leipzig! Unheard of! Disgraceful! What gentleman would want such a headstrong woman for a wife?

It was from Wagner's mistress, Cosima, whom Friedrich first heard of such whisperings, and he was certain that, as a mutual friend of Wagner, Gersdorff had been equally informed. He wondered if the rumors were the reason behind his sister's lack of an invitation to meet and visit with the Wagners. It was becoming increasingly difficult to leave Elisabeth behind at Basel during his sojourns to Tribschen. He would have thought Cosima, having first been installed as Wagner's mistress, to be above giving credence to such scandal. Still, he would not question her position on the matter, for her friendship had proved to be a beacon of light in his otherwise bleak existence.

He found himself often alone in Cosima's company. She was a true intellectual, well read, and able to debate matters of philosophical import with sound arguments that challenged his defenses. He put up defenses of a different nature in those times when his hostess questioned his attachment to his sister. Had he searched within himself to pinpoint the reason he had not forced the issue of Elisabeth's marriage? Was he unaware that he snapped at every gentleman who, out of mere courtesy, dared to inquire about the welfare of a young woman they had never laid eyes on? Was it necessary for him to begin nearly every sentence with "I often tell Lizzie"?

Friedrich's mouth gaped in response. Had he? Did he still? Of course not! Cosima had no idea of that which she spoke and he would thank her to refrain from diverting him with her taunting impertinence.

Cosima came to him then and took a seat beside him on the settee. She placed her fingers against his lips and quieted his protestations to her unseemly behavior. "Dear Friedrich," she purred, "you simply need the right woman in your life. I know what it is to spend endless nights alone, with Richard off and about so very often. Mayhap, I could introduce you to someone, or simply help you fill the void."

He watched her then as she stretched out like a cat and settled back against the settee. The Countess of Pforta's mocking laughter rung in his ears. He would not be so manipulated again. He would seize control of this situation.

With a sudden swiftness, Cosima found herself swept up in the arms of a maestro.

o o o

As if women of persuasion had some mystifying telepathic connection, Elisabeth presented Friedrich with a list she had devised for him of possible bridal candidates, directly upon his return from Tribschen. There were the Huffstetler sisters, both still unattached. Wilhelm Pinder's sister would do very well, though Friedrich had lost touch with Pinder before the war. The Vandermere girl several houses down seemed to be quite intelligent. And what of the girl he once fancied from Berlin?

Friedrich leaned down over the chair in which Lizzie sat and kissed her upon the nose. "And this is how you welcome me home? With a list that all but trumpets my shortcomings?" He plopped down in the chair opposite her and leaned down to remove his boots. "I'll not settle for anyone who pales in comparison to my Eli."

Elisabeth grimaced with a blush. "You must marry and settle down Friedrich. Now that you are established in your career, it's unseemly for you to remain unattached."

"And yet you remain unattached from your fiancé. Have you considered why? I fear I have at great length." He abandoned his chair in favor of the waning flame upon the fireplace grate, propping an arm against the mantel upon which to rest his forehead.

"For you see, matrimony does not necessitate attachment, nor does attachment necessitate marriage," he went on. "Take Oedipus, for example. Through him, Sophocles posits that every man's image of the perfect wife is derived from his mother. Never one for the company of others, I can't help but wonder if the tragic oracle ever gave consideration to conversation. I, for one, cannot imagine being shackled to a woman incapable of putting two thoughts together. Nor would I be able to tolerate any wife given to the notion that hers is a love so coveted that I shall relinquish command of my world."

He paused, shifting his gaze from the flames to the ceiling.

"A friend I would be content to take to wife. But then, a lasting friendship requires a certain amount of physical antipathy, given the tendency for sexual congress to transform cordiality into carnal contempt."

He craned his neck, peering over his shoulder at her. "No, I would rather have a lifelong conversation than a concubine."

Friedrich shoved away from the fireplace and ambled toward a brandy snifter on the sidebar, pouring a glass for each of them. "And therein lies the problem, don't you see?" He held her eyes as she took the proffered drink from his hand. "I fear my affections are hopelessly engaged to a conversationalist who will not give me the time of day. With her resides only antipathy in the darkness of an abyss from which I could save her, if I but willed it."

"But you cannot will what you will." Elisabeth interrupted the path of his thoughts before he spoke far too much aloud. "A tragic case, indeed. Have you a cigarette, darling?"

He patted the pockets of his vest in search of one, but came up short. Cesare Borgia he may be, but he was no Gersdorff, ever prepared to obscure her demons in a cloud of smoke.

"I fear I come up empty on that score. I have yet to figure out why the Americans commercialize their brand of virility through the exportation of those thin brown sticks. Whatever happened to a good European cheroot, hmm?"

o o o

In the weeks that followed, Elisabeth avoided thoughts of Gersdorff by turning her attention to helping her brother prepare for classes. They deconstructed scenes from *Faust*, debated the merits of Wagner's argument in *Das Judenthum in der Musik* (*On Judaism in Music*), and studied Spinoza, all of which were pertinent to the notes Friedrich had been compiling for his most recent literary endeavor, *The Birth of Tragedy*.

The ideology of Baruch Spinoza spoke to a need deep within Elisabeth's heart. The seventeenth century Dutch philosopher of Portuguese Jewish ancestry challenged traditional notions of Heaven and Hell. The Jewish concept of *Sheol* had long been the netherworld to which Elisabeth was convinced she would awake after death. A shadowy existence, disemboweled from God, in the darkest of pits known only to the despondently despaired. It would be no hardship, she reflected, to trade the earthly state of her soul for its preternatural equivalent. The monism of Spinoza, however, gave her hope that there may be something yet that could touch her soul, something that her being could touch, as well.

Birthless, deathless and changeless remaineth the soul forever, Krishna had told Arjuna. And so Spinoza offered that from the universe our soul was severed and to the universe it will return in congregation with all others.

"Harmonious refuge," she whispered to herself. "What an exquisite thought."

"What was that you said, Lizzie?" Friedrich inquired.

Realizing that she had unintentionally spoken her thoughts aloud, Elisabeth hesitated a moment before giving a reply. "I was wondering, is God a woman?"

"Well, that depends. If you believe in a god, then I suppose your creator's gender would rest with you. Tell me, are you proud of your sex?"

She gave a slow nod. "I would say that I am."

"Then most definitely, God is a woman! For you see, a proud people needs a god."

Elisabeth arched a brow at her brother. "Ah, then. So God is a *Jew*. How charming."

Friedrich barked out a laugh. "Here I have been angling for an invitation for you to meet Cosima, and you undermine my efforts by blaspheming the entire German race."

Elisabeth's gaze slowly sojourned up and down Friedrich's person. "And who is Cosima von Bülow to you that her Christian name should fall so frequently and so readily from your lips?" His silence spoke volumes. "I suggest you try harder to secure that invitation," she advised.

∘ ∘ ∘

CHAPTER XVI

∞

I increasingly find that, when hemmed in by pretension, ambition, and apprehension, I have no lasting inhibition.

∞

December 1869

The invitations from Tribschen continued to flow in, but still they included no mention of Elisabeth. Friedrich was torn. He could not continue to decline Cosima's requests, nor could he abandon his sister in Basel.

"The best I can do, Lizzie, is to make arrangements for you to stay with the Brockhauses while I pay a Christmas visit to Tribschen." Friedrich was pacing the floor out of nervous habit, those same nerves driving him to turn up his palms in supplication. "It won't be as bad as all that. In fact, the situation could not be better. Brockhaus's villa is just across the lake from Richard's manner. I will, of course, visit you, and we shall make merry at Christmas."

Elisabeth sought desperately for a winning argument. Staying just a ferry ride away from her brother's hosts was beyond mortifying. The baron's estate was not an option, as it had been closed up for some time due to his extended trips away from home. Her mother was out of town, caring for her dying sister, Ida, removing Naumburg from consideration— for the better, given that a visit to Naumburg would put her at risk of running into the Gasts and having them bear witness to her expiation during the holiest of Christian holidays. She laughed to herself. What irony was this? She had straddled both worlds, all the while a bridge constructed of gold, incense, and myrrh spanned the divide between conventionality and potentiality. Like a troll from a tale by *Die Bruder Grimm* she stood reviled and livid beneath the tress passage, good enough for neither existence, it seemed.

Worse, still, was that Friedrich expected her to accompany him into town at Basel to collect gift items compiled into a wish list commissioned by Cosima.

"You are not Cosima von Bülow's errand boy," she berated. "Why would someone of your stature allow another man's mistress to lead you about by the nose?" Her words resounded with an actuality she had long recognized.

Elisabeth sighed in resignation and consented to the arrangement.

∘ ∘ ∘

Mrs. Brockhaus's company had been so pleasant when first they met in Leipzig, but Elisabeth found it to be a bit grating on the nerves at present. She had taken to staring through a telescope focused on the Wagners' home across the way. Someone was making gay on this Christmas, and it certainly wasn't her, she seethed, as her hostess implored her to come away from the looking lens for the thousandth time. Who was this woman to scold one who, for all the world knew, would be a baroness?

"What do you suppose goes on within those walls?" Elisabeth asked aloud, and then cursed herself for showing weakness. She moved away from the window and laughed aloud at the absurdity of one who would hold onto the slightest pretension of pride while spying through a telescope for a glimpse of a world she could not but pretend to.

Within that realm of pretense, Friedrich was growing all too familiar with what occurred there. He navigated the rooms filled with merry-makers, Richard Wagner the merriest of all, deep in his cups. It would be another evening in which the composer would cajole some reluctant sot to take to the pianoforte only to be castigated aloud for his shortcomings, as if Wagner took personal offense to anything that did not satisfy his ear. By that measure, the man would forever be offended, Friedrich surmised wryly.

Several fingers fluttered at the nape of his neck, taking up a lock of his hair in a series of intimate, twirling caresses. "You have grown weary of our charades." Cosima's voice came on a coo to his ear.

"One or another of them, yes." He nodded without turning in her direction.

"Richard will retire to sleep off his drink soon. Perhaps we could remedy your weariness."

Friedrich clapped his hand about his forehead and began to massage his throbbing temples. If it were possible, his headaches were worsening. "I fear there is no remedy for what ails me but a good night's rest," he informed in a tone of warning.

Cosima came up on her tiptoes and stole a quick kiss from his lips. "In the morning, then." She retreated demurely.

Friedrich's sleep-laden eyes flew open in sudden surprise as nimble fingers played over his abdomen. By God, it was not morning, and she had defied him again! Cursing under his breath, he reached down and aggressively stalled Cosima's administrations.

She showed no surprise at his actions. "Did you know that you talk in your sleep?" Her words were more cautionary than an inquiry.

"I have been informed as much, yes. And whose company did I keep in my dreams? Was it Epicurus? Goethe? Schopenhauer? Montaigne? No, wait!" He snapped his fingers. "I wager it was Spinoza! I hold court with these and more, for I would like to have them advise me as to whether I am right or wrong. What's more, I would like to stand audience to them as they tell each other whether they are right or wrong."

Cosima brushed the practiced lips of a courtesan sensuously beneath his ear. "And what of your sister? Would you have her join the debate?"

Friedrich sat up on his elbows. "I would have my sister in company at the Christmas Eve gala."

Upon joining the house party the following day, Gersdorff seconded Friedrich's request. It was known only to Elisabeth and himself that their engagement was unraveling. That being the case, it would not do for him to stand in attendance without her by his side. There were a number of tantrums and a great deal of pouting — why? The baron could not imagine — before Cosima finally conceded to extend an invitation and have Elisabeth ferried over. A room was prepared for her as well. If she was coming at all, she may as well stay for the final days of the festivities.

No sooner had Elisabeth set foot in Tribschen than she began thoroughly assessing every aspect of the domicile. She was disappointed at first, finding the furnishings to be scant for such a grand home, a shortcoming that was otherwise overshadowed by the edifice's location atop a grassy hill, overlooking the beautiful Lake Lucerne, and an interior that boasted a grand red-carpeted stairway, elaborate crystal chandeliers, parquet floors, and numerous oil paintings of the master hanging about.

None of the paintings, however, could compare to the man who stood before her now: Wagner in the flesh. Elisabeth would later write to her mother of his breathtaking appearance in a "Flemish painter's costume—a black velvet coat, black satin knee-breeches, black silk stockings, a light-blue satin cravat tied in many folds, showing his fine linen and lace shirt, and a painter's beret on his head, which was covered with luxurious brown hair."

What she did not share with her mother was that her fingers itched to comb their way through his hair. Nor did she recount her gape of surprise when a beautiful woman dressed in red cashmere trimmed with pink flowers—a woman a great deal taller than the composer—came to his side and introduced herself as Cosima von Bülow.

Cosima's imposing height over her husband may have detracted from Wagner's allure, but Elisabeth gave it very little consideration as she carefully inspected the woman who had captivated Friedrich's tongue. Elisabeth knew to expect a challenge from this woman and received it before she could breathe a word of greeting to either of her hosts. Locking her own arm with Elisabeth's, Cosima took command of their first meeting, sweeping Elisabeth off and about the room as if she were a child in need of a governess.

"Do welcome our darling Friedrich's sister, Fraulein Nietzsche," her hostess cajoled one and all in a patronizing tone as she patted Elisabeth's hand. Cosima cast a glance across the room in Friedrich's direction, but instead met the admonishing eyes of Gersdorff, in response to which she laughed with manufactured gaiety. "Or perhaps, it would be more accurate should I introduce this lovely girl as the future Baroness von Gersdorff."

With this bit of intelligence, more than a few simpering ladies and dandified gentlemen fell in line to welcome the new arrival to their ranks.

One gentleman, in particular, drew Friedrich's eye immediately. He had made Paul Förster's acquaintance earlier in the week and found him to be insufferably puffed up with rabid anti-Semitic dogma and delusions of grandeur that placed himself, along with his brother, Bernhard, at the helm of Christ's cavalry. Handing his champagne glass off to a hired servant, Friedrich wasted no time in denying the madman the opportunity to defile his sister's fingers with his vile lips. As soon as he reached her side, Friedrich turned Elisabeth about and took her hands into his own, as if to showcase his greatest possession. "Paul," Friedrich nodded. "I see you have met my Lizzie, who has yet to get settled in." He then addressed Elisabeth. "We must remedy that immediately, love."

"Don't be ridiculous, Friedrich!" Cosima swooped in closer. "I will show her to her room myself. Besides, it's out of your way, darling. I have placed your sister in an upstairs room, you see, and have had your things moved to a guest room below stairs."

Yes, Friedrich did see, and one glimpse at Gersdorff confirmed that he did as well.

However, no one had greater insight of his mistress more so than Richard Wagner. The wife of Hans von Bülow, Cosima had abandoned their loveless union and taken up with Richard some six years before. The marriage was soon to be legally dissolved, and Richard supposed he would have to secure a permanent arrangement with his mistress, lest he

114

suffer Von Bülow's fate. Cosima was a handful, to be sure, and, for all that he was twenty-four years her senior, he was just arrogant enough to believe he could keep her in check.

Friedrich crept upstairs and padded down the dark hallway to Elisabeth's room. At 3:00 a.m. he'd suffered enough tossing and turning. He needed to caution his sister against Paul Förster. Though she seemed to have gotten past the heartbreak of her love for Peter, she still had a tendency to stiffen and clench her fists when within hearing distance of those who would cast aspersions against the Jews. It had crossed Friedrich's mind that he should refrain from forewarning her for the pure pleasure of watching her plant Paul a facer. But, then, that would not be fair to his Lizzie, whom he had promised to forever shield from public condemnation.

"Come," came her voice in response to the softest of knocks on the door to her chamber. It pleased him to no end that she had anticipated this covert visit. But then, why would she not? Distance and danger of discovery had never posed an impediment for him.

Friedrich stopped in his tracks upon entering her room. She was so beautiful, his Lizzie. With each passing year, she grew further into womanhood, exuding an air of poise that threatened to place her beyond his reach. He hated to think how influential Gersdorff had been in this regard. Indeed, the flames of jealousy burned deep within, gnawing at his ulcerous entrails. Friedrich shook off his trepidations, for it was he, not Gersdorff, who stood before Elisabeth in her bedchamber as she donned not a stitch of clothing, confident in her powers of seduction. He tore at his dressing robe as if he could not be rid of it quickly enough.

There would be no need for seduction.

∘ ∘ ∘

Composed as ever, Cosima swept into the dining room the following evening with a *frohe Weihnachten* (merry Christmas) on her lips for one and all. The table had been elaborately set

115

for a dinner of roast goose, stuffed with apples and chestnuts, accompanied by side dishes of red cabbage with onions, boiled potatoes and dumplings. *Stollen* followed for dessert. Elisabeth bit down into the sumptuous dessert pastry and savored it as she took in the room's festive décor. There was the tree, decorated the evening before with gingerbread ornaments. On each wall around them hung Advent calendars, constructed of fir tree branches with twenty-four decorated pouches hanging from their depths.

At the sight of the wreaths, a brief image crossed Elisabeth's mind of herself and Friedrich as children, anxiously awaiting the opening of one pouch a day for the 24 days leading up to Christmas. They took turns, wiggling their little fingers into the velvety folds to discover the mysterious treat hidden within. When it was Elisabeth's turn, she would, without fail, extract her greedy hand from the pouch, only to find it held a prize she did not want. When Friedrich's turn, it never failed that his hand would emerge with exactly the prize his sister insisted she had included in her prayers the night before.

Glancing in her direction, Friedrich's heart leapt. The smile on Lizzie's face mirrored that of the child-sister who had looked upon him as if he were God when he inevitably offered up his prize for her taking.

"My, my," Cosima broke the silence. "It's wonderful to see so many smiling faces this Christmas night. I rather thought there might be some tired-out expressions by this hour. But you, Miss Nietzsche, you and your brother look like you share the secret to happiness between you. And you, Baron, you don't look nearly as tired as one might think you should," she finished with a knowing wink at Gersdorff, who, in turn, looked from Elisabeth to Friedrich with an expression that communicated confusion. Elisabeth, too, was clearly flummoxed, for she looked upon him with what appeared to be nothing short of suspicion.

The odd tension at the table led the meal to break up sooner than planned, the women moving to the parlor for a bit of cider, while the men stayed behind for after-dinner drinks and cigars. Cosima waited for all of her female guests to exit the room before making her way over to Gersdorff, crowding him in so closely that her dress of velvet green brushed against his outstretched leg beneath the table.

"Do forgive me, Baron, if I caused you any discomfort just now. I certainly didn't mean to make poor Elisabeth blush so." Her laugh gave lie to her apology. Just as her sudden hand on his shoulder suggested a calculated deceit. "I suppose, having seen you leave Elisabeth's room at half past four in the morning, I just couldn't help but goad the two of you a bit. Why, you could barely pull yourself away from her! There's nothing I enjoy more than seeing two such passionate people in love." She drove the knife home on an exaggerated sigh.

Gersdorff's chair scraped out from under him and of a sudden he was gone from the room. No rejoinder, no *excuse me*, no *beg pardon*. Just the hoped-for reaction that would land Elisabeth Nietzsche on the earliest train back to Basel.

It was not often that the virtuoso had to take charge of the goings on in his household, but the sound of Baron von Gersdorff's raised voice halted Wagner's tracks in the hallway outside of the library. *You go too far, madam! I have exercised all of my patience to allow you to announce the end to our engagement in your own good time, but I will not stand by and be made to look the cuckold! For Christ's sake! You shame me, not with just any man, but with your own —"*

Richard stepped into the room, and all words ceased.

"Baron. Miss Nietzsche." He nodded to both in turn. "Forgive my interruption, but would you not prefer to join in the entertainments of the others below stairs?"

Without sparing another glance for his fiancée, Gersdorff offered his apologies to Wagner, and stormed in long strides toward the door, stopping just briefly enough at the threshold to ensure that "Tomorrow, Elisabeth" could be heard over his shoulder.

Elisabeth dropped her tear-stained face in her hands and began to sob anew. Tomorrow. Tomorrow she would have to broadcast herself as a jilt. She should thank him for that much, she supposed. He had the power to ruin her irrevocably, but he was giving her the opportunity to be seen as the one breaking off the marriage. While neither position was to be respected, it was better to be a jilt than the jilted. But then, a man of Gersdorff's caliber could withstand the condemnation of either label. It was she who would look the tart.

Masculine hands covered her own and gently pulled them away to reveal her face. Ashamed that she should be exposed thusly, Elisabeth rotated from Richard's view.

"Herr Wagner, I . . . I cannot apologize enough for the scene you just witnessed. I will pack my things immediately and remove myself from your company."

"And why deprive the rest of us your presence, Miss Nietzsche, just because your baron is out of sorts? He will come around soon enough."

Elisabeth shook her head. "No, I fear you are wrong. This is not the beginning of our troubles, nor will it be the end of them, so long as this farce goes on. Gersdorff would have me cut Friedrich from my life. Such an act would rip the very breath from my bosom, tear my soul asunder. Forsake Friedrich? My brother is the one constant in my life. And I should lose that anchor, for what reason? To put to rest the tittering gossips? To appease the jealousies of others? I know what they whisper of me, and yet I hold my head higher still."

Having collected herself, Elisabeth turned about and faced Richard with a composure that he would have thought beyond the mastery of anyone but Cosima.

"I believe it was your Schopenhauer, Herr Wagner . . ."

"Please, call me Richard."

"Very well. Richard, then. What was it that Schopenhauer said? 'Of inference all are capable; of judgment, only a few.'"

"Quite right."

"Well, Richard. I say let the many infer, for what harm is there really in that? And let those few who would dare claim divinity pass their judgment upon me, condemn me to the fires of Hell, even. They have no power over me, for I know that my Maker loves me. My relationship with God is my own affair."

Richard bowed in her direction. "I must say, you are a remarkable woman, Miss Nietzsche. The baron is a fool to let you go."

Elisabeth nodded her gratitude. "I apologize for going on so. You have been very kind. Do excuse me, I must return to my room and put myself to rights again."

As she exited the room, so did an air of majesty, imparting new inspiration to the safe keeping of the musician.

Despite Wagner's protestations, Christmas night did turn out to be Elisabeth's last night at Tribschen. She could no longer withstand the sight of Cosima fawning over both Friedrich and Gersdorff. Indeed, the farce was entirely too much to tolerate when, after Wagner had gifted his mistress with a performance of his heretofore unperformed composition *Siegfried-Idyll*, Friedrich stood and announced that he, too, had a present for Cosima in the form of his manuscript *The Birth of the Idea of Tragedy*—a manuscript he had not shared with Elisabeth, a manuscript she had not known he was working on. Her heart fell numb as she thought of all of the long, laborious hours she had put into researching, discussing, and debating Spinoza with her brother, only to find that *The Birth of Tragedy* was but a brain child to be revised to Cosima's liking. Hurt transformed into hysterics when Wagner stepped forward, seized the extended manuscript before Cosima could manage, brought it to his face for close inspection, and clapped Friedrich on the back in a show of gratitude.

"You have outdone yourself, Nietzsche! We thank you for your kind gift and shall enjoy reading it together."

Elisabeth stifled a chuckle behind the palm of her hand, but then quickly sobered when she saw that Gersdorff was doing the same at the expense of her brother's set down. "Do tell, Baron," she raised her voice to a pitch to be overheard by all. "What gaiety is this from one whose engagement has just been broken?"

An audible gasp went up in the room as Gersdorff raised his glass of schnapps in mock salutation, acknowledging that he had just been outfoxed, chastised, and publicly disclaimed with one masterful set down by a woman who, like the spirits in his glass, was at once bitter and sweet.

"It's really quite simple, Elisabeth. As ever, I was thinking of war, wondering what would become of us all if Atum and Sekhmet were to join their hands in matrimony."

o o o

CHAPTER XVII

∞

Baudelaire has declared war on Wagner. Truly, must Faustina defer to Valkyrie's judgment? What pretense is this?

∞

Spring 1870

At their mother's insistence, it was decided that Friedrich and Elisabeth should embark on an extended period of travel until the scandal of Elisabeth's broken engagement blew over. By the spring of 1870, brother and sister were spending lazy days in Clarens on Lake Geneva, a small village situated in and among the snowcapped Vaud Alps. Before their departure from Tribschen, Wagner made no secret of his esteem for Elisabeth, likening her beauty to the splendor of the royal courts of Europe. At the time, Friedrich had dismissed such uncharacteristic obsequiousness as but more of the composer's eccentric dramatics. But here, ensconced in Nature's majesty, he saw his sister as others must see her. Like the mountains, she stood stalwart, exuding an air of regality over all that resides beneath the heavens. Almost as if she were the mother of man. Of a sudden he was jealous of Christ.

Elisabeth and Friedrich came to a halting stop at the water's edge. The descent from their cabin a quarter of a mile above had been more of a brambling slide than a downward hike, sending them both into fits of fright, followed by laughter. They spread out a blanket and dropped to sit upon it as each collected breath. Falling to her back, Elisabeth shielded her eyes from the sun as she stared into the blue.

"Cloud gazing?" Of late, it seemed that Friedrich was not able to tolerate the companionable silence they had once shared in long intervals.

"*Da.* How far we are from Grandma Oehler's garden," she mused. "No shade trees, no ornate flowers, no wild foliage to provide us shelter from the world beyond ourselves. Just open skies, lording over the temples Nature has built unto God. No idle talk of virtue here. Here resides Truth's commandment, does it not?"

Friedrich leaned back on his elbows and tried to see the horizon as his Eli saw it. "*Thou shalt not lie.*" His whispered musings were followed by an eerie silence as if the Lord had truly spoken and there was an end to it. Just as quickly as the thought passed Elisabeth's mind, Friedrich rolled to his side and came down on one elbow to face her. "But then what is it to lie," he challenged her with a waggling of his brows, "when falsehoods are our only reality? Truth requires inquiry. Where social convention is concerned, inquiry is inconvenient, for the individual it is but self-invention." Searching her face, he reached down and gently brushed a curl behind her ear. "To cease lying is to cease living."

"And if honesty should bring one to the brink of darkness, to the brink of death?" She whispered her query as his lips hovered just centimeters above her own.

"Then you, sweet Lizzie, have relinquished yourself to another's Truth."

His lips fell hot on hers, and she knew in that moment that God was no celibate. Immaculate Conception was but another lie.

o o o

From Clarens, the siblings travelled to the Bern Mountains, where they were joined by Friedrich's friend and colleague, Franz Overbeck, before journeying on alone to *Axenstein bei Brunnen.*

Like a predatory fiend, Cosima von Bülow managed to trek alongside them via her correspondences that found them at every stop. No one understood better than Elisabeth that no greater deceiver was there than a woman who coveted all which she could not have. She felt for Cosima, particularly given the pathetic pretenses under which she wrote to Friedrich: Did his tooth still ache? She recommended extraction. Might he be willing to pick up a copy of Durer's *Melencolia* for her to gift to her lover for his birthday? Speaking of melancholy, was her dear friend lonely? Mayhap he should get a dog.

Elisabeth jotted off a response, informing Cosima that she had given both brother and sister a fit of the jollies with her latter suggestion. *Darling girl, if you would like a lapdog, you need*

not hint around about it. We shall make a present of one to you when
next we find our way to Tribschen.

Spring turned to summer and no sooner had the travelers made their way to Tribschen than France declared war on Prussia, just weeks after receiving news that Prince Leopold would indeed assume the Spanish throne. Bismarck had played his part in the carefully engineered provocation, successfully rallying the German states to Prussia's side. Both Austria and Switzerland announced neutrality, though the Swiss retained a fully equipped defense force. In spite of it all, life at the Wagner abode was the same as it ever was: impervious to reality. A truth? A lie? Or just an illusion? Elisabeth gave it a moment's consideration and then determined she would embrace whichever best suited her in any given circumstance.

"Miss Nietzsche, we are honored to have you with us once again." Here was an illusion, she decided, for there was nothing decisive about the man bowing over her hand. To some the composer represented a disciple of Truth, a beacon lighting the way to Christ's unblighted right hand side. To others he was a devious despot, peddling discord, marketing an elixir for despondency, perpetuating pogroms. A man who stood for everything and nothing. What must it be like to hold such power over individual perceptions? Elisabeth was intrigued.

With each passing day of their visit, Friedrich grew more concerned over the amount of time that the composer spent in company with his sister. Their solitary rides on horseback grew longer, and the need to "take fresh air" more frequent.

"Tell us," Friedrich spoke over dinner, "what wisdom has my sister imparted that holds you so enamored of her companionship, Richard?"

Both Elisabeth's and Cosima's widened eyes shot to Wagner, awaiting his reply. "Friedrich, you of all people should know how enlightening Elisabeth's conversation can be. Brazen, this one." He nodded in Elisabeth's direction.

124

"Would you believe just this afternoon she had the temerity to ask me if I believe myself to be a Jew? 'Confess it,' she said to me. 'How could one so wise in the ways of the world not know his secret self? Is it not reality to which the anarchist protests too much?'"

Wagner laughed heartily and slapped his knee at the memory of her bald-facedness. "I know now, Friedrich, the secret ingredient to your high spirits. Refreshing, is your Elisabeth."

Cosima stood abruptly from the table. "Yes, invigorating," she intoned. "Elisabeth, dear, if you have finished with your dinner, I propose that we take coffee in the garden this evening."

"Sounds lovely to me! I, for one, don't care to be spoken of as if I'm not at all present."

"Come now, Elisabeth," Richard called to her departing figure. "Pray, do not blame a man for forgetting himself in your presence. You make blessed fools of our sex. Imprudent men will imprudent acts commit," he laughed jovially.

"Indeed," concurred her brother, "Lizzie has a way about her that reconciles a man to the world."

The men's joint laughter carried through the parlor and out into the garden, stoking Cosima's ire and stroking Elisabeth's ego.

"I'm so sorry we were unable to find a dog for you," Elisabeth attempted to cut the tension between them as she and Cosima winded their way along the gravel path in and around the shrubs in bloom.

"Don't be silly, dear. What would I want of a pet when I have two such good friends as you and Friedrich?"

Elisabeth's lips took on a ruthless smile. She had no doubt that she was the dog and Friedrich the pet in this cutting analogy. Cunning as Cosima's words were, Elisabeth had long ago found herself to be immune to such attempts at cruelty. Having been denied control beneath Gustav's bulk and stripped of her dignity by Peter's treachery, she was beyond the reach of another's manipulation. Nothing took hold of Elisabeth that she did not summon forth herself. On this evening, she beckoned the fortitude of Faustina.

Friedrich closely eyed his sister and Wagner on the coming morning. She had not come to him last night. Nevertheless, upon careful inspection, he was satisfied that she had not made a Caesar of Wagner. He thought of the Bridegroom in the Garden of Eden, and realized that his friend, having once made a fiend of himself, would not hesitate to take yet another man's wife as his mistress. He was relieved that Cosima would soon be made as honest a woman as could be expected, yet aggrieved that his sister would never know such peace. Not fair! He chastised himself. Lizzie knew him better than any, and so she would be privy to Truth. Goliath to man's ignorantly false and falsely ignorant construct of honesty.

° ° °

CHAPTER XVIII

∞

He had been granted wings — could have taken flight to any realm of existence. But like Orpheus, Mephistopheles looked back, and God was mad with revenge.

∞

Though Friedrich had always insisted that true heroes had no cause for battle, he petitioned the Swiss government for permission to serve in defense of his native Prussia against the French scourge. Permission was granted with the caveat that, as a citizen of the neutral nation, his service would be confined to a medical transport unit. Thus, in early August he accepted an assignment as an orderly, stopping first in Erlangen for training before joining the front near Worth.

Elisabeth returned to Tribschen during this time, assisting Cosima in the final preparations for her wedding on August 25. The couple's two young illegitimate children, Eva and Seigfried, were to be included in the wedding party, a snub against convention even greater than the adulterous relationship that produced them. Elisabeth doted on the children.

Recognizing the wistful look of what-might-have-been in Elisabeth's eyes, Cosima developed a growing affection for the Fraulein Nietzsche and tried hard to forgive her idolatrous infatuation of Richard. After all, a woman filled with guilt must have a god to confess her sins to. Cosima, having two such confessors, decided to be charitable and relinquish a severance of her attention. For while she would marry one, she preferred the other, and what better way to keep a rein on both than to have Elisabeth ever present at her bosom.

"And what news is there of Friedrich these days?"

Elisabeth glimpsed up from her position on the floor where she now pinned the hem on a dress from Cosima's trousseau and wondered if she looked the veriest vulture she, herself, had once frowned down upon. "He has developed a bit of a chest ailment. It is not unlike Friedrich to dismiss the seriousness of such a predicament, but I do so wish he would take his health seriously and come home to us."

Cosima arched an eyebrow. "Home? To us? Do you consider Tribschen home, dear? Oh, do say it's so! The children just adore you, and I would love nothing more than to be a sister to you. To help you find such happiness as is ours." She swept her arm about her, drawing attention to all that she and Richard held together, instantly regretting her words as she realized that Elisabeth's gaze had fallen on the children playing on the floor. She placed a comforting hand on Elisabeth's shoulder. "Your happiness will soon come, darling. We will find you a virtuous man, constant in his affections."

Elisabeth nearly choked on the laughter gurgling in her throat, threatening to trumpet the irony of Cosima's proposed quest. *And you, Miss Nietzsche? Are you virtuous?* When she finally spoke what she heard was "Truly, Cosima? Why should I settle for a virtuous man when I possess the virtue to claim God for myself?" She tapped her chin in pretended thought. "Brazen temerity, I believe your bridegroom called it." Then she laughed the laugh of one who was on intimate terms with the mad . . . and Cosima was afraid.

Diphtheria. Elisabeth folded the missive she had received that morning and clutched it close to her heart. The diagnosis meant that Friedrich would have to be moved to a care facility without delay. The postscript included a line from Baron von Gersdorff, assuring her that arrangements were underway to move Friedrich to the Hotel Walfisch in Erlangen until further transport to Naumburg could be arranged.

Though there had been little contact between them since Christmas at Tribschen, Elisabeth had diligently scoured the broadsheets for any news of the baron. He was fresh from the front of the Battle of Gravelotte where more than 20,000 Prussian troops were either killed, wounded, or went missing during the bloodiest battle of the war. For him to take time to see to the well-being of her family now filled her eyes with tears and her heart with regret.

Elisabeth dashed the falling tears from her cheeks and steeled herself for what must be done: making immediate arrangements to return to Naumburg, where she would oversee Friedrich's convalescence.

° ° °

Celebrations went up in the streets of Naumburg upon word of the Prussian victory in the Battle of Sedan. Down, but not out, the Prussian forces had devastated the French army, forcing Napoleon the III to call off attacks. The next day the emperor was captured along with some 80,000 of his men, wreaking havoc in Paris and launching premature proclamations of victory in Berlin. All celebrations across Prussia would come to an end once word spread of the regrouped and revitalized French militias, soldiering on without their emperor.

Elisabeth looked about her and noted the heightened disparities between the classes since last she was in Naumburg. The division of wealth that all knew of and none spoke of was now somehow . . . blaringly blatant. There was no veil thick enough to cloak or condone pleas of ignorance. The power of Prussian patriotism gave indisputable voice to aristocracy and clergy, while stripping the peasant and the Jew of the right to even form opinions. There were clearly defined borders between the territories that belonged to the merchant classes and those of peasant workers. And then there was what could only be described as ghettos, relegated for those Jews not rich enough to pose as pretenders. Was this to be Prussia's future? A German confederacy, pieced together through war, ripped apart from within?

Elisabeth reached the door to Weingarten 18, inserted her key, and entered to find her brother already in residence, lying on the parlor couch. He turned his head toward her and she sucked in a sharp breath. From her position in the foyer, she could see that he was gravely fatigued and burning with fever, his chest rattling with the cough of a consumptive.

"So, Eli, you have come for me at last."

Attempting to conceal her shudder at his condition, Elisabeth removed her bonnet as she advanced into the parlor. "Of course I came, darling." She pulled a stool up to the couch and pressed her hand against the scar on his chest. "Where else would I be when my heart bleeds?" she asked softly.

Friedrich placed his hand over hers and held it tighter to his chest as if he were entreating her to reach through the old wound and touch his heart. "No matter how I may try, I'll never be a battle-hardened hero." He meant to laugh, but the only sound that came forth was the cough of one whose throat was constricted by toxins. His fit calmed and his eyes quieted as he fixed them in her gaze, lifting her soft hand to his lips. "Tell me, love. Are you actually able to draw breath in Naumburg? Does the stench not make you gag?"

Elisabeth smoothed the fevered tendrils of hair from his forehead. "Shh," she soothed. "The fever has you talking nonsense."

He turned his head away from her. "I have been talking nonsense my entire life; the whole world speaks nonsense." He shifted his head again, looking to the ceiling and crumpling his nose in offense at the inanity he found just above. "And it stinks of shit. Of the decomposing excrement shat upon man nearly two thousand years past." He turned his face back to his sister. "And so what do you make of it, Lizzie?" he asked almost frantically. "Prussia has crowned herself God. Hence, the Jew swims in a sea of sewage." He reached up and caressed her cheek with the backs of his fingers. "And you? Will you sink or swim?"

His laugh resounded raw, wild, maniacal. For a brief second, Elisabeth's own laughter rang about in her ears, and then all faded to a fugue of lilac.

It had been some time since she had suffered such a spell. Yet here it was—here they were: Gustav, Peter, Gersdorff, Friedrich, and . . . Paul? Why had he tormented her so of late? She searched her mind for a ghost of a memory, but came up blank. She shuddered and shoved the unpleasant torment of thought back into its sepulcher. Vaguely aware of Friedrich's weak fingers combing through her curls, Elisabeth came fully awake to find herself on the floor, her legs tucked beneath her, her head resting on the couch, her neck extended in expectation of the stroke of her brother's hand. The sudden horrific image of an executioner flashed before her eyes, prompting Elisabeth to jolt to her feet and retreat from the room in a state of freakish frenzy.

Somehow, somewhere, someway, there was another someone. She swiped her hand across her forehead, and then lowered her sweat-drenched palm beneath her gaze. Her head swam in synchronicity with the rivulets that rolled across her skin. "Dear God, there must be another!"

Friedrich heard her shouted plea from the stairway above.

Elisabeth lay abed, trenching the depths of mind and soul in search of an explanation for Paul's reemergence in her thoughts. What had she done to him that she could not recall or vanquish from memory? Had she been too forward, too needy? Was he so disgusted by her lust for a Jew that he could not even now reach out to her? Was it necessary for her to assume that she had lost her friend to anything but the call of God? She surmised it was possible that Friedrich had simply warned him off.

Remembering one of Paul's many favored quotations from the *Bhagavad Gita*, Elisabeth demanded order of her random thoughts. *The mind acts like an enemy for those who do not control it.* She whispered Krishna's admonishment aloud to herself. Pulling off the coverlet, she swung her legs to the side of the bed and took to her feet. The floor beneath her was cold, but there would be warmth in the spirits she sought from the study. Her progress was arrested just outside her designation. Hell and damnation! There stood Friedrich taking solace from a drink of his own. She rushed forward.

"Friedrich! What on earth are you doing out of bed in your state?" Her gaze roamed his form, propped as it was against the desk for support. "You can hardly stand on your own," she chided as she scrambled to place her weight beneath his.

Friedrich allowed her to drape his arm over her shoulder before drawling out, "Come now, Lizzie. It's not all that bad." He pressed his advantage, pulling her closer still and bringing her forehead to meet his lips. The alcohol on his breath was too strong for one so weak in constitution.

"Friedrich, stop this now! We must get you back to bed immediately."

He stroked her hair in response. She knew he meant to be tender, but the drink had rendered him heavy of hand. "I will go to bed, my love, as I always have done, after I see you content in your slumber."

Elisabeth expelled a breath in acquiescence and carried his weight to her chamber.

Something was terribly, terribly wrong. In a hazed state of awareness, Elisabeth grew frantic at her failed attempts to disengage herself from her opaque oppressor. She screamed aloud, yet there was no sound. She swung her arms in fight, yet they lay limp by her side. She began to cry, yet the dry tears on her cheeks were not her own. With great struggle she lifted her heavy lids, and took in Friedrich's concerned eyes as they searched her face for some sign of sanity. His rims were red from tears shed hours past. Friedrich retreated as Elisabeth struggled to purchase perch upon her elbows.

His gaze grew deeper in concern as he cautiously cupped her cheek with shaking hand. "You hate me," he blurted out on a sob. "Are my hands so despised as you say?"

Dazed, Elisabeth lifted her hand to cover and hold his own closer to her cheek. "Don't speak so Friedrich. Where does this come from?"

He pulled his hand free and passed it over his face. "From your own lips, Lizzie. From your very own lips." Her attention transfixed on the trembling forefinger hovering before her lips. Slowly, as if he were in pain, as if his limbs were as heavy as her own, he traced her bottom lip. "You questioned why I touch you so. 'God above!' you shouted, 'Am I so beneath your contempt that you would rape me barren?'"

Elisabeth gasped as her fingers flew to his lips, silencing his words. Tears streamed down her cheeks. "Oh, Friedrich, forgive me," she breathed out. "Those words were not directed at you."

He gently removed her fingers from his mouth. "No, I would give you an answer." He closed his eyes almost as if he could shut out the sound of his own words by isolating himself within the darkness known only by him. *Friedrich! How did you find me?* He flinched before resuming speech. "There is nothing contemptible about you. More still, there is nothing beneath or beyond my grasp. Yours either, I would wager. Sex, the lust to rule, selfishness — not one of us can hide from God's curse and man's temporary burden." A low laugh escaped him as his eyes came open. "Temporary, only because the Almighty covets power high and low. He would rake Eternity's womb to harvest and hoard unto himself the spawning seeds of Truth sown by the Antichrist."

Friedrich looked down and realized he still held Elisabeth's fingers enclosed in his hand. He brushed his thumb over her knuckles in deep contemplation, working up the courage to ask her the one question to which he dreaded the answer. "Who has raped and robbed you of that which God delights in, Lizzie? Tell me, and I shall reap his beating heart from his barren soul."

Elisabeth scrambled from the bed, shaking her head sorrowfully. "I suspect it was myself." She covered her face with her hands, unable to suffer his pitying gaze. It was all too much to stomach. He looked upon her as the Holy Father would a lost sheep. She needed a diversion, a superficial rock to forfend the test of Truth. Yes, she was needy, and forward, if need be. A sudden thought occurred to her. "Get yourself well, Friedrich, and we shall return to Tribschen."

○ ○ ○

CHAPTER IXX

∞

Forever indecisive – stagnated even – Honir still has no real conviction, and so it is left to Artemis . . . à vivre à travers lui.

∞

By the time Paris surrendered on January 28, 1871, Friedrich was well enough for travel once again. With plans to visit Tribschen at a later date, he and Elisabeth journeyed to Lugano for a six-week stay. An awakening grew in Elisabeth during this trip, a dawning comprehension of the power of ideology. Why had she not seen it before? For as long as she could remember, she had taken Friedrich's every philosophical leaning to heart, felt his convictions, and appreciated the links between the history that shaped those convictions and the future that could be shaped by them. Missing from her awareness was the developing journey between that once envisioned and its actual culmination.

She imagined how she must have looked, eye pressed to a telescope, peering across the waters to Tribschen, longing to be a part of the Wagners' elite circle. Then she thought of Richard Wagner and all that he endured during his exiled years, his music a direct result of his having stood up for what he once believed in. She had wasted years nodding her head in agreement with men of logic, hoping she might, in this way, gain entry into higher circles. Why should she not have ideas of her own? Why had she relegated herself to the role of troll when she should be fighting her way across the bridge? Notoriety was not to be had by hanging on the coattails of those who had made history, but to be among those who forged a new narrative.

As she and her brother sat now in a quaint café across from the equally loved and despised "Beating Heart of Italy," Giuseppe Mazzini, a chorus of *either books or babies* played in her head. Her choice for babies lay long dead. No, it was time she had books, ideas, and social standing of her own devise. Just what those ideas were or how they would come to fruition, she had not yet determined. For now, it was enough to have made up her mind to acquire them. Friedrich had always said she was a quick study, and here before her was an opportunity to learn something beyond that which was limited to knee-level.

When Mazzini first wandered over to their table, Elisabeth eyed him warily. Clothed in a threadbare jacket, faded breeches, shoddy boots, and — was that hat moth eaten? — he looked to be a beggar. He sat, presumably at Friedrich's invitation. Unlike Friedrich's, her Italian was not what it should be. She sat in complete ignorance of their conversation, nodding her head at appropriate intervals as a proper lady should, until Mazzini flashed a staying hand at Friedrich. Entreating a pause, he inclined his head toward Elisabeth and addressed her in German.

"Fraulein Nietzsche, how rude we are to exclude you from our conversation. We speak of the Carbonari. A dangerous topic of conversation, no?"

Indeed it was, Elisabeth pondered, recalling what she knew of the radical secret societies of nationalists who had been known to form alliances with Jews and organize riots to illustrate their strength in demand for the reformation of the political structure. Particularly in Italy. After years of exile Mazzini had all but won his battle. With the capture of Napoleon III, word was that Italian sympathies were leaning toward the radicals and cries for a stronger citizenry. Yes, it was a hazardous topic, but Elisabeth did not want to kick off her intellectual independence by coming down on the losing side of history. She launched into what she hoped was a response of which her companions would approve.

"Dangerous it is, Signore! But what a thrill it must be to see the budding fruits of your labor. A unified Italy, strong and revered," she mused. "Exactly the result we seek of our German Confederacy." She raised her glass in a toast. "To nationalism."

Glasses clinked. Elisabeth and Mazzini sipped in honor of victory as Friedrich contemplated just what his sister's idea of nationalism entailed. He received his answer when he heard her warn Mazzini against allying with the Jews.

"Better to know where their loyalties truly lie," she intoned.

Built at the site of a sixteenth century convent, the *Hotel du Parc* in the Italian-speaking region of Lugano, Switzerland, was everything and more than what Elisabeth had imagined it to be. Though the cabin in Lucerne had its appeal, the *Hotel du Parc* offered up an ambience of antiquity—just the right setting for one who sought the formula for enlightenment.

She was beyond delighted when she espied the renowned photographer, Francis Frith, setting up his equipment on the wharf. Grabbing Friedrich's hand, Elisabeth rushed him in the direction of the photographer. Busy adjusting his equipment, Frith broke concentration at the sounds of gaiety and joyous abandon that preceded the couple's approach. The photographer spoke first. "You are here for a photograph, and it would be my honor to capture the rapture of your love for all eternity."

Friedrich laughed and shook Frith's hand amiably. "A bit dramatic, don't you think?"

"Life is a drama, my dear boy. 'All the world's a stage.' Shakespeare would accept nothing less than for the artist to write the script, *as you like it*." Frith nudged Friedrich's elbow encouraging him to join him in his joke.

"An artist with wit and a way with words. As a philosopher, I concede the match to you." Friedrich bowed in mock reverence, and then extended his hand to Elisabeth. "May I present my sister, Mr. Frith?"

Frith's eyes widened. His face flushed red with embarrassment, before he quickly recovered. "Ah, but of course. Siblings. I should have guessed. I mistook the brilliant innocence of exuberance for the equally consuming fires of passion." He positioned them before the camera and looked into the lens, bringing brother and sister into focus. His head came up immediately at what he saw there. "Or perhaps I was not mistaken."

Friedrich smiled with an attempt to make light of what the photographer picked up with his keen eye. *"Vivre sa vie!"*

"Indeed, it is your life to live." Frith disappeared behind the camera's curtain and snapped their picture, sending flashing light and a purplish smoke into the atmosphere.

It came as no surprise to find the photograph hanging on the hotel guest board the next day. It was a daily ritual for patrons to file by to see themselves and the images of others who could say they had seen and been seen at the fashionable resort. Nonetheless, as she stood by her brother's side, Elisabeth could not spare a gaze for any photograph but theirs. She leaned sideways to bend his ear.

"How abstemious you look beneath that hat!" She made her point by employing her severest impersonation of his voice.

Friedrich's lips quirked upward. "And here I expected you to say that you could see nothing beneath my hat except for my mustache."

Elisabeth scrunched her nose up at the offending shrub enshrouding his upper lip. "It is atrocious, you have to confess. I will never understand why men insist on sporting what positively looks like dead vermin on their visages."

"But it does give one pause for thought, does it not? What grander achievement is there for a philosopher than to at once arrest and provoke the machinations of the mind?"

Elisabeth punched his shoulder. "Well, I can concede this much. For all its severity, your expired rat does reduce the sickly countenance you have had since your illness." She reached up and brushed a curl back from his forehead. "You have had such a difficult time of it, dearest. It does my heart good to see you enjoying yourself."

The smiling Friedrich turned serious once again upon the evening. Choosing to take their dinner in the hotel restaurant, he and Elisabeth found themselves seated with members of General Helmuth von Moltke's immediate family. Upon introductions to Frau Maria von Moltke, her father John Heyliger and his wife (and Helmuth's sister) Augusta, polite conversation was exchanged. Friedrich expressed his admiration for the general's service to the crown, his ingenious military skill, and his widely published essays and articles that detailed his years organizing armies in the Ottoman Empire.

The family could wholeheartedly appreciate such praise. He was certainly not alone in his commendation given that—should the family dare divulge? But, of course! There could be no harm in it. Word would get out soon enough—the general was to receive the title of Count for his valor. How good it was to be victorious over France at last! The prospects for the German Confederation were indeed without parallel despite a unified Italy.

More pleasantries were exchanged before the conversation turned to the future of Germany; a topic few of their countrymen had come to an agreement on, much less the small group at the table.

"Do not be deceived into believing the war to be over," the general's wife confided, imparting her husband's words of wisdom to the diners. "'What our sword has won in half a year, our sword must guard for half a century.' How remiss we would be if we let ourselves become complacent in the face of those who would threaten to dismember our nation. We must preserve the peace."

Elisabeth prayed in vain that her brother would restrain his tongue.

"Come, now. Let us not pretend that any nation maintains a ready military for the sake of peace. Hobbes had the right of it. The only way to ensure peace is to lay down the sword for contracted survival. I would take it even further and posit that it is not enough to lay down the sword, but to break it." Holding his glass aloft, Friedrich watched the wine within swirl as he twirled the stem between his fingers. From the way in which his companions looked at him, he may as well have been an apostate—*or an Antichrist with disciples*, he laughed inaudibly. "No, as long as we have need of defense, we have need of war. With pride grows an appetite for greater power and more war. Have we the guts to break the sword, or is it beneath our pride?"

Once again he took in the incredulous looks frozen upon the faces of his tablemates. "No answer, I see." With that he placed his glass upon the table, rose without excusing himself and sauntered out of the dining room.

Elisabeth was mortified.

"I'll beg you to forgive my brother's passions. Strong in his belief that it is the men of letters who shall forge our future, he holds ideals that, while laudable, are not necessarily realistic given the unholy assault our people are currently under. He once told me that unity of man, free of compromise, ready to sacrifice everything to Truth, was at hand. Christian principles are, of course, what he's really advocating," she lied. "'Love thy neighbor,' and so on. Unfortunately, I'm sure you'll agree, our neighbor is not always in want of God's love. To break the sword would be to break faith with our Lord."

Pleased with the self-determining ring to her words, Elisabeth nodded her satisfaction to the occupants at table, all of whom were working hard to hide their discomfiture at her baffling speech. Did she speak of the Jacobins or the Jews? Did she even know of what she prattled on about?

○ ○ ○

CHAPTER XX

∞

He offers freedom from the foils of life and the spoils of war. Freia, it must be considered, may be nothing more than Froh's Phantasie.

∞

Elisabeth had known they would inevitably cross paths again. Still she had not fathomed how painful it would be to lay eyes on Gersdorff for the first time since the dissolution of their engagement. Caught up in the delight of their return to Tribschen, Elisabeth turned over her pelisse and bonnet to the manservant who welcomed her and Friedrich into the Wagners' home. Hugs were exchanged all around before Richard caught hold of Elisabeth's hand, tucked it within the crook of his arm and escorted her to the sitting room, Cosima and Friedrich lagging just behind.

"Come," the composer urged. "You must share with us every detail of your sojourn. I daresay I was quite envious — and dare I say insulted? — when you wrote to Cosima without sparing a single line for a jaded radical in need of fresh inspiration.

"I have lived among the snow-capped Alps for an eternity, Miss Nietzsche, but I've no doubt that a glimpse anew through your eyes would infuse me with a new score-worthy perspective."

As they crossed the threshold to the sitting room, Richard held his hand out in front of them, his thumb spread apart from his fingers as if he were framing a vision. "Imagine the melody resounding from Nature's fortress. What sweet serenity! What agonizing anguish! On the whims of the wind, she plays us all for fools."

Elisabeth could attempt no reply at the moment. Indeed, her feet were like clay, weighted to the floor. The vision before her was much like the one Richard had just described. But instead of majestic mountains, she saw before her the unmalleable stature of Karl von Gersdorff, leaning over the snapping fire that filled the room with energy. Yes, here was serenity and agony. And she was definitely a fool.

Following the direction of Elisabeth's thoughts, Richard attempted to divert her attention back to him. "Friedrich, dear boy! We should like to see the pictures from your trip."

Friedrich wasn't exactly sure when he had become "dear boy," but he understood the meaning behind the *nom de guerre* quite well. If there was to be war between the two of them, Wagner would cast him as a lad, too green to satiate a woman of complex yearnings. "I believe Cosima has possession of one or more of our photos."

Having yet had his presence acknowledged, Gersdorff stepped over to the coffee table, plucked up the photo taken by Frith at the *Hotel du Parc* and examined it closely. "Here is one, I believe. It would be worthy of a frame were it not so tattered." He pointed to the bottom right corner, bent, worn and discolored by fingers that had held it overly long.

Cosima cleared her throat and retrieved the photograph the baron extended in her direction. "Ah, there it is," she trilled. "I had put this aside with the express intention of speaking to you Friedrich about that ridiculous hat. Could it not have been removed for the photograph? Why would one cover such lovely locks? I declare, you are set on making yourself old before your time! Elisabeth, how on earth could you condone such poor taste?"

Intervening before she could answer, Richard took Elisabeth's right hand and clasped it between his own. "My darling," he said to Cosima, his eyes locked with Elisabeth's, "why should one as breathtaking as the scenery around her take into account her stodgy brother's attire?" With a flourish he brought Elisabeth's hand to his lips and kissed the tips of her fingers.

Gersdorff moved forward and clapped Wagner on the shoulder. "I see you are at your flamboyant best, Richard. What say you we spare the ladies' their swooning hearts and have a bit of a smoke?"

Elisabeth thought she had successfully bitten back her smile, but realized her folly when she caught a wink from the baron's eye. It had been directed at her, hadn't it? She looked over her right shoulder to find that Cosima had caught the wink and was in response casting him a cat-like glance of either seduction or sedition. Either way, Elisabeth was willing to bet that the two of them were in bed together. Oh well, she mentally shrugged, better him than Friedrich, or even Richard, for that matter.

"Dinner went tolerably well." Richard approached from Elisabeth's right and offered her a glass of sherry.

They stood alone in the parlor as the others remained in the dining room to take their after-dinner drink. She could smell the familiar smoke of the baron's cigarette.

"I suppose you could say that, though I dare say there is a murderous tension between Karl and Friedrich."

"And can you blame them?" Richard took a sip of his drink and visibly savored it as he swallowed. She suspected he savored all things in life just so. "What a man won't do for the woman he loves," he finished with a distracted tone of voice that jolted Elisabeth to the realization that she had been staring at his throat as he swallowed.

Just as suddenly as embarrassment washed over her it was replaced by a courage as crimson as the sherry on her tongue. Old images came to mind: she, clad in red, waltzing about in Peter's arms, her mother looking beyond her in search of a girl that may never have existed.

Elisabeth laughed almost provocatively. She was just about to employ the flirtatious glance she had witnessed Cosima using earlier, when her squinting eyes landed on the vision of her hand beneath Wagner's lapel, palm flat against his chest. She was becoming a wanton.

Before she could snatch it away, his hand clamped over hers and held it possessively against his chest. "Don't assume Cosima's wiles, I beg of you, Elisabeth. Your unrehearsed reaction to passion is intoxicating in its innocence."

Elisabeth arched an eyebrow in dubious inquiry. "Do not fool yourself, Maestro. I am far from innocent and very well-rehearsed, I might add."

"Mayhap." Richard dipped a finger into his glass and then traced her plump bottom lip with its sherry stained tip, as if to paint her a harlot. She winced and flinched aback, hurt that he had made no further argument in favor of her innocence.

"You misunderstand me," he rejoined in response to her repel, still mesmerized by her lips. "Your mouth appears to me as a clean canvas on which to paint the hue of German blood; the richness of Christ's blood."

Elisabeth jerked her face away. "Stop," she shouted on a tormented whisper. "You blaspheme!"

Richard chuckled. "What? You can accept such tomfoolery from the Antichrist's mouth, but not from the Composer's soul? For you see, I do have one, Miss Nietzsche. A soul, that is. And I would come to your bed and breathe it into your being, were not I afraid of whom else I might find there."

Elisabeth gasped and nearly threw her drink in his face before determining to instead rise to the challenge that she found on his countenance. She cast him a rueful smile and slew him with a feline gaze that he found far more enticing than his wife's tired-out wiles.

Feeling as wicked as her red lips must look, Elisabeth placed her index finger beneath his chin. "For one reputed to be so brilliant, you cannot be ignorant of when your wife's bed is otherwise occupied. In which case, mine is empty." With two taps beneath his upturned chin, she turned and glided from the room like a swan unfettered.

Once in her chambers, bravado gave way to misgivings. She wondered what Richard would say had he known she had bled the blood of a Jew.

∘ ∘ ∘

When a knock came on her door several hours later, Elisabeth found herself hoping that it would be Richard, but felt only relief when Friedrich entered her chamber. Shrugging off his robe, he climbed into bed beside her, wrapped his arm around her and tucked her head beneath his chin. When a girl, she had referred to this pose as the *comfort cozen*, singular in that it conveyed the affection of a brother, not the lust of a lover.

For a long spell he rested quietly with her before finally broaching the subject of his thoughts. "Our meeting with Gersdorff could not have been easy for you today. I'm truly sorry for it." He stroked her hair as if to salve her wounds. "Had I known he would be here . . ."

"Don't, Friedrich. You could not have known, and it was an inevitability. I'm glad it's behind us. Perhaps we can put our discomfort aside and be friends once again." She tilted her head back and studied his face. "At least I hope you and he can remain friends. It pains me to think that my selfish heart may have caused an irreparable breach between the two of you."

"Shh, Lizzie. You forget that my heart is equally selfish." Friedrich chuckled. "Besides, the baron hardly endeared himself to me or Richard, for that matter, with his endless heroic tales of his exploits on the front line, unmanning a composer and a brigadier in one fell swoop."

Elisabeth laughed softly in return. "Yes, he can be quite the braggart. He once told me that he would snatch the prize of victory from the hands of God and keep it for his own. At the time he claimed I was that prize, but, in the end, he did indeed prove to be the victor. For the prize, you see, was not worth the effort." She sighed and snuggled in closer. "But still, he put a great deal of effort into bringing you home to me when you fell ill. While I would like to think it was done out of consideration for us both, it was for you alone, I'm certain."

Friedrich tilted her head back once again and brushed his lips over hers. "You are the grandest of prizes, Lizzie. The baron's dilemma has simply been that he could not snatch from the Antichrist that which is too hot for the hands of God to hold."

Elisabeth lightly smacked at his chest and blew out a frustratingly fatigued sigh. "I should berate you for your blasphemy, you know? But I am tired. The lot of you have frayed my nerves today."

"Unjust!" Friedrich protested. "The sherry on your lips tells a different story. You, dear girl, are tired from drink." He slid from the bed and retrieved his robe before bending down to kiss her once again. "Sleep well."

It wasn't until another knock came on her door a short time later that Elisabeth resigned herself to a wakeful night. She heard the door creak open, despite a lack of invitation to enter. She buried her face in her pillow. The clink of glasses and what sounded like a decanter lid being lifted prompted her to roll up tighter in her blanket.

"Oh, for Heaven's sake! I thought you said I had had enough drink for one night."

"One can never have enough drink, I always say."

Elisabeth's eyes flew open to find Richard standing over her, a glass of sherry extended in offering. He was still dressed in his evening wear, though his jacket, waistcoat, and cravat had been discarded, and his shirt sleeves were rolled up to his elbows.

"What on earth possessed you—" she demanded in unfinished protest.

"As you said, Elisabeth, when my bed is empty, I shall find you in a similar predicament. Oh, and I hope you don't find it too presumptuous of me to use your Christian name. I am standing in your bedchamber, after all."

"No, of course not. We are old friends, it seems."

Richard offered her his arm as if they were in a packed room of polite company. She stood from the bed and allowed him to lead her to the cramped seating arrangement before the crackling fire that warmed her room. Even in spring there was a chill at Tribschen. She took the seat opposite him, seething at the image of Friedrich in Cosima's arms. Was it because she had rebuffed him?

Richard sipped his sherry before addressing her unspoken thoughts. "I notice that you do not wonder as to whom it is that has put me out of my own bed. You assume Friedrich. Why not the baron?"

"Because Gersdorff has too much honor."

"Honor." He repeated the word as if it tasted like ashes on his tongue. "What is honor, but bourgeois lassitude?" Richard leaned forward, propping his elbows on his knees. "Do not fault them, Elisabeth. By your own admission, you are far from innocent yourself. And by my own admission, I am naught but an old whore willing to play any game to get what I desire."

He stared into the fire as he spoke, almost as if he expected the flames to pay heed to his imparted wisdom. "A doxy *and* a revolutionary. What do you say to that? Shall we make love or shall we make war?"

"And where has waging war gotten you, Richard, except exiled?"

"Quite right." He nodded his head deferentially. "Who knew that a few published articles, and acquaintances with August Rockel and Mikhail Bakunin, could cost a man his country?"

Elisabeth eyed him over the rim of her glass as she sipped in consideration of his question. "I suspect that it is your acquaintance with the design of a hand grenade and your willingness to launch the device that rendered you *persona non grata*."

He smiled appreciatively at her. "And so it was. All worth it, I assure you."

"I have no doubt. As a matter of fact, I am filled with awe and envy when I think of the determination it took for you to stand ready to battle for your convictions, even in the face of blazing Saxon guns, no less."

"And Prussian muzzles," he amended. "Over the resounding report of which the people still have a right to be represented by a constitutional form of government." He took a final swallow of his sherry and set his glass aside with ascertained finality behind his gesture. "Or no government at all," he added. "But let us not talk of government. I prefer the ungoverned topic of love. Have you an argument in favor or against it?"

"I will tell you as much as I have told Friedrich. Love is such a spiteful concept, particularly when it is mistaken for lust." Elisabeth pulled her legs up into her chair and tucked her feet beneath her gown. "And you, sir, are nothing if not a liturgist of lust."

"A polemicist, you mean."

"In your case, I'm willing to wager that they are one and the same."

Richard barked out a laugh, wholly unconcerned over being heard in the corridor. "My god! *Phantasie* hardly does you justice. I shall compose you anew."

Richard rose, scooped Elisabeth up in his arms, and made for the bed. She looked about the room in search of the Silent Specter. She assumed the menacing shadow would intervene when God had reached the end of his patience with her. Until then, she would live the life of another, a life worth viewing from afar.

As was the case when in Friedrich's arms, she was met with only silence. The decision left up to her, she would take a chance on actually being composed anew this time.

° ° °

CHAPTER XXI

∞

"Hell is empty and all the devils are here." If I could but contact The Bard, I have no doubt he would warn me against carnal relations.

∞

Richard was surprisingly vigorous for a man thirty-three years her senior. But, then, it should have come as no surprise, given the adventurous life he had lived. Like Friedrich, he was strong in his convictions. Unlike Friedrich, Richard had been willing to take up arms, to risk life and limb, for the betterment of his people and the human condition as he saw it. He was a provocateur in and out of bed, and Elisabeth felt torn in her allegiance.

Friedrich's commitment to Truth was grander in scope. He would take on the world at once: provoke all of mankind to see beyond themselves, to look to a universe as fathomless as eternity for the meaning of existence.

Richard, on the other hand, had her nearly convinced that one must first form borders within which Christian brothers could come together, strengthen an alliance of German stock, worthy of forging a path for all existence.

Both men lived by the words of Schopenhauer, selectively drawing on those of his philosophies that suited their respective causes. Where Richard hung his actions on Schopenhauer's belief that a man of wisdom will see through the superficiality of the thoughts of others and correct their way of thinking, Friedrich found credence in the idea that man's most unassailable right was complete ownership of his own life and person. One took a nationalistic perspective, the other a cosmic perspective.

There was merit in both arguments, she recognized. On whose side should she take up position? In the arms of a thinker who would someday do? Or in the arms of a revolutionary who had done? She mentally shook her head in dismay. Had she not just recently made up her mind to do for herself?

The nights that followed were a study in scandal. Having taken to assuming that there would be no room for him in his bed, it was becoming a nightly routine for Richard to settle himself by the fire in Elisabeth's chamber. She had no doubt that Friedrich knew of these rendezvous, as surely as she knew where he could be found in these hours. She was not adverse to him seething with a little jealousy. As she was learning from Richard: for every wretch there was a rotter; and if the composer's life were any example, there was much to be salvaged from the decay of depravity. Suddenly his broodingly dark compositions made sense.

During his years in exile, Richard had upended the sheets of nearly every woman whose acquaintance profited him. In Switzerland, he had taken up with a close friend's wife, despite his continuing marriage to the actress Minnie Planer. Julie Ritter's patronage went beyond financial support. So intrigued was she, an introduction was made to a friend, Jessie Laussot, with hopes that she would be able to make her own financial contribution toward the realization of Wagner's dream achievement *Der Ring des Nibulungen*. It was to be a four-opera cycle, a compilation of several finished works and several more in progress. Madame Ritter's patronage lasted beyond his stay in Switzerland, while that of Madame Laussot's came to an end after Monsieur Laussot uncovered Richard's plan to elope with his wife.

On it was, then, to Mathilde Wesendonck, wife of the silk merchant, Otto Wesendonck. From Wagner's tale of this affair, Elisabeth gleaned that Mathilde had been the inspiration for *Tristan and Isolde*. Whatever tonic Wagner had in mind to remedy the malady of their respective marriages, it had clearly worn off when Minnie intercepted letters from Mathilde, putting an end to that particular affair.

Never one to be dissuaded, Richard gallivanted his way through society and on to his next conquest: the wife of the Austrian Ambassador to Paris, Princess Pauline von Metternich. What an inspiration she had been! From that *affaire de coeur* was born *Tannhauser*, Wagner's musical rendition of the sacred and the profane to be discovered in the despot, Love.

Little could shock Elisabeth in these days. Nevertheless her eyes widened and her conscious murmured misgivings when he revealed the truth behind his relations with King Ludwig II of Bavaria. The eighteen-year-old monarch had reached out to Wagner in a letter, which opened with an expression of deep affection for and admiration of his "beloved one," his "adored one." There was financial gain to be had, Wagner explained to her, and even one of a deviant sexual persuasion could be sexually persuaded in turn. The pretense was no hardship, he assured his paramour of the day. For Ludwig had been a thing of ethereal beauty, as mesmerizing as melodic transcendence, with his dark, wavy hair, his boyish good looks, and his effeminate physique.

Most definitely, there had been much to gain from that quarter with still more to come. Why, even Tribschen had been a gift from Ludwig!

"You jest!"

"Assuredly not! Why would I purchase a home that I can scarcely afford to furnish?"

Elisabeth looked to the ceiling. With all of the goings on beneath this roof, she should have known that it had been built as shelter for sexual congress. With sudden curiosity, she eyed her companion speculatively, trying to determine if she was but another hardship among a string of many conquests, and if her brother had ever found himself in this very position.

° ° °

Elisabeth sought out Friedrich first thing the next morning. As expected, he was found in the drawing room writing one of many letters to his colleagues. One, already sealed and addressed to Basel, was a missive requesting an extension of his leave of absence from the university; his health still not being quite up to par. She suspected that he had made up his mind to permanently limit his associations. Increasingly, he seemed to prefer writing over personal interactions. Socials and even small group gatherings were becoming more and more difficult for him to endure. Most academics, she reflected, were socially awkward, but her brother seemed to have withdrawn from all attempts to interact outside of his small circle of friends. All of the debates that he once relished now took place in his mind or on paper. It was almost as if he were posing an argument on behalf of one not his equal and feared he may lose the internal debate. Elisabeth hated to interrupt him in these moments of concentration, but she simply must speak to him about Richard.

"You need not tell me what you were up to last night." Friedrich spoke without a single interruption to his present occupation. "I need not even guess. As I once told you, I'll always know where my soul lay, and last night it lay with a master."

He turned then and watched as Elisabeth's eyes darted disconcertingly about the room. He could see the wheels of wile turning in her brain. She was desperately scrambling for a response.

For a brief moment she wondered if he meant to tell her that he, too, had succumbed to the "master." "May I have a word with you?" Her voice was unsteady.

"Proceed."

"How many are there—I mean to say, is it true—"

Friedrich laid his pen down. He was angry, but not cruel enough to force her to suffer her folly alone. "You want to know about the king of Bavaria. 'Tis true enough," he nodded almost mournfully. "Even now your lover drafts a memoir for the boy-king. He has asked me to look over it for him, and I must say it is so full of heart I have committed the sin of coveting." He waved his hand airily about. "Coveted his spouse, coveted his lover, or perhaps both. If I were but a boy-king." Friedrich meditated into space for a moment before resuming his train of thought. "Deussen was a firm believer in seizing every experience in search of enlightenment. I have seized and you have seized. Do you feel enlightened this morn?"

Elisabeth turned away so that he would not see the tears threatening to spill from her eyes. Once composed, she spun back around to face him. "Enlightened. Indeed I do feel enlightened. Paul Deussen has haunted me of late. Never once did he touch me."

Friedrich furrowed his forehead at this enigmatic vein of conversation. He cleared his throat. "Gersdorff has offered to accompany us back to Basel. I propose we leave this afternoon."

"Do you think it wise?"

"Given the circumstances, I think it better for you to be seen leaving with the baron than sleeping with the Bavarian."

Elisabeth gasped.

"He bought the house, Lizzie. You cannot be that naïve."

"The devil resides here." Elisabeth's expression was one of pure panic. Wringing her hands together, she looked as if she might collapse. "We must leave with deliberate speed."

Friedrich nodded. He must remove her before she lost herself to the darkness that was Wagner's appeal. Better the Antichrist you know than the devil you desire.

o o o

CHAPTER XXII

∞

And a god emerged from the Black Forest to discover that every sun-dried bone from Bayreuth to Bavaria had been picked clean.

∞

Friedrich is certainly the most talented of our young friends—often, however, rather morose because of a somewhat unnatural reservation of his behavior. It is as if he is protecting himself from the overpowering impression of Wagner's personality.

Richard placed Cosima's diary back in her sewing basket where he had found it conspicuously open to the page he had just read. If Friedrich had kept to himself during this past visit, then he was sorry for Cosima. He was not, however, fooled. His wife's true concern was not the effect his "overpowering personality" had on Friedrich, but rather on Friedrich's *geheimnis der liebe*. Surely Cosima had figured out by now that her lover's affections were elsewhere engaged, though she need not worry about losing him on that score.

Richard's new paramour, however, was a different matter altogether. She had fortitude of spleen, a courageous constitution that drove her near recklessness. Richard smiled to himself. He had pricked every object of his fancy, but no one had dominated his imagination more so than Elisabeth Nietzsche. Friedrich may perceive the way of things, but it was she who possessed the will to power. She just didn't know it.

Richard turned his thoughts from the empowered to the powerless. It would not be just to say that Ludwig II was powerless, for he held the future of a nation within the clutch of his inexperienced palm. Indeed, he may very well be holding Richard's future in contempt as punishment for his lack of attentions these past few months. Jealousy was not an emotion the composer could easily abide, and so he must assuage the boy's hurt feelings. He was set to tour Germany to promote his festival for the presentation of *der Ring* in Bayreuth, tentatively scheduled to commence two years hence. A side visit to Bavaria would only serve to assist his cause. Without the king's financial support, Richard's life-long ambition may never reach fruition.

From the Jewish quarter of Leipzig, young infamous Wilhelm Richard Geyer had clawed his way to the upper echelon of society. At fourteen, he had changed his name to the now famed Richard Wagner, under which name he became a man of affluence and influence. From Semite to revolutionary to Royal Saxon Court Conductor, Richard Wagner had succeeded in putting Shakespeare and Goethe to music. Thriving on lust, he had procured financing, land, and even an opera house, all purchased by his talent for charming the masses. Expelling a growl of frustration, he retrieved his travel bag from the closet. Time to charm the man-child of Bavaria.

o o o

"You play a dangerous game, Elisabeth."

Elisabeth rolled her eyes in exasperation. Good God, she had not even had time to remove her cloak, wrinkled from their arduous trip back to Naumburg. How many times would she have to have this conversation? "Do leave off, Baron. You and Friedrich certainly have curious objections for two men who toady up to Wagner so."

Gersdorff's posture drew up straighter, if that were even possible. "Neither of us are sycophants. Can the same be said of you?" He walked over to the sidebar to poor a brandy when the thought occurred to him that it was not what Elisabeth had to gain but what Wagner had to gain. He snapped his middle finger against his thumb as realization hit home. With the purposeful strides of a commander, he came up before her and grabbed her by the shoulders. "You gave him money, didn't you?" Elisabeth stood mute, feeding his barely restrained temper. "Answer me!" he shouted, shaking her in his grasp.

A sleeve slid off her shoulder, drawing the baron's attention to her low-cut bodice. He passed a hand over his eyes, squeezing his temples before swiping it down his face, like a curtain from behind which he thought to emerge unruffled.

She stood and stared at him, heedless of her state of dishabille. From her eyes darted daggers of hatred for the man who once presumed himself lord and master of her fate. She grabbed hold of her fallen sleeve and yanked it back into place. And then she laughed. At *him*. "There was a time I looked at you and saw Chaos, Truth in the form of a puzzle, that, when built, brings to life a modern Prometheus. I once thought you were the fire of life, but you are naught more than a soul's assassin, set on gifting fire to some and vanquishing it in others." She circled him then, her gaze perusing him from head to toe with determined disdain before finally honing in closer as would a bird of prey.

She halted before him so close that, had she been taller, her lips may have brushed his. His eyes fell on those lips he had once possessed. He leaned down to claim them once again but went cold at the words she spoke against his mouth.

"Well, Prometheus, Pandora stands before you by the command of another, and I shall burn wherever it so pleases me."

"Well, and what did you expect to come of such a conversation?" Friedrich asked his friend over cigars that evening.

Gersdorff leaned forward to use the ashtray, sparks fading to ash as they fell from the tip of his cigar. "I suppose I thought to play the gallant that I once was in her eyes." His eyes lit in self-amusement as he inhaled another drag of smoke. "A military man should always know when to retreat." He laughed.

"There is no retreat from the mystery that is Lizzie. She has a tendency to disturb a man—body, mind, and soul. It amuses me even today when I think of Krug and Pinder chasing her about as if she were a butterfly rife for ensnaring. Ah, but she flitted, make no mistake about it. Resign yourself to it, Baron. She has escaped your net and fallen into a tangled web of the maestro's weaving. He will dash her heart until it is as dark as the forest he now broods in." Friedrich pointed his still burning cigar in Gersdorff's direction. "But she will survive it. Passion thrives on hope, and Lizzie gives Menoetius nothing, if not hope."

○ ○ ○

Dearest Elisabeth,

You write of accompanying the Wagners to Bayreuth, and I must absolutely forbid it. Your brother has allowed you to run wild long enough. It is not for a woman to roam about in the company of artists, particularly those who must form societies to raise funding for their projects. I hear the most scandalous things about the Wagners and their circle. You cannot mean to take up your brother's penchant for making scandal broth. You will have to marry, after all. You must return to Naumburg at once. There are a number of eligible gentlemen still agreeable to making your acquaintance, despite the rumors that follow in your wake.

With much affection,

Your Mother

P.S., Do encourage Friedrich to write. Our entire circle looks forward to more word of the delights of Tribschen (and Bayreuth, now).

○ ○ ○

Dear Mother,

I would have Elisabeth accompany me to Bayreuth. Further arguments will not be entertained.

Friedrich

○ ○ ○

Son,

The shame you bring upon your sister will be her undoing. You once told me that it had been unfair of me not to marry after your father died. Yet now, because you would look to yourself, instead of any other, you condemn your sister to a life of solitude. Your obsession with her is not natural. Have you not been warned of it before?

Mother

Elisabeth took up a letter from the salver, saw the return address and immediately deposited the missive upon the fire grate.

Friedrich peeked over the spread out newspaper he was perusing, an inquisitive expression on his face. "Will you not read it?"

"I see no purpose in it. Another letter from Mother that I can, no doubt, recite word for word without lifting the seal." Elisabeth placed the back of her hand over her forehead, imitating a swoon. "*You have brought shame to the House of Nietzsche*! As if there were such a house," she said sotto voce. "Apparently a broken engagement to a baron constitutes ennoblement of the most meager among us." She resumed her swooning pose. "*Your prospects are running thin, though I have done everything in my power to quiet rumors flying about. Some call you a jilt, while others say the baron jilted you for your perfidious nature*. And so on, and so on."

"Yes, she writes me much the same. She is right, of course. You must marry at some point."

"As must you."

"That's arguable." Friedrich snapped the newspaper closed. "Neither scenario suits me at this time."

Elisabeth smiled to herself knowing that there should be no difficulty in seeing to it that he remained so disinclined — even if it meant getting in bed with the king of Bavaria. As Cosima had taught her, a man will share his bed with more than one, but will share a lover with none. Elisabeth counted on just such an outcome on several fronts, for hers was a jealous god.

° ° °

CHAPTER XXIII

∞

Lohengrin requested only that I break my brother's mysterious hold on me. Had it really been too much for him to ask?

∞

Bayreuth 1872

The construction of an opera house on land donated to Richard Wagner by the town council brought new life to Bayreuth. German broadsheets were filled with accounts surrounding preparations for the much anticipated *festpiele* for the debut of *Der Ring*. As he took in the crowds gathered along the construction barriers, Friedrich could not help but think back to the hopeful faces that once gawked at the pompous performances put on by the horse guards of his brigadiers unit. The present-day onlookers wore similar expressions of wow and wonderment. It was a bit jolting to think that one man could garner the allegiance of a nation that once took an entire army to acquire.

If any further proof were needed of the nation's pride in their composer, it could be found at the construction site of the Wagners' new home in Bayreuth. One wing of the house had been completed, while another was still under construction. It was here that Friedrich and Elisabeth would be staying for the next several weeks. *Wahnfried*, Wagner had elected to call it. A home, he liked to explain, where delusions and madness conjoined with peace and freedom. As he looked about, Friedrich saw the former while Elisabeth, he noted, found there to be merit in the latter.

However, peace and freedom proved to be short-lived for Elisabeth when she came face to face with the king of Bavaria, who had settled in a week prior to her own arrival. Having once decided she would bow to no man, Elisabeth dipped her head, as regal as a queen, in acknowledgment of their introduction. If Friedrich noticed the slight, he covered it well, whereas Richard's cheeks burned bright red, and Cosima bit her pink lips to suppress what appeared to be a smile of admiration.

The boy-king was as beautiful as Wagner had described: practically girlish with his long dark curls, delicate bone structure, and—judging by his attire—his penchant for buoyant colors. Elisabeth found it difficult to tear her eyes from his blue-violet waistcoat, the sight of which made her feel in some way violated. For a man reported to be a recluse, Ludwig was certainly given to flourish in Richard's presence. She looked upon the boy almost pityingly as she recalled the way in which Richard once described him to her: *So soulful and lovely, that his life was in danger of melting away in this vulgar world like a fleeting dream of gods.*

Elisabeth insentiently tossed back her head, took in the forming roof above them and held no doubt that beneath it were housed two dangerous, vulgar gods. She flicked a shrewd gaze in her cohort's direction. "Cosima, darling, will you join me for a turn about the grounds?" With a knowing laugh, Cosima heartily agreed to do just that.

Ever the consummate counselor, Cosima chose this opportunity to share some background on Ludwig known only to Richard via letters from the king, and only to Cosima by virtue of astute prying. "The first rule to survival: always know your competition, Lizzie."

Elisabeth laughed gaily as she locked arms with her improbable friend. "Do you mean to tell me that we have not buried the hatchet between us?"

"You know very well of whom I speak." Cosima chuckled in return. "Richard, you see, is not the only one in possession of a wandering eye. The king has his own share of side interests, enough to keep my husband's jealous attentions trained upon him. If you hope to maintain a hold on any part of Richard's affections, you must make sure he has reason to keep an equal eye on you."

"Hmm . . ." Elisabeth pondered allowed. "Are you suggesting that I seduce the boy?"

"Good God, no! There are plenty of men for that job. I would suggest you find a bit of a . . . diversion, as they say. *Elsewhere.*"

"I cannot imagine that you are suggesting I stick to my brother's side this visit, as that assuredly would not benefit your schemes." Elisabeth raised a provoking brow at her friend.

"You must show me how to do that some time."

"Do what?"

Cosima attempted to lift her right brow. But, finding she lacked the muscle coordination to pull off such a feat, she relented and held it aloft with her finger.

Elisabeth fell into a fit of laughter, swatting her friend's hand downward. "Stop that! You look ridiculous!"

"Ridiculous was not what I was aiming for. There's something regal in that ability that you have. A look of damnable daring, and, could it be?" She reached over and pushed Elisabeth's eyebrow upward. "Ah, yes! There it is. *Derision*." She let Elisabeth's brow drop and then patted her hand as would an approving old auntie. "Regal, darling. Absolutely regal. Wear it well, love, for Peter Gast joins us on the morrow, and I hear he tires of his wife."

○ ○ ○

Peter's arrival came far too early for Elisabeth's liking. Cosima knew her to be a late riser, so surely there could be no harm in her staying abed until at least noon, she reasoned. Venting frustration at her prickling conscience, Elisabeth huffed out a puff of air in the direction of the unruly curls plastered to her forehead after a night of fitful sleep. As much as she would prefer to remain hidden in her room, she was no coward. So determined, she kicked aside her coverlet and padded over to pull the sash back from her window.

In the street below was a flurry of activity surrounding a lavish coach marked by a crest that advertised the obscene wealth of its owner and trumpeted a future increase in prosperity. Elisabeth stared at the engraving of crossed swords, a phoenix framed between them as it rose from a banner aflame with the motto *Nondum Intellexit*. He had *chutzpah*, she'd give him that. A threat? A promise? *Not yet realized*, indeed. Fearing that she would be caught gawking,

Elisabeth stepped away from the window. She would dress and join the company. It was time for a little self-realization.

Peter's heart constricted when he saw Elisabeth descend the stairs. She was stunning in her gown of royal blue, her head held aloft, nodding only slightly at the greetings that met her. Such poise, such grace; she far outshone the dandified king of Bavaria—and perhaps even stirred his admiration. Not a man in the room was left unaffected. The composer not the least of all, Peter thought enviously.

"Mr. Gast, how do you do?" Elisabeth stopped short and offered up her hand, which he promptly seized and pressed to his lips, lingering overly long in the formality.

"I am as well as ever, Miss Nietzsche. Gentlemen," he turned to the others, "what more agreeable company can a man find?" He drew their attention to both Elisabeth and Cosima.

"And what of your wife?" Elisabeth cut in before the others could second Peter's obsequious flattery. Only nerves as taut as her own would induce him to comport himself in such an unctuous manner.

"Hadassah does well, thank you. It is, of course, a disappointment that she could not accompany me on this visit. She remains behind with the children, you understand?"

Elisabeth tilted her head back and appeared to be looking down her nose at him as if she were taller than he. "I fear I have no experience with such matters, Mr. Gast. Perhaps it has escaped your notice that I have no children of my own."

That stung. "And what of the baron? He is well, I hope?"

Cosima stepped forward. "That will be enough from the both of you. I'll not have my guests verbally jousting."

"Perhaps a good joust is exactly what I need." Elisabeth took in the shocked faces of the men around her, looking from one to another as if she were in the midst of making one of the most important decisions of her life. Her intent gaze finally settled on Ludwig. "Your Majesty," she purred as she advanced upon him, attaching her hand to the crook of his arm. "Would you be so kind as to afford me a lesson in fencing this afternoon? You do fence, don't you?"

"But of course. What monarch does not?" He smiled the boyish grin of a born charmer. Oh, yes. He could be made as excellent a confidant as Cosima.

"Swords or epées?"

"Epées, my lady. Swords are made for barbarians."

"But that cannot be, Your Majesty!" Elisabeth's voice carried over her shoulder as the king escorted her into the breakfast room. "For I just spotted two swords on the crest of one of the finest carriages I have ever laid eyes on."

Cosima's own eyes twinkled with pride as she turned to the remaining of her guests and beckoned them to follow the king's lead. A *boy*! Her protégé had just successfully used a boy to bring three men to their knees, each with an eye out for Elisabeth's attention.

Miss Nietzsche's antics of the afternoon provided the perfect topic for conversation over dinner that evening. "Out foxed by the strategic maneuvers of a mere baron — untenable!"

Elisabeth lowered her fork from her lips and bestowed her most winning smile on Ludwig. "The baron hardly does anything by halves, Your Majesty. He is one of the few men I have ever known who believed a woman to be as capable as a man. That, and he thought Friedrich could use a good defeat from time to time. Thusly, I was trained."

Laughter went round the table as Friedrich dabbed his napkin at the corners of his mouth in preparation for a response befitting his sister's opening salvo.

"What is this? Are you telling me that the good baron was averse to calling me out himself?"

"Perhaps you have forgotten, brother, that you would break the sword rather than wield it."

"But my dearest Lizzie, is not the pen mightier than the sword? Am I to believe that the baron has been no more to me than an intellectual impostor all these years?"

Elisabeth pointed her fork accusingly at her antagonist. "This is precisely why the baron thought I might have need of a sharp weapon."

Richard responded with a hoot. "Indeed, that sharp tongue of your brother's could use a good rest. Will you cut it out then, Elisabeth?"

Elisabeth pretended to consider his question. "No, I should say not. My Lord tells me that I should turn the other cheek and leave all things in His care. If the Almighty chooses to suffer Friedrich—" she shrugged "—well, then, so be it. As Friedrich is fond of saying, 'God, too, has His Hell.'"

"Then the baron shall have good company," Ludwig asserted.

All eyes darted in his direction.

Cosima was the first to overcome her shock. "Why, Your Majesty! Did you just wish the Baron von Gersdorff to perdition? You sound as if you are jealous!"

"Of the baron, yes. Of Elisabeth, no."

Richard visibly winced at the truth of the wisdom he had imparted to Elisabeth not so very long ago: *even one of a deviant sexual persuasion could be sexually persuaded in turn.* Perhaps he could turn Elisabeth's cheek to his advantage.

"A king must marry at some point," Richard encouraged Ludwig as they strolled through the garden later that evening. It had not been easy to tear the boy from Elisabeth's side. Had it not been for Friedrich not so subtly insisting that his sister was tired out from the day's events, he may never have had this opportunity to speak alone with his benefactor.

"You cannot be serious."

"Why ever not? You were engaged once before."

"The only thing that the Duchess Sophie and I had in common was our love of you."

Richard examined the boy's earnest face and nearly felt a cringe of remorse for the way in which he had strung the lad along. He gently took the boy's chin in one hand and softly caressed his cheek with the other. "Do you fear Hell, my boy?"

"I fear madness more. My brother and my uncle plot to have me declared insane. Perhaps it's true. I have provided for your every whim and here you attempt to use me to secure your Elsa from her Gottfried. But, unlike me, he is no longer a child. Besides," Ludwig said, lifting his own hand and caressing Richard's cheek in return. "You should know better than anyone that it is the Jew who requires watching."

Richard smiled and motioned for his companion to return to the house with him. "Believe me you, Gottfried will see to that."

○ ○ ○

CHAPTER XXIV

∞

Ishmaelite: A Jewish deserter? Or a deserter of Jews? Just as Abraham denied his brood, the boy-child has claim to neither the Antichrist, nor the Jude. So be it — they shall have their lie!

∞

Peter treaded quietly toward Elisabeth's chamber. She had not invited him, but he simply would not rest until he found evidence of the girl she had once been. He tapped lightly upon her door, certain that he had heard a faint commotion within. But no answer came.

"Would you mind telling me why I find you outside my sister's bedchamber in the dead of night?"

Peter spun on his heels to confront his inquisitor. "I may ask the same of you."

"No, you may not. We are good friends, Peter, but I had hoped not to be forced to revisit this disagreeable scenario. Leave matters alone. We are, both of us, Ishmaelites. What matters who planted the seed?"

Peter looked upon his friend with a weary sort of disillusionment. The aging falsehood had taken its toll on his spirit, and perhaps even his mind. Friedrich stood in silent awe of the ague upon Peter's face as the words of Sir Walter Raleigh tripped off his tongue:

Tell fortune of her blindness;
Tell nature of decay;
Tell friendship of unkindness;
Tell justice of delay.

Friedrich picked up the thread of the poem, quoting his own favorite verse from the selection.

Tell zeal it wants devotion;
Tell love it is but lust;
Tell time it is but motion;
Tell flesh it is but dust.
And wish them not reply,
For thou must give the lie.

The two men briefly clasped their arms around the other and parted ways, each heading back to his respective quarters, both knowing that Elisabeth had long given herself up to the lie.

Richard watched as Elisabeth brushed out her hair and then lifted her hands to her shoulders, attempting to rub the knots out of her sore muscles. "I have never seen anyone cut such fine a figure with an epée than you, my love." He drew up behind her and gently brushed her hands aside, taking it upon himself to soothe her ache.

Elisabeth glanced at him suspiciously in the mirror. "Not even the boy?"

"My darling, the boy was too enamored with you to pay heed to his own fine form."

Elisabeth shooed his hands away. "I should have guessed there was more behind your attentions tonight than your ardor. Nothing you do comes without a price. Let's see; you have my money, my body, and you'd have my soul, were it not already held in contempt by another. No, you would have me extract something from the child, to secure his lifelong devotion."

Elisabeth seated herself insolently on the bed, leaning back on her elbows to better taunt her current tormenter. With one in the room and two, perhaps three, more just beyond the threshold, she was suffocating beneath the weight of past transgressions.

Richard moved forward, nearly trapping her to the bed. "And how do you know that my goal is not your lifelong devotion?"

She kicked out her foot playfully, knocking him backwards. "I find that hard to believe." She laughed. "No, thanks to you, I now have pockets to let. It makes no sense that you would have me over one who so readily and freely parts with his riches."

Richard fell onto the bed beside her and tweaked her cheek. "Sassy wench! Perhaps I would have it *all*."

Elisabeth rose, walked over to the door and laid her hand on the knob. "Then you best go and pay attention to your king. He may be but a boy, but he is not, however, without the pride of a man."

Richard looked her over long and longingly before giving way to her advice and passing through the door she now held open for him.

Unfortunately, sleep would elude her once again upon his absence.

"I half expected to find you in the nursery. At the very least I would have thought the one in need of nursing would have come to you."

"And are not you standing in my room in the dead of night, to nurse your wounded pride?"

Friedrich dropped to Elisabeth's side, the mattress creaking beneath his weight. "If my pride has been wounded, it was at your hand, Lizzie." As he spoke the words he brought her hand to his lips as if to sear the mark of betrayal deep within the snow-white skin of her manipulative fingers. He took her index finger between his forefinger and thumb, examining it as one would an exotic specimen. "Imagine, something so delicate and slender as this single member has the power to control a man's fate. It beckons as often as it banishes." He took her finger into his mouth. Once dislodged, he examined it further. "It strokes innocently as often as it stabs viciously. It wields an epée as often as it wields a sword." His gaze slid from her finger to her eyes. "It awaits the bidding of no other than its commander." His hand cupped her cheek as his thumb caressed the line of her porcelain jaw. He was gentle, yet she was afraid. "Tell me, love, where is your commander now?"

Friedrich looked about the room as if in search of someone, but returned his attention back to his sister when he found nothing but the Specter in company with them. His next words flowed tauntingly close to her ear. "I suspect by now he has resigned himself to teaching another to wield an epée. Who, then, is the vanquished?"

Elisabeth squeezed her eyes closed to restrain the tears that threatened to weep forth from her gutted soul. "Perhaps he wields an epée; perhaps he wields a conductor's baton," she bit back. "Either way, where my soul is concerned, I fear God has his work cut out for him."

Friedrich rolled over, nearly pinning her to the bed. She defiantly withstood his scrutiny as he peered into her eyes.

"From my point of view, I see no soul." He lifted Elisabeth slightly and then released her with a near violent shake of her shoulders, gruffly dropping her back to the bed as he rose and abandoned her to his cruel words.

Once alone, Elisabeth finally addressed the Specter. Her old speechless companion was cloaked in a shroud of pale purple, clearly vying for her attention. "*I am the vanquished. It is he, with his iniquitous desires, that has robbed me of all decency.*"

° ° °

CHAPTER XXV

∞

One so thunderous as Thor can harrow even the highest of priestesses.

∞

As they walked through the park, Elisabeth looked to the gentlemen in her company, Peter on her right arm and Ludwig on the left. She vividly recalled being in a similar position before, only then she stood between Peter and Paul. But that had been for her own purposes at a time in life when her most pressing obligation was to find a husband.

When had she marked her soul for sell? She walked now between two wealthy men who, whether they knew it or not, were paying dearly for her attentions. The perpetrator's words resounded in her head: *I am naught but an old whore, willing to play any game to get what I desire.* Elisabeth laughed aloud and then realized her guffaw had been out of sync with whatever it was the two men had been discussing around her.

"Miss Nietzsche, you laugh at the notion of marrying?"

She masterfully dodged the question. "For goodness' sake, Peter, let us not regress. I am Elisabeth to you." She turned to her left. "And to you, Your Majesty. One can hardly address a fencing master so formally."

The king laughed merrily. "Ah, my lovely Elisabeth. I let you win, you know?"

Elisabeth yanked her arm free of his, as would a petulant child, handily employing the art of coquetry. "'Tis not true and you know it well, sir! I can wield a weapon as meticulously as any man. Shall I demonstrate with my grandfather's dueling pistols?"

"Ho, now!" Peter reached behind Elisabeth and slapped Ludwig on the back. "Careful before you answer, man. A sharp wit, a sharp bite, and a sharp shot, she is. I confess I have fallen victim to all but her bullet."

"Pity, that," responded Ludwig. "For then I might have the pleasure of escorting the beautiful Elisabeth without you in tow." Yes, indeed. She was made of stern stuff, as would be expected of his queen. Ludwig shook the possibility away. He had no doubt that she would keep his confidence in exchange for title and power, but his nation was still smarting from the loss of autonomy. It would never do to ask them to bow to an Imperialist.

"Gentlemen, please," Elisabeth chided with a practiced pout. "You are both as arrogantly flattering as our host." She knew she had hit her mark when she felt Ludwig stiffen at the reminder that Elisabeth was no ally, but an adversary, who threatened to unsettle his relationship with the one he truly loved.

Elisabeth turned on her next object of prey. "Speaking of our host, Peter, what is all of this increasing talk of Christianity that he has taken to? Has Richard, like you and Friedrich, not been an ardent admirer of Schopenhauer? One would think he would ascribe to atheism! I vow I have prayed fervently enough for his soul."

Peter smiled despite himself, amused by her deftly feigned ignorance. "It's quite simple, you see. A composer is what it suits him to be in any given situation. For example, my first duty when penning a scale is to be true to myself. What is it that my soul sings? And once its sentiment is sung, will I truly be brave enough to bare it naked before a crowd? It is not an easy decision to come to, and is more often than not resolved by allowing the listener to make of it what they will. As it is now, Germany would make a Christian of every heretic. Hence, our dear friend transforms."

"Like the *Norns* in this *Götterdämmerung* he is to debut, our Wagner weaves the rope of Destiny through deception." Ludwig nodded thoughtfully, surprising even himself by his sudden insight.

Elisabeth sighed in longing. "Now this transformation of Destiny I must see!" She allowed her exuberant expression to drop to one of consternation. "Whatever will we do if the Wagner Societies cannot drum up enough funding to bring such a masterpiece to the masses?"

Ludwig faced her then and grasped her hands in reassurance. "We shall see that it is done. Will we not, Mr. Gast? *Nondum Intellexit*, no? Let us yet realize this German dream." He bowed low over Elisabeth's hand. "Elisabeth, you are a shining jewel among your countrymen. You will go far."

Peter watched the two wander off, wholly forgetful of his accompanying presence. Several moments went by before he recognized Friedrich's attendance just behind him.

"Köselitz, what goes on here?"

Peter turned to his friend and chuckled. "It's strange that you should choose this moment to use my birth name. It turns out I have not been invited here as a composer, but rather a benefactor. The maestro will cast aside his hated name, yet take my filthy money all the same." He turned a questioning eye on Friedrich. "Not much better, now am I?"

The evening was spent devoted to one composition or another. At the present moment it was Friedrich's turn at the pianoforte. As his fingers ran up and down the keys in warm-up, he caught everyone's attention with a single mention of Cosima's former husband. "What you are about to listen to, my friends, is a composition that I wrote for Hans von Bülow. *Manfred-Meditation*, I call it. And do you know what he did upon playing it? He dashed off the nastiest of missives, questioning my meaning behind this 'undelightful and anti-musical draft.' He decried it a parody of the future." Friedrich halted his play and looked over his shoulder at his audience. "Now that hurt!" He nodded his head in serious jest.

Richard approached the piano bench, leaning over Friedrich's shoulder to scrutinize the score. "The composition itself is not so bad," he pronounced his verdict. "It is only that you play like a professor. Music is not rational, Nietzsche; it is passionate."

Friedrich stumbled on a note. "Ah, but passion must be left to the fairer sex that motivates us to put the 'woman,' so to speak, in our music."

Cosima felt a pang of jealousy when Richard's eyes alighted on Elisabeth at the mention of passion. She moved forward to join her husband at Friedrich's back. "It sounds very much like Hans to tweak a man's pride so. Here, let me." She reached forward to turn the page for Friedrich, as her husband slipped off in the direction of Ludwig, who had also gravitated toward Elisabeth.

Peter emerged from the quarantine of the corner he occupied across the room. "Good God, man! What woman inspired you to torment that instrument so?"

Friedrich abandoned his play and addressed no one in particular. "I call her the Holy Spirit, the High Priestess who holds art in hostility. Her touch promises nausea and disgust, darkness in every form of Christian faith. I should prefer the thunder of the Old Testament. At either turn, the result is the negation of life. And so it is from a tortured instrument that one can hear the cacophony of annihilation. What? Is it not a crowd pleaser?" Instigated on by the discomposed faces about him, Friedrich lashed out at the weakest among them. "What say you, Peter? Christ anointed feet with oil, but did he lick boots? I suspect you would know, for your people have long been stuck beneath their soles for all the ages, have they not?"

Elisabeth shot from her seat. "Friedrich! That is enough! Clearly, you have had far too much to drink."

Richard motioned for Elisabeth to hold her temper. "No, it is a fair question. Mr. Gast, would it not be preferable to permanently remove the Köselitz from the bottom of your shoe?"

Peter proffered Richard a contemptuous nod. "It would be about as rewarding, Richard, as you scraping Geyer from your own. The difference is that I choose to be realized."

Richard looked to Ludwig, raising his eyebrows in mock astonishment. "And to think it is I who am being honored tomorrow at the ribbon cutting for the theater."

○ ○ ○

Elisabeth opened her door and yanked her night visitor into the privacy of her room. "Thank God, Ludwig!" she hissed through gritted teeth. "I could not have borne it had you been any other."

Ludwig's wide, white grin only served to make him look more boyish. "You are safe, Elisabeth. Your other callers are otherwise engaged. Richard is in his own bed, for once, and your brother and Mr. Gast are reconciling their differences over another round of drinks."

"Do you mean to tell me that Friedrich means to get drunker still? He would be quite wise to keep his distance from me for at least the foreseeable future." She motioned for Ludwig to take Richard's customary spot by the fire as she took the seat just opposite.

"Ah, but if it had been your brother at your door instead of myself, you'd have let him in."

Elisabeth squeezed her eyes shut, acknowledging the truth of his words. "I have no choice. I am all that he has."

"Are you? It seems to me that he has no shortage of companions in this house."

"Here, yes. Elsewhere, no." Elisabeth turned her attention to the flames in search of exactly what it was that troubled her so. "Something is happening to Friedrich. He has no interest in socializing outside of this small circle. I'm not even sure if he ever plans to return to Basel." She turned to the king with an imploring look. "At least not alone."

Ludwig raised his hands, indicating that he wished to ward off the direction of her thoughts. "Surely, you do not expect me to . . ."

Elisabeth leaned forward and swatted his knee. "No, of course not! It's that Cosima prefers to keep me about—to help with the children, you see. Richard leans on me as Napoleon would his armory." She huffed in frustration.

"And Friedrich torments you for the fortification of his soul."

Elisabeth stood to pace about the room, wringing her hands red, a symptom of her agonizing anxiety. "We are a torment to each other. Our hopes and dreams pinned on the happiness of the other, the problem being that neither of us truly wants the other to be happy. This is what Friedrich means by the negation of life."

"Then you are the Holy Spirit for whom he composes?"

Elisabeth grimaced remorsefully. "I suppose I am. Friedrich calls me by many names: Elisabeth, Lizzie, sometimes Llama—a childhood nickname—and Eli. Do you know what Eli means, Your Majesty?" At the shake of his head she explained. "It is a variant of 'God' in Hebrew, Arabic, and Aramaic. The Eli of the Old Testament was a high priest. So, yes, it would seem that I am the source of his nausea and disgust. The feeling is mutual, I assure you. There is solidarity in our solitude, for neither of us will ever experience the comfort of life and love beyond the confines of our conjoined shadows."

Ludwig reached out his hand to grasp hers in reassurance.

"I suspected you would understand," she whispered. "Now, do grant Richard his funding. I wish to return home."

° ° °

CHAPTER XXVI

∞

A Teutonic victory, an assimilated Jew, and an aphorism for the dumb. "Life wants deception," as he is so fond of saying when we meet out of season.

∞

By home, Elisabeth referred to Naumburg. The fall months were upon them, and Friedrich had decided to take to the Swiss Alps for a solitary hike, formulating and revising what would later be published as *Untimely Meditations/Thoughts Out of Season*; a title which Elisabeth found particularly amusing, given that he was writing amongst the changing leaves, the backdrop of which was exactly *her* season.

Germany's victory over France could prove to be a dangerous outcome, he had told Elisabeth. Triumph often leads man down a path of arrogance. Indeed, protestations of the superiority of German culture had cultivated a false sense of invincibility among his countrymen. The role that the arts played in this deception began to sit uneasily with Friedrich, particularly as he developed a distaste for Richard's commitment to propagandizing such false allusions. Friedrich suspected that these percolating anxieties may have been behind his rude outburst at Bayreuth. Once again, he begged her forgiveness as he had done countless times since their departure from the Wagners'.

Elisabeth set aside Friedrich's latest letter in consideration of his words. Yes, citizens of The Confederation might have grown a little over-confident since the war, but was not this just the sort of awakening her brother had advocated for all of these years? Perhaps he had forgotten the words of Spinoza: *Peace is not an absence of war; it is a virtue, a state of mind, a disposition for benevolence, confidence, justice.* Elisabeth firmly believed that man, German or otherwise, could do great things so long as he was confident that justice could be attained for the greater good. She knew that, were Friedrich there, he would challenge her to form an argument as to who and what constitutes the greater good. She wasn't sure what her answer would have been to such a question, but she was certain that she shared in Richard's vision for a nation solidly united through a shared heritage, expressly that of Teutonic origin, brought back to life on an unconventional stage—a forum set apart from venues owned by bankers and businessmen—where an authentic German could make his case without taint.

Well, enough of such ruminations. There was the festival to think of, as confirmed by the number of letters she had received from Cosima. She plucked one from the top of the stack.

Elisabeth, darling . . . You have managed to thoroughly seduce the boy! He speaks of you incessantly — asking goodness knows how many questions about you — to which Richard stupidly answers in great detail, too great for the boy's liking. (And mine, I might say.) What followed was some sort of argument about Richard not paying enough attention to his benefactor, as the one filling his purse might expect. Of course, nothing is ever said in front of me . . . I came about this information the usual way.

I believe the child means to withdraw his support! He degraded Richard's hard work in the most demeaning of ways, referring to the project as nothing more than a "fool's dream," and insisting that he would not be proved the greater fool for funding it. It was a most terrible insult!

We will have to take another tour to drum up funds, lest we allow the whole festival to fall apart. I hope we can count on you to return to Bayreuth to watch the children. Do send me word in the affirmative.

By the way, Richard speaks of petitioning Bismarck to grant your brother a post. What better way to remedy Friedrich's disillusionment with the German spirit than to call him, once more, into the service of his country?

Elisabeth refolded the letter, a quiet laughter rising from the back of her throat. "What little they know of Friedrich," she mumbled to herself, just before she penned a reply confirming her availability to return to Bayreuth while the couple traveled.

○ ○ ○

Friedrich returned to Basel in time for the fall semester. Just viewing his schedule brought a slump to his beleaguered shoulders. Aside from his regular course load, he was to give a series of lectures on Greek and Roman Rhetoric, the Homer Question, and Sophocles. His shoulders slumped even further when he found his courses to be low in enrollment and his lectures to be sparsely attended. Either he had made himself absent for too long, or the reception of his literary efforts was quite poor. He concluded that both were most likely at the heart of his continued solitude. He could join Elisabeth in Bayreuth, but he was simply unable to reclaim the motivation he once had and the unbending respect he once held for Wagner's project.

A grand diversion presented itself to Friedrich in the form of Lady Malwida von Meysenbug, first introduced to him by Cosima. The daughter of a French baron, Malwida was a self-made writer who, in 1869, published her *Memoires of an Idealist*. The author remained anonymous to all, except those of her French, German, and Italian circles.

With her on this visit, she brought Paul Rée to make Friedrich's acquaintance. The two men had much in common. Both were devout students of Schopenhauer, both had attended the University of Leipzig, and both were fond of committing their philosophies to paper in the form of aphorisms. It didn't hurt either, Malwida considered, that Rée was the son of assimilated Jews made wealthy by business and land ownership.

What a joke on society! So many of them believed they could, with a sniff, separate Jewish money from "honestly earned" German currency—*money* really was such a crass word, as crass as the sensory organs refined to ferret it out. Now the very same who proclaimed to abjure gains that had passed through Jewish hands clambered to be among those included in the Rée family's inner circle. It was an unspoken understanding that if one of a certain standing did not look, act, or profess to be a Jew, then no one must let it be known if they held knowledge to the contrary. Even the Wagners, to some extent, managed to keep their noses from turning upward in disgust when in Rée's company. Only very slightly, though.

Malwida's eyes twinkled as she observed Friedrich and Rée in deep discussion. She knew that Friedrich understood all too well the game that was played, as surely as she knew he was *not* playing it.

The same could not be said, she reflected, of the young man's sister. Malwida had observed Elisabeth at a number of Bayreuth gatherings and, in her, saw a spirit adrift. Like so many women, the girl was torn between an independence of mind and an inbred dependence on the thoughts of others. What was needed was an educational system that would provide a quality education to all, regardless of gender. Then women need not garner bits and pieces of their lives and times by bending over sewing, making a pretense of not listening to what men will impart. Malwida thought she may have heard Elisabeth crying out in her sleep on more than one night of a Bayreuth stay, the pleadings of a woman in desperate search of a portal. A way in? A way out? The answer varied according to the dreamer, though one did not exclude the other. In fact, she had heard quite similar night disquiet from her friend the Baroness Brüning who—devoted to the plight of the oppressed as she was—remained oppressed by choice via self-attachment to her husband's side.

Choosing to ignore Rée's possible involvement in such an enterprise, Richard had assured Malwida that she would find a kindred spirit in Friedrich who was equally as committed to universal suffrage. Point of fact, the two Nietzsches had happened upon Lady von Meysenbug's own dear friend, Giuseppe Mazzini, a year or two back. Yes, she could imagine that, and more.

Having, over the years, become a champion of émigré causes, Malwida thought she saw something beyond revolutionary in Friedrich. Where many of her compatriots, Richard included, held on to some past impetus running out of steam, the philosopher before her was the creator of the dynamism that empowers the future. Others of her revolutionary set—Graf Reichenbach, and Gottfried and Johanna Kinkel, to name a few—would appreciate such gravity of mind in one who made no apologies for his views and clearly harbored no false humility.

Indeed, the only sign of weakness readily seen was the philosopher's obvious failing health. He spoke lightly of having recently been unexpectedly called upon by his former professor and current colleague, Wilhelm Ritschl, who—with great pain in his eyes—spoke of Friedrich's growing unpopularity among the students at Basel. It troubled him, Malwida perceived, that his poor health and long absences were gaining him a reputation of being unreliable, even unstable, perhaps.

The latter charge, no doubt, resulted from the number of recent failed, or unpopular, essay publications. It was no wonder that he preferred to write in aphorisms—as men and women of high intelligence will do—for prophetic thoughts are not only "out of season"; they are well outside the bounds of conventional reason. Grand ideas are often obscured in lengthy narratives devised so for the purpose of talking down to those assumed to be dumb. An aphorism was more like a word to the wise, a methodology of placing an idea in the human hand and trusting that it would grow in possibility. It was possible that Friedrich put too much faith in man's ability, or that he had none at all. He was quite the paradox, perfect for the challenge she hoped to present him in the near future.

o o o

CHAPTER XXVII

∞

Do I speak Italian? Not as of yet. No, I have naught but a German tongue to wag womanlike over a proper kaffeeklatsch.

∞

Bayreuth, Spring 1873

"I cannot decide who is the crueler—Friedrich for sending you, or you for following his dictate."

Gersdorff laughed as he helped Elisabeth sift through an assortment of pamphlets to be distributed as part of a fundraising effort for the festival. There was a definite pall over the party at Bayreuth, as prospects were slim for presenting *Der Ring* within the time frame that Richard had hoped. Ludwig had made good on his threat to pull funding. All direct contact between the two men had come to a halt, placing Malwida von Meysenbug in the unenviable position of go-between. Gersdorff felt a bit like an emissary himself, an envoy dispatched by Friedrich to maintain Elisabeth's good graces toward her absent brother. "I can well understand your disappointment, madam. I am no equal to your brother."

Elisabeth's eyes shot to his as the barb hit home. "What compels you to take such a caustic tongue with me? I have never understood your objections to the love that a sister holds for her brother. What sister would not be loyal to a brother who puts her protection above all else?"

"Come now, Elisabeth. Loyalty is one thing. Love, as it is, between a man and a woman is something else entirely."

"You speak nonsense. I loved you with all of my heart. Perhaps I still do. No matter, it does not signify now." Elisabeth's eyes shyly found his again. She laid down her pamphlets and pretended to busy herself with a list of donors. "Nothing good ever comes of love. It has been my experience that men cannot tell the difference between the heart and the passions. I learned in the most difficult of circumstances that I am no exception to the rule, and so I have decided to make my own rules." With a lighthearted laugh that rang false, she brought the unpleasant conversation to what she hoped was an amicable end. "All the more reason that it's better I am not, after all, a baroness."

"Tell me, are you still having episodes?"

Not the turn of conversation she had hoped for. But, then again, only three people had witnessed her night terrors, and the man before her now was the only one unashamed enough to speak of it outright. "By any chance have you read Dostoyevsky's *The Idiot*?" At his affirmative nod she continued. "I often feel like quite the idiot myself, for what woman would let such a man go?"

"Good girl! Well done. You have dodged the question, but answered it all the same. I'm sorry to hear that you still find yourself in such a state. My thoughts were constantly with you while in attendance at your brother's birthday party in Naumburg, surrounded, as I was, by three fugitives of fugue. You could remove yourself from the sources, you know?"

"Yes," she retorted jauntily, "but I will never be able to escape myself."

"Leave them be, all of them. The darkness will lift, and you will find yourself again."

"According to my woman's education, there *is* no me to be found outside of a man. In fact . . ." She tilted her head in consideration of her thoughts. "There have been only two men who have sought my company solely for the benefit of engaging me in good conversation. And one of them prefers his own kind! Now doesn't that just say it all?"

Elisabeth laughed the laugh of one who held no fear of Fate, which begged the question: what exactly did she interpret as her fate? Gersdorff fervently hoped that she would, indeed, succeed in escaping herself.

o o o

"You need not convince me," Friedrich assured Malwida. "I have long confided such a wish to my sister. A commune of the minds — rich, poor, male, female."

They spoke of opening a free school in Italy, just the type of revolutionary endeavor that Malwida thrived on.

"We would have to include my sister, you know," Friedrich went on. "She's a smart woman. I have always thought that she would make an excellent teacher of domestic skills."

The enthusiastic expression slipped from Malwida's face. "I have had occasion to share conversation with your sister and have found her to be ambitious beyond domesticity. She has a prodigious mind, capable of a great deal more than etiquette training. You would have girls learn the arts and sciences but deny Elisabeth's mastery of the subject matters?"

Rising to take his leave, Friedrich extended his hand for a parting shake of Malwida's. It had never occurred to him to lay his lips on her fingers. "Perhaps I'm just afraid she may outsmart me," he said with a wink. "Nonetheless, in the end, Elisabeth always has her way, for I deny her nothing."

"Now there's a good brother." Malwida smiled approvingly, he thought.

Elisabeth shook her head in amusement when she received her brother's next letter. He waxed poetically about a groundbreaking institute of learning to include girls, and saw nothing ironic about proposing to call it a Modern Convent. No, but he must recognize how aptly sardonic such a name was in its preposterousness. But still she knew as well as he that parents would flock with children in tow for the opportunity of a free education, no matter what name was emblazoned upon the building. Funding would come from Malwida von Meysenbug and Paul Rée, of course; that was of no concern.

What worried Elisabeth was the undertone of resignation in Friedrich's letter. He spoke of making arrangements for the future as might be expected of an invalid, envisioning the life of a quiet school teacher; a wise alternative, he argued, to the pressures of his professorship. Altered, too, was the manner of his address to her. He opened his letter with a formal "Elisabeth," not Lizzie, nor Eli, and his closing was equally distant. "In old brotherliness," he had written. She knew that Gersdorff was in company with Friedrich now, helping him compensate for his poor eyesight by taking notes for the second *Meditations*. Had he broken faith with her? Had he revealed his knowledge of the secret once known only to The

Specter? No, never. *Gersdorff has too much honor*. Those had been her words and she felt them still.

She turned her attention to the postscript. Malwida would soon join her at Bayreuth to assist in the fundraising efforts. Elisabeth could hardly wait to receive this paragon that held the admiration of every man of Elisabeth's acquaintance. She crinkled her nose. Hopefully Malwida would not be accompanied by that odious Paul Rée! She was sure he was a Jew, and there was an acquaintance she had no wish to make, an unjustifiable disdain for the race growing stronger within her.

It was not Paul Rée, but Friedrich and Gersdorff who showed up at the door with Malwida. The women greeted each other with a kiss to the cheek. As if they were old friends, Elisabeth observed. She mentally shrugged; such was the benefit of being Richard's mistress. Her gaze moved to her brother with what appeared to Malwida to be a sense of trepidation.

A bit taken off guard, Malwida took Elisabeth by the arm and adeptly turned the young woman's attention away from the two men, between whom a palpable resentment had sprung up upon crossing the threshold to Bayreuth. Against one another, against the master of the house, or against Elisabeth, she could not determine. Malwida pushed the thought aside. No matter who was in residence, tension abounded at Bayreuth. She was determined to break it. "I hope you don't mind my entourage, Miss Nietzsche—"

"It's Elisabeth, please."

"Elisabeth, then. I hope you don't mind the presence of these two sour faces, but the baron would insist on coming, and Friedrich would not hear of being left behind, avowing that he could not leave his sister alone in the presence of such a rogue."

Gersdorff looked at Friedrich as if he might call him out, so fierce was the blazing menace in his eyes. "I am hardly one to take liberties that are not mine to take."

The deep red that flushed Elisabeth's face was not plea enough to arrest Friedrich's temper. "You would do well to remember that, old chap. Never forget that I still hold her purse strings."

It was an outrageous accusation to make, as brother, sister, and baron knew that Elisabeth managed her brother's money, some of which Friedrich had just borrowed from Gersdorff. *Old brotherliness.* He was behaving as if her heart and her fate were his for the gifting. He was as good as omnipotent.

"Let us have some coffee and catch up," Elisabeth suggested evenly.

○ ○ ○

CHAPTER XXVIII

∞

The Prince of Salemo is all sadness . . . The ring doesn't fit.

∞

"Ludwig will join our party on the morrow."

Elisabeth rolled to the edge of her bed to find her brother pouring himself a glass of sherry at her sideboard that once stood empty of alcohol. She had taken to drinking lately, exchanging one fugue state for another. "Do you suppose Richard and Cosima expected us to hold court here in their absence? "

"I expect the king comes at their begging." Friedrich offered to share his drink with Elisabeth. When she declined, he placed the glass on the bedside table and slid in beside her. "As angry as he is with Richard, he'll not allow the project to fall through. Malwida has given me to understand the boy wishes to seek your advice before he makes a final decision."

Elisabeth turned her face to his, eyes widened in surprise.

"Don't look so shocked, Lizzie. Never forget that you make a man see the world differently. There is a certain persuasive power about you. You are a Nietzsche after all. Embrace it."

Friedrich wrapped his arms around Elisabeth's waist and pulled her to him, her back against his chest. He had come to protect her from Gersdorff, but there was no force present to protect her from him, or from herself. Since her earliest memories, he had been the only force in her life. She chided herself for the greatest of weaknesses, but then gave in to the rite of sanctuary. It was her decision to make, was it not? In one moment she was Diana, innocent huntress, in the next Cynthia, huntress of the innocent; both providing passage to a man's immortal aspirations. She was a pagan, and Friedrich her idol. Why must she abuse herself so? Could not her bitterness be directed elsewhere?

They lay in quiet solitude for a long spell. Elisabeth turned a questioning eye to The Specter, which, in turn, signaled permission for her to break the peace. She trailed her fingers up and down the arm that encaged her. "I despise you, you know?"

"Hmm" was his only reply, having long ago assumed her sentiment to be a given between them.

"You promised to safeguard our secret, that my reputation would go untouched. Yet you accompany Gersdorff here with a jealousy that falls far outside the bounds of brotherly affection, leaving me open to idol gossip and speculation."

"A fine job of that you've done for yourself, Lizzie. It is well known that you are Richard's mistress, a position you have made little effort to conceal. If men will line up at your bedchamber door in search of pleasure or conversation, it has little to do with me."

"You say that, yet you stand watch outside my door like Charon. I wonder, would the Jew not pay for his passage? Is that why he was banished? It's certainly not a question of *could* he not pay. I don't expect to find him wandering the banks of the river Styx for a century-long penance." The venom behind her words surprised them both. Her heart was weighted by darkness.

"No, that never-ending punishment is reserved for him on earth. Besides, you should know by now there is no amount of coin that would induce me to release your shining soul."

"Ah, then you are not Charon, but Erebus, chaos coursing through your veins as you guard the secret passage to Nyx's lair. That's more apt, wouldn't you say?"

Friedrich gently released her and placed a final kiss on her nose before leaving the bed. "I would say you need some sleep. Heed me, or I shall, indeed, summon the son of Sin to stand guard once more."

∘ ∘ ∘

It had been a long time since Elisabeth had experienced such levity that she now found in Ludwig's company. He had truly become a trusted confidant and commiserate. "Thank you, Your Majesty, for reinstating the funding for the festival. Richard can be so trying, I know, but we must forgive him his passions, for he has so many." This caused Ludwig to laugh as she knew it would.

"Was there ever any doubt that I would do so at your request? No one else would dare approach life — or a king, I must add—with quite the undaunted frankness as you, my dear Elisabeth. I am charmed and refreshed in your company."

She locked her two arms around his left as they strolled along the garden path. For the life of her, it was as if this man—one who would never demand more from her than friendship—were a life vest to be held tight to, for fear of drowning in blue ocean waters mucked with sand, troubled by the treading feet of the wrathful and the sullen.

"And my brother would have me teach etiquette to the Italians. Could you imagine such a thing? Pent up all day, as the students would be, with Friedrich and myself as their teachers, they would have no hope of surviving polite society."

Ludwig placed his hand over his heart as if having been struck smitten by Eros. "Marry me, Elisabeth, for I, too, am unfit for polite society. And may well be mad," he continued *sotto voce*, "as my family claims."

Elisabeth's eyes twinkled with merriment as she swatted Ludwig's hand down from his chest. "Just when I was beginning to enjoy your company. Don't you go making a fool of yourself, too!"

"No, never a fool, only insane."

Elisabeth suddenly looked sullenly about the garden, as anxious as a caged bird. "I shall go mad myself, if Cosima and Richard do not return soon."

"What? You don't care for the renovations I am making to the garden?" Ludwig swept his arm in an arc before them.

"Oh, I most certainly do! I am particularly fond of *Wodanaz* in all his mantic glory." Elisabeth pointed to a water pond graced with a statue of the mythological German prophet positioned in just such a manner that he looked down upon a group of dancing *nikwuz*, rendering him the vision of chaos in poetry, rather than in war, as was the more traditional depiction. Clashing images of Friedrich and Richard filled her mind's eye, though the roles in which she would cast one or the other remained unclear to her.

"I fear I am a fool of Fate, dear Elisabeth."

"Or a self-defeatist," she responded as if there were nothing unusual in suggesting such. She caught a glimpse of the concerned eyes that were now fixed on her face. He'd find no emotion there. *From my point of view, I see no soul.*

Ludwig turned her chin so that he may see into her eyes, the look in his own so ill-omened it nearly made her flinch. "What is it that you see?" she asked while fearing the answer.

"I see a kindred soul, one as helplessly drawn to destruction as I myself am. We cannot suffer a Jew in the bramble. Very well, we will see that the festival takes place. If I must tolerate the Kaiser, I will do so with you by my side."

Elisabeth threw her unbound hair arrogantly over her shoulder and sighed. "I'm afraid, Your Majesty, that the maestro has already charged me with keeping Dom Pedro of Brazil company."

"Here's a plan, my reluctant queen. You busy yourself diverting his wife, Teresa Christina, and I will endure the burdensome company of Dom Pedro. I hear he's quite beautiful."

The laughter that filled the garden drew Friedrich's attention to the window.

"I have been asked to write an entreaty to the citizenry in support of the festival." Friedrich's concentration remained on his dinner as he spoke, his knife and fork scraping against the plateware.

"What a fine idea. And will you do it?"

"I will. And I'm glad you approve, Elisabeth. I'll have to beg a great deal of your assistance in keeping notes for me— my bad eyesight and all. I'm afraid it will be quite time consuming."

Ah, it was a trap and she had just placed herself squarely in the middle of it.

Friedrich studied his companions. "Malwida, gentleman, you will understand that I must keep our dear Elisabeth to myself for a period while I play the propagandist?"

Ludwig looked as if he may protest, but Malwida cut him off. "Of course, Friedrich. We must all do what we can for our cause."

Even if one cause varies greatly from the other, Elisabeth thought bitterly. "Let's not forget that I am here for a very specific reason." She looked about the table as if selecting a prize recipient to fill her shoes. "Baron, how do you feel about children?"

Friedrich nearly choked on his food.

Gersdorff lifted the hand of command. "Calm yourself, Nietzsche. She speaks of the Wagner offspring. She is here, after all, to see to their welfare. You may keep the strings of your money pouch tightly laced."

Elisabeth found her own concerns mirrored in Ludwig's eyes. If Friedrich—both father and brother to her—were to stake a more blatant claim, Straparola would most assuredly greet her as Doralice in the next world.

Elisabeth signaled for dessert.

o o o

CHAPTER XXIX

∞

I saw the flaming path to Hell last night. Imagine my surprise to witness myself the avant-garde, shining a light on the fragments of God! In His Afterlife, perhaps he will reveal to me just how many vagabonds can be spared from one pound of flesh.

∞

By the autumn, Elisabeth had resigned herself to remaining at Bayreuth for the long haul. The Wagners remained at large, joined now by Malwida. Friedrich had returned to Basel, Ludwig to Bavaria, Gersdorff to Leipzig, and Elisabeth to lonesomeness. It shouldn't bother her so. Had not the sorrow of solitary confinement branded itself upon her bosom while assisting Friedrich with his fundraising pamphlet? *Assisting* was perhaps the wrong descriptor for what Friedrich had required of her. Her thoughts and opinions had been of no importance to him; all that was required of her was to reinforce his views.

Where once he had encouraged her to seek Truth, she was now given to understand that he had already discovered the key to the door of The Absolute and would have opened it had he not decided that entry by such simple mechanics was beneath him. No, he would delve deeper still within himself to unleash the will to command the door open. He reminded her of Turgenov's Bazarov, obsessed with finding Truth by disavowing its existence with each encounter. She had recently read *Fathers and Sons* aloud to him. Did the pages call to him? Did he find himself within their folds — dispersed in bits and pieces, sowing the seeds of Nothingness, like the god of Egyptian lore?

Elisabeth redirected her thoughts back to the letter from Cosima she now held in hand:

We are most assuredly cursed! Ludwig's betrayal has cost us dearly. I thought you had brought him up to scratch, so to speak . . .

Elisabeth stalled here. If only Cosima knew how close she had come to literally bringing the king "up to scratch." She could be a queen even now. She resumed reading.

The Friends of Wagner Societies have outright rejected Friedrich's pamphlet, "Mahnruf an die Deutschen." An Admonition to the Germans, indeed! Malwida says you assisted in this. What were you thinking, dear girl? One does not admonish those who carry purses with loose strings. But that is neither here nor there at this juncture.

Another writer has been employed and we shall see what becomes of it.

Elisabeth put the letter aside. "True," she said aloud, "one admonishes neither God nor Greatness, for Friedrich could not debate himself and win." She jolted to a stop in her trek toward the red-carpeted stairway that she so admired. When had she replaced her faceless image of God with Friedrich's visage? When had the absence of that visage become such a relief to her? A moment ago she had felt lonely, now she could barely breathe due to the oppressive heat emanating from the crowd in her head. Elisabeth fell to her knees in fervent prayer, but her entreaty to God could not be heard over the echo of Friedrich's voice. *She will be the mortar that holds a broken man in repair. When she has pieced him back together, she will guide him along the path to deliverance.*

At the remembrance of this prophesy, her hands fell unclasped as her head raised up. Had she just bowed before the memory of a broken man after once promising herself to bow to no man? Elisabeth looked frantically about her, certain that she was going mad. She must beg of Malwida to return to Bayreuth posthaste, else she might find the children taking care of her.

Elisabeth flew into Ludwig's arms when he arrived two weeks later. "I expected Malwida, but secretly hoped it would be you who came to my rescue!" Peppering his cheeks with kisses, she squealed with delight.

Ludwig gave her a brilliant smile. "It was better this way, for I am in hiding, you see—as, I suspect, are you." He turned Elisabeth about and steered her by the shoulders into the main parlor as if giving her a personal tour of the home she had come to think of as her own. "What better place to hide than beneath your tormentor's nose?"

"Do I torment you, then?" The shock on Elisabeth's face hastened him to explain.

"But, of course you do, my love. You haunt my dreams, my every waking moment."

Elisabeth's face fell, his words bringing the misery of her night terrors into the light of day. She shoved them back into the depths of darkness and struggled to catch up to what Ludwig was now saying.

"I tease you, of course. Like you, it is Richard from whom I hide. My excuse is all of the tiresome panhandling from one who is increasingly becoming a vagabond."

The image of Giuseppe Mazzini and the rise of a nation materialized in Elisabeth's mind's eye.

"Why do you hide, Elisabeth?"

Her response was delayed by her self-mocking laughter. "If I were as cunning as you, Your Majesty, I would be at Basel this very moment." On second thought, she shook her head. "No. No, I am wrong. There is no amount of cunning that would serve me in hiding from one who is everywhere in every moment."

"We speak of your brother, I presume? An exercise in futility, to be sure."

"Futility, fury, misfortune. I am like a moth flying foolishly toward a flame." Elisabeth placed a gentle hand on Ludwig's cheek. "I think often of your proposal. How easy it would be to accept, to spend my life in comfortable companionship with such a dear friend." She dropped her hand to his shoulder. "But I have never been one to take the sensible route." *She watched dumbly as Gustav led her by the hand.*

Ludwig fondly squeezed the hand she rested on his shoulder. "But this is because you are brave and filled with fearless vigor." *And you, Miss Nietzsche? Are you virtuous?*

Elisabeth ducked her head, but she failed to conceal her remorseful smile from his gaze. "Yes, it seems that I am quite reckless, devoid of honor." *What is honor but bourgeois lassitude?*

He lifted her chin, forcing her eyes to his. "There is no sin in that. History is riddled with recklessness. Order is born of Chaos, and you, dear Elisabeth, possess an inoculation for ennui. I cannot deem myself worthy to put order to your chaos." *If you spurn the seed, you will be left with the chaff. Or perhaps with nobody!*

Elisabeth shook with a sudden chill. It was as if a vulture had just blocked the shining sun. "My goodness, we talk so seriously for two friends who have been starved for good company! Now, enough of this nonsense. If I promise not to panhandle, perhaps you would escort me to tonight's performance of *La naissance d'Osiris*?"

"Happily so," he nodded with a grin. "But you will beggar me all the same."

"Most likely," she slyly concurred.

° ° °

Returning to Bayreuth far sooner than expected, the Wagners were most pleased to find Elisabeth and Ludwig in company together. Maestro and reformed mistress had made every imaginable plea for subsidy, accepting as their due even the most measly of pittances from the work-worn hands of the miserable. Where was this rise in national esteem that victory in war had so promised? The masses had invested blood and now parted with their money for a guaranteed return of social justice that was to be messengered by way of the maestro's melody.

It was a mesmerizing tune, Ludwig knew, just as assuredly as he knew that Richard's surprise in finding him at Bayreuth was feigned. One glimpse of his shared skepticism written plainly on Elisabeth's face was a measure of the waning wiles of one who proudly confesses to be "an old whore." The violet-misted veil was slowly lifting, revealing the mucky sand trap of straightforward charm.

The very second the realization dawned on Ludwig, Elisabeth recognized it, too. She skittered from his side and called the kettle black. "Richard Wagner, how dare you presume to play us for fools!" She patted his cheeks with both hands as if she might kiss him, but then swiftly released him in favor of Cosima, kissing the air beside her cheek instead. "You cannot possibly expect us to believe that you are ignorant of the goings on at Bayreuth." She surveyed their faces as would a mother trying to divine which of her children had been naughty.

Ludwig made a futile attempt to conceal his awe-filled smile. Friedrich was fond of saying that Elisabeth was too hot for even God to hold without mittens. Well, the gloves were certainly off. *Now let's see how God charms his way out of this*, he thought uncharitably.

Richard bowed over Elisabeth's hand. "Ah, dear lady. You cannot accuse me of being base-born and then chide me for knowing where every *pfennig* to be had is squirreled away."

"You mean to tell me, you searched the world over and found yourself back here, at Bayreuth? Are you home or are you in exile?"

Cosima lost the battle with her heretofore-controlled mirth. "A bit of both," she managed to say despite her strangled laughter. "Like the hand grenades he himself once devised, our Richard is ready to explode in the face of every stalwart to his project."

"I have witnessed such an affliction in another." Elisabeth cast a knowing eye on Richard. "Like Friedrich, you would blast the door down rather than simply open it." She paced the floor and then sharply turned about, all eyes on her as if she were a schoolmaster. "I would ask what you might do should you find yourself looking upon the shards of a door you might want to close again. But, then, that would be very Friedrich of me, now wouldn't it?" Elisabeth briskly brushed her palms together in imitation of one dusting off dirt. "Why not just walk through the door?" She raised a brow in inquiry, the one that both Cosima and Ludwig knew to be the agent of Disdain. "Hmm?"

Richard moved forward and placed a fond kiss of dismissal on her cheek. "You know how I enjoy your banter, but you have the tongue of a scorpion, and I am weary."

Elisabeth curtseyed her appreciation, as husband and wife exited for their chambers.

"Very well done of you, Isis," Ludwig whispered in her ear.

o o o

CHAPTER XXX

∞

"If in truth ye anoint me king over you, then come and put your trust in my shadow: and if not, let fire come out of the bramble, and devour the cedars." And so the bramble would burn, for the people preferred Abimelech to Jotham.

∞

Bayreuth March 1874

Neither will nor warmongering answered Wagner's demands from a nation he increasingly looked upon as one of his own creation. When Elisabeth was little, she had imagined, as only a child could, the Corsican evolving from David to Goliath as he marched across the map. In his hand was a particular brand of constitution, rolled up like an ancient scroll and tied with a neat red bow. She never thought to query of her fanciful mind what might be written upon that fictional scroll, and as she looked at Richard now, she intuited that this Napoleon would burn the scroll before allowing anyone to unravel and gaze upon the invisible ink scribbled on the vellum.

Seated in the parlor, Elisabeth shared a commiserating glance with Cosima as they listened to Richard ranting and raving at His Majesty in the study just down the hall. In the face of what Richard referred to as Ludwig's "obstinacy," the composer had attempted to circumvent the king, taking his case directly to the Bavarian secretary, who outright refused his request for financial assistance for the festival. Ludwig now stood accused of attempting to undermine the rise of the German, of God himself, Richard angrily proffered as he waved a fuming finger heavenward. What seemed to be an interminable rant came to an abrupt halt at the barely audible sound of what may have been the most ominous voice either lady had ever heard. It took only the briefest of seconds for the two women to come to the conclusion which Richard, too, surely must realize by now. The boy-king had grown up.

o o o

"He will give 100,000 Thaler from his personal reserves, contingent upon my providing the king with an account of every expenditure."

The king had been said with no small amount of contempt, Elisabeth noted. Her bedchamber taking on a greater chill with each passing night, she tucked her feet beneath her gown, prompting Richard to stoke the fire. "What is this I'm hearing from you?" Elisabeth goaded. "Was it not you who taught me that even one of a deviant sexual persuasion could be persuaded by the opposite sex?" She examined her nails as might a queen who tired of the court jester.

Richard pinched the bridge of his nose and then dragged his hand down his face with a long sigh. "I told you to endear yourself to him, not to conscript him."

"As I recall, you *asked* me to keep him in good temper with you. It has been quite some time since I have done as any man has *told* me to do. Friedrich, case in point."

Richard gave a low laugh as he brought his brandy snifter to his nose. "And how is the prodigal Antichrist faring?" He waited patiently for her response as she drew on a cigarette. Pure elegance. Only Elisabeth could make such a nasty practice appear graceful.

"Malwida tells me that he does quite well. I find myself to have fallen out of charity with him since undertaking your *request*." She leaned forward and tapped out her fag. "It seems that Ludwig is no longer to his liking."

"Nor mine," Richard interposed.

"That is because he is no longer a malleable boy. No, he has become quite the man, a man who actually lives the life that you and Friedrich only preach about."

"Preach, by God!" Richard sprung from his seat and crouched before her like a panther ready to pounce. He held his hands up before her eyes and turned them slowly about for her full inspection.

Elisabeth could not turn away from the mesmerizing sight of them, for in them was the representation of another set of hands . . . no, not hands, but a set of arms that encased her in a garden, many arms, in fact—Gustav's, Peter's, Gersdorff's, even Friedrich's. And she had allowed them, had countenanced each and every embrace that left her bereaved of self at every turn. She mentally cursed herself as among the weakest of fools. "Whatever point you're trying to make with those hands, however composed they are, you'll find they have no sway over me. You think to threaten me with them?"

Her own hands were brave in that moment, as she clasped them around his right hand. "Hmm?" Rubbing first the back of his fingers and then stroking his palm with her thumb, Elisabeth conducted an inspection of her own determination. "Not so long ago I thought this hand could offer me my every want and desire." She cast it away from her in contempt. "If I had a *pfennig* for every time I've made that mistake, you'd not need Ludwig's financial backing. But you see? I find that I am no longer content with accepting that which is given to me on condition. I intend to have my due, outright."

Richard drew back. He had never known her to be so fierce, so filled with hate. He had thought, initially, that Ludwig had made her soft, but he knew now that it was she who had hardened the king.

"You are wrong," Elisabeth intercepted the path of his thoughts. "He is his own man."

Richard sat mute as she tickled him under the chin as if to underscore the difference between boy and man. His own mother had not condescended to him so! "I begin to wonder, Elisabeth. Which of you is truly mad, you or your brother?"

A throaty laugh emerged from deep within her. "Well, that is our secret, now, isn't it?" Elisabeth stood up and circled around to the back of the chair Richard had just fallen into. He felt the increasing heat of her breath on his neck as she leaned over him: the breath of a dragon. "And one I'll not share. Perhaps you should meditate on it, as Friedrich does this very moment."

He mistook her meaning as an inference to Friedrich's latest installment of *Untimely Meditations*. He reached back, clasped her hand and circled her around before him. "And tell me, love," he cajoled as he brought her fingers to his lips. "How many of his meditations are of you?"

Elisabeth stared hard for what felt to him like an eternity. "None, I should say!" She spoke with a finality of voice that matched Ludwig's disturbingly quiet command of earlier. "Unless, that is, either of you believe me to be Abimelech."

Richard took in the length of her as she appeared to tower over him. By damn! For all he was worth, she might *yet* be the ancient King of Gerar.

○ ○ ○

Friedrich's *Meditations* vexed Richard in more ways than he could count. Does history shape the man, or does man make history in the process of defining himself? "Well, both!" Richard muttered fiercely. Had he not taken up a grenade and gone into exile as a result of history? Had he not, by doing so, then made a history worthy of future adherence? Friedrich would have the generations to come put all of that aside, to seek the meaning of existence through self-agency. It was the philosophy of an idealist. Indeed, for one who despised the simplistic thought of man, this Friedrich—a man he no longer recognized—put too much faith in his brethren's ability to respond to the rapidly changing world around them.

"But of course they need to know history before they can even identify the changes around them!" Richard shouted, even as an unsettling thought niggled at his conscience. He knew well that Friedrich was painting him as a pied piper of some sort, leading the band down the path of history as he would have it written—past, present, and future. No, he was not wrong, he assured himself as he reaffirmed his assessment that Friedrich was placing too much responsibility in the hands of those who knew not what to do with it.

The immature rantings that lay before him in print reinforced Richard's view that his old disciple had buried his head in books for far too long. It was lamentable, for Friedrich had possessed such promise. *Every master has a disciple destined for mastership.* These oft spoken words of Friedrich's stung as they reverberated in his head. Yes, Richard was in agreement that every disciple must rise from follower to leader. But Lucifer be damned! He'd not allow Nietzsche to go unchecked. With a curse he threw the crumpled paper aside and determinedly strode to his writing desk.

"My goodness, someone is out of sorts. 'A corpse is a pleasant thought for a worm, and a worm is a dreadful thought for every living creature.'" Cosima's voice grated on Richard's nerves as she quoted from *Meditations*. "I wonder, are you the worm or the living *creature*?"

Richard angrily threw his pen on the desk, knocking over a bottle that now spilled ink as dark as his mood. As dark as Elisabeth's soul was growing. He shuddered. "That is enough, madam! It is time for your ne'er do well lover to settle down. A wife would be just the thing to bring him to order."

"If his Lizzie will allow it." Something about the way Cosima suggestively stroked the wooden frame of the settee set Richard's teeth on edge.

"It's time that she married, too. Why have you not turned your love of match-making on her?"

"Ha!" Cosima's guffaw was incredulous in its daring escape. "What need has she of my skills? She nearly wed herself to the boy-king! Besides, perhaps I enjoy the distraction that Elisabeth provides so well."

Richard turned a speaking look on his wife. "We should throw a house party as a sort of promotion for the festival. You'll take the opportunity to invite a bevy of eligible bachelors and women capable of reining in the headstrong brother-sister duo. It's also an excellent opportunity to raise more funds." Pleased with his plan, Richard sauntered to the door, turning back to his wife with a final thought. "Make those marriage prospects individuals of means, my dear."

∘ ∘ ∘

CHAPTER XXXI

∞

If Hesiod's Catalogue of Women had been transferred from papyrus to paper, it would surely lay next to Debrett's on every gilded table. Perhaps then, the judges of the underworld would know their parentage.

∞

In his state of further declining health, keeping company with anyone—marriage prospects or otherwise—was the furthest thing from Friedrich's mind. Wasting away at Basel, he found it difficult to concentrate on writing, on class preparations, even on study. Gersdorff had offered to come assist him with a third *Meditation*, but Friedrich had declined, noting that his incapacity had gone beyond the hurtle of his vision to a fagged concentration of mind. He had high hopes that the start of the summer semester would prove invigorating. Nonetheless, news of the cancellation of his courses for low enrollment left him oddly relieved, despite an undercurrent of dismay that coursed through his veins. He would have to make a decision about his seat at Basel soon, a decision that could best be made on a solitary sojourn.

He discovered himself on the banks of Rheinfall just outside of Neuhausen. On the journey there, he confessed himself a coward for running away just as he declined Wagner's request to write *Aufruf an die deutschen Frauen (Call to German Women)*. It had enraged him that the composer would even be so bold as to make such an entreaty after passing over his first pamphlet and writing off his *Meditations* as unreasonable and unreadable. He had very nearly dashed off a response to inform the composer that the work would naturally be considered "unreadable" to the unenlightened. Upon further consideration though, Friedrich reasoned that he was above such base reactions that made humans so commonly human.

Standing, as he was now, in the far-reaching mists of the fall, he was reminded of a poem written by just such a one as he—Eduard Morike, a theologist who played the philologist, though, admittedly, he probably was better served than Friedrich in that he actually turned to the church before putting screws to it. The rushing water spewed and roared its serenade as Friedrich quoted Morike's words aloud:

Near and hard
To grasp
Is the God.

But where danger is
Deliverance also grows.

He felt those words, Friedrich did. They sat like a burden on his shoulders. "Marry," men of the world had told him. But as he looked out on Nature's pure majesty he could not help but wonder, *but what do they know of the world*? No, it was Lope de Vega's optimistic truism that steeled his spine: *Yo me sucedo a mi mismo.* Yes, that was it. Like de Vega, Friedrich would be his own heir. All other paths were fraught with danger—the Cross not excluded.

He looked now into the mountains upon the *Schloss Worth* castle, a testament to the puppetry of History, a theatric manipulation of injustice that reasoning minds could rewrite . . . if he did but will it.

From the Rheinfall, he traveled to Bergun, a municipality of primogeniture where one castle after another graced every mountain and lakeside. It was what could only be described as a thing of beauty in portentous harmony: a far, far cry from the dirty street and stinking ghettos of the real Germany. Friedrich took in the sight of noxious wealth and drew in a deep breath. *Does the smell not make you gag? It stinks of shit.*

Elisabeth had joined him in his sentiment in Naumburg, but what would she say to this? There had been a time in life when she would have coveted such a lifestyle, but Peter had changed all of that. For a period it had seemed as if Elisabeth might stand in defiance of History's claim to divine right of rule. But then Wagner had made himself divine, the perfumed air around him masking the foulness of what History has to offer.

Was this why Wagner's music had begun to play false in Friedrich's ear, the notes as sour as the canker of his being? Ever-present bile burned the back of his throat. With another look at the palatial portrait of pomposity hovering over his nation, Friedrich spat putrid phlegm upon the hallowed ground.

Having taken a room at the Hotel Piz Aela, Friedrich settled in to concentrate on his writing. His room proved to be a bit confining, prompting him to take pen and pad outdoors for his ruminations. Seated at a bistro, he had a breathtaking view of a crystal blue lake, made bluer still by the reflection of mountains of blue granite. The scene was oddly familiar. Perhaps *odd* was the wrong descriptor, for it was not odd at all for Elisabeth's spirit to accompany him on every lonely trek. He saw her now at the Hotel du Parc, reveling at the magnanimity of Nature and thrilling at having their photograph taken by Frith.

The photographer had indeed caught something magnanimous in that photo—Elisabeth on a precipice he could not quite name, preserved now for the ages. He would study the photo again as one might a puzzle . . . or a map.

"You look quite content. Might you share your secret?"

Friedrich's attention snapped back to the present and the woman now sitting at the table next to his. Like him, she was clearly in the process of researching: books and notes spread about on her table, her fingers covered in ink. "Forgive me, madam. I am Friedrich Nietzsche."

"Bertha Rohr," she offered, a wide smile lighting an intelligent face, framed by light brown hair.

A bit thinner and she could have easily been Elisabeth, Friedrich observed, and then found himself startled and annoyed that he should compare every woman to his sister. "Pleased to meet you, Bertha Rohr. And what is it that occupies your attention?" Friedrich nodded toward her array of materials.

"Now, I'll not answer that question until I know your position on women as doctoral candidates."

"No crypticism in that answer, now is there? Would it please you to know that I am on a committee at Basel University where we are now undergoing a process to accept and enroll female candidates?"

Bertha rose and approached Friedrich's table, reaching for one of his books. "Of course, you're a professor. I should have recognized it straight away judging by your reading material . . . Schopenhauer, Spinoza," she began to tick off his references one by one. "And —" she picked up another book. "Nietzsche? That is you!" she exclaimed. "But why have I not heard of your work? I am studying contemporary philosophers, after all."

Friedrich laughed. "Perhaps it is because I am so obscure as to be insignificant. Besides, it can be costly when one's publisher has to write-off the bulk of unsold books. Oh well, another age, perhaps." He waved his hand as if to dismiss invisible recalcitrants.

She gave him a quizzical look. "Another age?"

"In My Afterlife."

"And do you expect to have an afterlife?"

Friedrich's nod was decisive. "If I will it."

"Oh, I see then. The secret to your contentment . . . the will to live."

"The will to will, more like."

Bertha laughed with delight, despite the far off look in Friedrich's eyes. "Can you will my dissertation into acceptance, then?"

"I can will myself to read it." He grinned. Appallingly aware that she was still standing, Friedrich motioned for Bertha to join him. "Where are my manners? Please do sit. It will take a while for me to read your dissertation, after all," he teased, in no way expecting her to produce it on the spot.

Bertha sat and plucked a small stack of papers from her attaché. "Not so very long." She chuckled as she held out her meager offering.

∘ ∘ ∘

She is one of the most intellectually engaging women I have ever met. I cannot countenance it, Lizzie, but I damn near asked her to marry me on the spot . . .

"Absolutely not!" Elisabeth shouted at the letter in her hand. Why in God's name had Richard and Cosima set their minds to marrying Friedrich off? It would not do for him to choose a bride without her counsel, for only Elisabeth truly knew what type of woman would make her brother happy. Said woman would have to be intelligent, of course; caring; understanding; and capable of encouraging Friedrich in his pursuits. There would be lifting and soothing of spirits to accomplish, a strong bond of friendship to be formed, for that is all a wife could expect to have of him.

She slapped the letter down on her writing desk. No, no, there was not such a woman to be found without her help. Taking up her pen, she wrote a reply to her brother, reminding him of his poor health and his even poorer ability to make such decisions of import. He must join her in Naumburg immediately, as the holidays were fast approaching and Mother would be sorely disappointed if he did not spend them at home. Confident that she had made her case, Elisabeth sealed her reply and then lifted the lid of her desk to deposit Friedrich's letter into the overstuffed treasure drawer.

o o o

Christmas turned out to be a somber affair. The family dynamic had transformed from a state of intangible tension to one of intense strain. Silent messages transited the sitting parlor as mother, son, and daughter sat in the subdued glow of the Christmas tree. Elisabeth was painfully aware of the quiet of the company. Friedrich's defense weapon of choice was a day-old newspaper, Franziska's a cup of coffee, and Elisabeth's a poorly stitched embroidery. Good God! When had she devolved into her old pastimes? She cast her sampler aside and began massaging her neck, sore from bowing over her stitchery. A shudder racked her body as an image of her kneeling before an anonymous entity skittered across her mind.

"And what do we hear of the baron these days?"

Ah, and bow she must. "Very little, Mother. I'm sure he has much more important things to keep him occupied than correspondence with Friedrich or I."

"He is in Berlin attending to parliamentary business," Friedrich offered from behind his paper.

"Berlin? For the holidays?" Somehow it did not sit well with Elisabeth that her former fiancé stayed in such frequent touch with her brother. She very well nearly felt violated. *What game do you play with your brother, Miss Nietzsche?* For an uncharitable moment she wondered if Friedrich had taken a new lover.

"Oftentimes men feign business for the arms of a lover."

"You read my mind so effortlessly then?"

"Children!" Franziska chided prudishly. "We do not speak of such things in this household!"

Friedrich snapped his paper closed. "No, I suppose we don't," he acquiesced as he made a futile attempt to ease the pain in his head by squeezing his temples. "Otherwise, Lizzie would have had a much-needed father."

Elisabeth jolted from her seat. "God's teeth, Friedrich—"

"Elisabeth! Your language!"

Her mother's admonishments had long ceased to stay Elisabeth's temper. She was about to flay into Friedrich with a vengeance, but he cut her off short.

"Elisabeth is right, Mother. God has teeth, and the bite of Conscience teaches man to bite back."

"You have no conscience," Elisabeth snapped.

"Whatever do you mean, dear girl? I am ever conscientious."

"I will not tolerate this sniping," their mother insisted. "At Christmas of all times!"

Brother and sister sat stoically as their mother practically slammed her coffee cup on the side table and stormed from the room.

"And where are God's teeth now?" Elisabeth asked as she lay in Friedrich's arms a short time later.

"Right now they are concentrating on your conscience." His jest was cruelly seductive as he took her earlobe between his teeth with a gentle tug.

"Always my fault, is it? You say I have no male authority figure. Why, then, do I suffer like Europa?"

o o o

CHAPTER XXXII

∞

Amnesia or no, with the right setting and the right lighting one would think Siegmund would recognize his own twin in Sieglinde. Ye Gods! She could identify him solely by his scent.

∞

January 1876

Having requested and received relief from his teaching duties, Friedrich wrote to Elisabeth of his plans for extensive travel. It in no way surprised her that he should choose to gallivant around Europe rather than finish what he had helped start at Bayreuth. He would join Malwida and Paul Rée in Italy where one might presume he would turn his mind to the school he had been so enthusiastic about, but, in her heart, Elisabeth knew that this would be yet another abandoned project. Friedrich's growing weaknesses grated on her mind and struck discord in her soul. Where she used to look upward when thinking of her brother, she had now fallen into the habit of staring at the floor in consideration of him. He clearly thought equally as low of her given that he had no reservations about tossing out Peter's name at her as if he had no notion of how deeply it cut.

The carnival in Basel is more than can be borne, he wrote. *I will be leaving for Geneva as soon as I can pack, and will forward my address as soon as we arrive. There is a distinctive restlessness in this year's celebratory commotion. What was once pure mirth is now underscored with rage. Peter has summed it up best, I believe — "a barbaric spectacle of students, beating their drums like pagans, as if to bring down the walls of Jericho."*

"Well, if anyone should know about paganism, it is Heinrich Köselitz and his Jewess," Elisabeth muttered meanly.

"And what is a Jewess to a German thoroughbred such as yourself?" Elisabeth startled at Richard's unexpected embrace as his arms snaked around her waist, his hands settling at her ribcage.

"Really, Richard," she half-heartedly admonished, "it is not at all the thing to compare women to horseflesh in our day and age."

Richard stepped back and placed a hand over his heart as if an arrow had pierced his feelings. "Horseflesh? I protest!"

"I'm sure you do. Now, where is Cosima?"

"I could not tell you. Now, why are you changing the subject? You cannot accuse the most tender, most amorous of lovers of treating one so dear to him as an animal without giving him satisfaction."

Elisabeth moved past him to peer out the window, as if she were expecting someone of consequence to arrive any moment. "I am not up for our usual banter today, Richard."

Gently massaging hands found their way to the back of her shoulders. "I don't doubt it." His whisper was filled with unvarnished concern. "You had a particularly difficult night. I was unaware that you still suffered so. You called his name, you know?"

The raw sound that emerged from Elisabeth's throat was almost . . . animal-like. "And whose name would that be? Which tormentor denied me a peaceful slumber?"

"Who do *you* think it was? I should make you guess for the satisfaction of better knowing your mind."

"Don't be cruel, Richard!" she snapped with thinning patience.

He sniped back. "Cruel, my love, is uttering your brother's name while you are in my arms."

Elisabeth hugged her own arms about herself, drawing up as would a porcupine prepared for attack. "Who else's name would it be? The weight, the weight of it! You say you want to know my mind? Only Friedrich knows my mind and so it is always to him that my mind wanders. It's a dark path I tread, with a dark guide as my sole companion. If I had a name to put to my specter's face, I should, no doubt, call it in my sleep in hopes that it would for once carry a lantern." Elisabeth stood on her toes, straining to identify the carriage making its way toward the house.

"Many are expected today, Elisabeth. Who do you look for so intently?"

"Ludwig. He carries with him a lantern."

"I cannot believe it has been over a year!" Elisabeth exclaimed when she finally had Ludwig to herself. She clapped her hands on each side of his face and lovingly squeezed his boyish cheeks. "Be still, let me kiss your beautiful lips." And she did. Elisabeth was one of the few women that he allowed such a familiarity. She was the sister that Ludwig had always wanted, and the one that Friedrich Nietzsche clearly did not know he had. Such a waste of good fortune!

"What a tedious year you must have passed!" Ludwig set Elisabeth away from him and twirled her around, examining her form as if to see if she had grown. Or aged, considered Elisabeth.

"I dare say I have thoroughly debased myself, for you are looking at one of the most productive of panhandlers." She brought the back of her hand to her forehead in dramatic despair. "I wanted to be a stage organizer, but what's a girl to do when there are not enough funds to build a set?"

Ludwig sighed heavily. "You need not turn your beggar's eyes on me. I assure you Richard has the funds, and needs only my approval to spend them." He withdrew a piece of parchment from his pocket, shaking it out for her inspection. "What is your opinion of the figures assigned to these requests?"

Elisabeth studied the columns of numbers circumspectly, her eyes finally settling on the expenses for her particular projects. "Oh, definitely the *Die Walkure* set," she informed him as she assumed the mask of one who possessed an opinion born of long experience in such matters.

"My, my, aren't you quite the Sarah Siddons?"

Elisabeth shot him a winning smile, and then quickly pulled a sobering visage. "Shhh." She put her fingers over his mouth; another familiarity only she was allowed. "If Richard even heard you jest that a common actress was worthy of his stage, he'd throw your money back at you, and then we'd all gladly take ourselves off to hell just to save ourselves the misery of hearing him wish us there for years to come."

"You make a good point." Ludwig shuddered comically. "I wouldn't want that, for you know," he tapped her chin, "wherever you go, I will follow." He looked unto the horizon as if considering a location for a vacation. "And I can't particularly say I would enjoy such a destination."

Elisabeth swatted his chest. "Be serious! We were talking of what I want."

"Of course, madam. Pray continue."

"The costumes need a bit more flare – Sieglinde's, most importantly."

"I see. And does Siegmund need an extra touch, as well?"

Elisabeth waved her hand to indicate that Sieglinde's brother was of little consequence to her. "No, no. Anyone who dies so soon into the tale does not deserve to be remembered."

o o o

Grandma Oehler: Now there was a woman who had lived her life to the final act. Despite Richard's pleas, it was Naumburg that Elisabeth returned to after her grandmother's funeral. Her mother needed comfort that Friedrich could not be counted on to deliver. Well, to be fair, Elisabeth had been feeling a bit spiteful toward her brother when she received news of their grandmother's death and had delayed notifying Friedrich. She supposed she didn't really want him in residence with her.

Both joy and sadness filled Elisabeth's senses when she thought of Grandma Oehler. There had been life at Pobles, life in the garden tableau of God's creation, but death in the soil hidden beneath that floral façade. Elisabeth's head spun as hollow memories forced their way through her relative calm. Lilacs, she smelled lilacs. The sickening scent filled her nose and propelled her to vomit. Sweat pouring from her forehead, Elisabeth looked about frantically for a cloth to wipe the taint from her mother's carpet. Having seized a handkerchief from her pocket, she set to dab at her mess, but then stilled her cloth-clad finger in its effort to wipe away that which would forever reek. As if suspended in time, her arrested finger hovered just above the floor, pointing accusingly at her putrefied viscera.

Sometime later she awoke with the startling realization that she had fallen face down in a muck of her own making. Bayreuth, Hell, or Basel—what were her choices? At this point, she thought she might rather prefer Hell, if only her specter would spare her a lantern.

o o o

CHAPTER XXXIII

∞

Machiavelli spoke for the Jew of Malta. Who, then, speaks for the Woman of Purpose?

∞

Though her reprieve from the stresses of Bayreuth was much appreciated, Elisabeth fervently missed the whirlwind of diverting social functions she had enjoyed there. To occupy her time, she had taken to vigorous study of English, Italian, and French. She taught Sunday school and took courses in darning so that she may assist the poor. *Wasted energy*, her mother had called it, insisting that her efforts would be better spent in trying to find a husband. It didn't help that Cosima seemed to be of the same mind:

Elisabeth, darling, how droll your days must be away from Bayreuth! I try to picture what you might be about and, inevitably, the image of a spinster hunched over a crotchet pops into mind . . .

Espying her darning in an old chair by the window, Elisabeth snatched it up, angrily threw it into her sewing basket, and shrouded it beneath a blanket as punishment for the affront it presented her.

. . . But not to worry, my dear. I have just the thing — or man, rather — to cheer you. Dr. Bernhard Forster is a teacher at the "Friedrich's Gymnasium" in Berlin. He is visiting his mother there in Naumburg and has made me a special promise to visit you while in residence there. I must say, he's quite handsome. Just your style, in fact. What a fine conversationalist he makes! Do take advantage of this visit and all that Bernhard has to offer . . .

Elisabeth expelled an exasperated sigh as she plopped into a chair with the flagging determination of the demoralized. A man. Would she forever be fated to follow the lead of a man? "Do take advantage," Cosima had written, but it was Elisabeth's unfortunate experience that the man always held the advantage. No sooner had the conviction overtaken her than she dropped her head in her hands and cried.

Once in Dr. Forster's presence, she could not fathom why she had wept. As she poured him coffee, she nearly made a mess of the doily lining the serving platter, so beautiful was he with his blond hair, intelligent green eyes, and determined jaw. Were his hair a darker shade and his lip covered with a mustache, he could almost pass for Friedrich. Was Cosima aware of it? Caught in the act of gaping, Elisabeth quickly diverted her eyes, a heated blush creeping up her cheeks.

Bernhard cleared his throat. "I am deeply sorry for your loss, Miss Nietzsche. I understand from my mother that your grandmother was the kindest, most upstanding of women, every bit a parson's wife. That is something, I imagine, both my mother and yours can lay claim to understanding."

Elisabeth sipped her coffee quietly and carefully. "Indeed." She nodded her head in measured approval. "There is no greater responsibility than that of a minister's wife, always a shining witness ready to bring every soul unto Christ."

Bernhard's ears perked up considerably at this. He had not expected a friend of Cosima's to take such a traditional perspective. "I'm glad to hear you say so, Miss Nietzsche. Women like you—women of purpose—are at the backbone of our great nation. The mothers of Prussia, one might say."

It was Elisabeth's turn to pay heed, for he had referred to their country as Prussia. Not Germany, not The Confederation, but *Prussia*, the mother of Germanic existence. She set her coffee cup aside. "It's strange, is it not, that just within a few years after the war, we find ourselves indistinctly known as Germans? As if we have no identity, as if it were not Prussian blood that paved the way for the confederation the states now enjoy."

"Hear, hear, madam. You have gone directly to the heart of the battle that is ours to undertake. It is the way of capitalism, communism—the way of the Jew—that lures individuals behind a curtain from which they will emerge indistinguishable as they join the masses. Not surprisingly, it is the Jew, Karl Marx, who leads the band with Aryan annihilation in his sights."

It is the battle cry of Nationalism to which the feet of the Wandering Jew will once again tap. Elisabeth's body nearly shook with anger at the memory of Peter's words. She had been such a fool for so many years, duped into believing that it was the Jew forever retreating when in fact they were an advancing army of increasing numbers with a golden calf at the helm. She pictured the calf now, fierce and impenetrable, with a blanket of royal purple across its back, Europa atop the saddle. Elisabeth remembered herself just in time to hear the tail end of what Bernhard had been saying.

". . . And I would be so honored if you would agree to attend my speech next Tuesday evening, as my special guest, of course. I expect to be able to gather enough signatures to form our own Wagnerian Society here in Naumburg by using the composer's own words, no less." Bernhard jumped to his feet and stood tall as if he were already at the lecture podium: *The Jewish race is the born enemy of pure humanity and everything that is noble in it.* I heard him say those exact words to the King of Bavaria, who didn't quite seem to side with his beneficiary on the matter."

"Ludwig doesn't really care for such divisive language." Absent-minded of her words and her actions, Elisabeth propped her chin in her right palm, and drummed her fingers against her lips.

"*Ludwig*? You call the King of Bavaria *Ludwig*?" The realization of how useful this connection could be pleased Bernhard to no end.

Elisabeth's mouth dropped slightly open as she stammered, "I—forgive me, I misspoke. The king and I are on rather close terms, but perhaps such familiarities would best be saved for my private conversations with His Majesty." She knew as soon as she'd said it that her guest had taken affront.

"I'm sorry, madam, if I have given the wrong impression. I would never presume to overreach." He stood and collected his coat and hat. "On the matter of Tuesday's lecture?" He looked her way expectantly, awaiting her acceptance.

Elisabeth stood with him. "It would be an honor to attend, even more so as your special guest." Even in her *spinster* state, the art of flirting had yet to fail her, as evidenced by Bernhard's mollified expression.

She was, indeed, a woman of purpose, a dark and deadly tempest brewing in her breast

° ° °

Good evening. My name is Dr. Bernhard Forster, and my father was a pure Aryan. Thus began every one of Bernhard's lectures, the positive response of the crowd growing in resonance with each event Elisabeth attended. She was enrapt by his words, his looks, and the force of his convictions. Her thoroughly enjoyable hypnotic state was broken when Chaos, or the ghost of Chaos, came to her side.

"You find this sort of talk appealing?"

"Baron . . ." Elisabeth gritted out as she proffered a curt nod in Gersdorff's general direction. "And how do you do this evening?"

"I was doing quite well until I spotted a woman of particular intellect falling prey to a prowler."

An incredulous *hummphh* found escape through her nose, as she smirked in her tormentor's direction. "If you dislike him so, then why are you here?"

"I am a soldier, a philosopher, and a lord. It would be remiss of me to turn a blind eye to that which is brewing in the cauldron."

Elisabeth turned a peevish eye upon him. "And why have you not travelled on to Italy with my brother?"

"I fear I am not cut out to mend broken hearts, or minds for that matter. I have commitments to my title and country and have not the luxury of being amongst the *Free Spirits* your brother and his friends have now taken to calling themselves."

Elisabeth shook her head as if she didn't quite follow him. "What is this about broken hearts?"

Gersdorff laughed incredulously. "I should have known your ears would stop working at the mention of your brother's heart. If you really must know, then prepare to have your own broken. We met a music director in Geneva by the name of Hugo von Senger. No sooner had we made his acquaintance and that of his intended, Mathilde Trampedach, than Friedrich proposed to the fair Mathilde. He has quite an opinion of himself, your brother, offering his hand to a spoken for woman he barely knows and then smarting at the inexorable rejection."

Ah, so this is why she had received very little protest when she insisted Friedrich need not rush back to Naumburg in the wake of their grandmother's death. Elisabeth straightened her spine. "I don't know why you think it should break my heart," she rejoined nonchalantly. "I should say any woman would be most fortunate to have him. He grows in national popularity by the day, thanks to Richard. And Bernhard, of course. Great minds are drawn to Friedrich's philosophy."

"Great minds . . ." Gersdorff's tone rung superior in her ear. ". . . have a propensity for recasting every mold to fit their way of thinking. Little do they know that Friedrich makes it his mission to keep man in eternal limbo with his expertise in cogitation. And this Forster you have fallen in with . . ." He pointed toward the podium with a flippant finger. ". . . is a bad seed. You've met his brother. What would draw you to such a disagreeable sort?"

"I don't find him disagreeable at all, Baron. He wears his Prussian uniform in such a stately manner—"

"Deceptive, you mean. He's an arse, Elisabeth, and you're a fool if you can't see it."

"Yes, that's exactly what I called myself upon meeting him. *A fool.*"

o o o

My dearest Friedrich . . .

What is this I hear about you proposing to a woman you have only just met? For the life of me, I cannot make you out these days. First it was some young woman in Bergun, and now Geneva. Was it not you who always said that only a fool offers his hand too quickly? What is your hurry of a sudden? And why must I suffer the embarrassment of such tales?

I do wish you would return home. Naumburg is enjoying the insight of Dr. Bernhard Forster. (You may recall that we met his brother at the Wagners' some years back.) Anyway, Dr. Forster has taken to the lecture circuit and, as a result, we are all reminded what it means to be Prussian, to have Teutonic blood coursing through our veins.

As leaders, we must take up the mantle of Christ and bring morality back to a Hell-bound civilization. We have made it our Christian duty to take the Jew under our wings and usher him unto Christ. But what to do with those who simply do not want Christ's love? Those who would perpetuate and propagate a lineage of heretics? "Go therefore and make disciples of all the nations, baptizing them in the name of the Father and the Son and the Holy Spirit" is Christ's Great Commission. I see now, brother, that we have gone about it all wrong, mistaking Christian charity for duty. Our nation suffers beneath the weight of our sins.

Indeed, Dr. Forster is a man of great intellect and foresight. You would most assuredly like him upon introduction.

Speaking of which, whatever you may hear from Gersdorff on this subject, you must disregard it. He is only jealous, and, perhaps, at a loss for grasping the significance of our Lord's message as channeled through Dr. Forster. As teachers, both you and Dr. Forster know a little something about trying to reach those with inferior understanding.

Do say you will return home soon. I can't wait to introduce you to him!

Your Lizzie

∘ ∘ ∘

My Dearest Lizzie,

I have never known Gersdorff to be anything less than honorable in all his dealings, besides which there is nothing he could possibly say that would alter my opinion. I am glad that you enjoy Dr. Forster's "insight," as you put it, but as you'll recall, we do not think much of his brethren.

The language you used in your last letter was quite strange to me . . . perhaps you were fatigued? You have confused religion with race, and believe me, Dr. Forster's concern is one of birth. No amount of religious conversion can wash away bloodlines, and *something tells me that your Dr. Forster would not accept it even if it were so. If all were equal in the eyes of his god, what value then would his Teutonic heritage hold for him? Think on it, love. If you believe your New Testament, then Christ the Jew hung on a cross for you. Would you repay him for his troubles by bleeding out his entire race?*

As for any understanding that you believe I could possibly share with Dr. Forster, I'll remind you that teachers and professors are a wide world of wisdom apart from one another. Never settle, dearest girl.

Your loving, if disappointed,
Friedrich

○ ○ ○

CHAPTER XXXIV

∞

From which side of the theatre is a pogrom best viewed? God has, once again, broken my lorgnette.

∞

Bayreuth
August, 1876

Elisabeth was thoroughly disappointed when Ludwig made good on his word and departed Bayreuth before the opening of the festival. There had long been tension between the Bavarian king and Kaiser Wilhelm, both refusing to attend the festivities if the other was expected to be there. When forced to choose, Richard chose the Kaiser. Ludwig was behaving like a child, the composer insisted. Bavaria would simply have to stop laying its inability to stand alone at the feet of the Kaiser. A part of The Confederation it was, and with The Confederation Bavaria would remain, no matter how loudly they squalled and squawked about autonomy.

Deprived of her closest confidante, Elisabeth had to make do on her own, though she had to admit that the royal entourage from Brazil was quite fascinating. As she looked upon the beautiful Dom Pedro and his equally lovely wife, Teresa Christina, she was reminded of how Ludwig had assigned her to keep company with the wife, while he chatted up the husband. A scandalous thought occurred to Elisabeth that it would be no hardship to curry favor with either one. A crisp image of Ludwig lighting the way to Hell, lantern held high in one hand as the other squeezed hers reassuringly formed in her mind. No, it was unjust of her to hang him for her crimes! A woman of purpose, she had carried her own torch since meeting Dr. Forster.

She spotted his striking blonde head now as he made his way down the aisle of the darkening opera house. A man of pure splendor, if ever there was a talisman of German superiority, it was he. He was the epitome of a Norse god, prepared to stand in judgment of this evening's performance, *Die Walkure*. Elisabeth craned her neck to find that the god had chosen her for his particular favors and was weaving his way in her direction.

"Miss Nietzsche," Bernhard greeted her with a nod. "How lovely you look this evening!"

"And how fine you look in your dress uniform, sir."

He straightened his jacket and lifted his chin higher. "I thought it rather befitting for the occasion."

She took him in with admiring eyes that just as quickly expressed confusion, as she recalled the tale of an emperor with new clothes Friedrich read to her as a child. Clothed as Bernhard was now, Friedrich had written to her once: *Who is more vulgar in this scenario? The oaf taken in by such an elaborate display of ceremony, paid for via levies he can ill afford, or the extravagantly clad piper, prancing about on a Trojan horse?*

"Miss Nietzsche, are you unwell?"

Elisabeth quickly pasted a smile on her face. "I am quite well, thank you. It just seems a tad bit stuffy in here."

"I have always been told that I have a tendency to suck up all the air in the room, but you may rest assured that I would breathe nothing but life into you."

Elisabeth gasped as the baritone of her favorite voice boomed over her shoulder. She was out of her seat in less than a second. "Ludwig! But I thought you had fled."

The angry flush on Bernhard's cheeks did not escape Ludwig. In that moment he found that he quite enjoyed the novelty of rendering a man jealous over a woman. "I do not flee, madam," he teased, as he brought her gloved fingers to his lips. "I only hide," he continued in a muttering jest. "From the Kaiser, that is." Elisabeth laughed gaily, a sound of genuine joy Ludwig well knew was once reserved only for Friedrich.

Elisabeth scooted over a seat, making room for Ludwig between herself and Dom Pedro, her mouth nearly dropping to the floor when Bernhard made haste in taking up the seat instead. He had guts, this one.

Grinning like a cat, Ludwig took the seat to her left, settling himself close enough that they may make their usual mischief without causing too much of a commotion. "It seems your friend Dr. Forster recognizes a thing of beauty when he sees it."

Elisabeth covertly cast her gaze to her right, observing Bernhard in the act of ingratiating himself to the Brazilian emperor. An unlady-like snort escaped her nose as she rapped Ludwig's arm with her fan. "You are nothing short of a scoundrel," she chided.

"Speaking of dashing scoundrels, where is your brother?"

"I do not recall saying you were dashing, and I believe my brother is off in Sorrento or there about. With Paul Rée," she added belatedly. "A gentleman who, Cosima assures me is — upon closer examination — a Jew. Ironic that she's just now figured that out."

Ludwig attempted to cover his smile as he drew in a gasping breath of feigned shock. "Never say so! Your brother taking up with a Jew? Why, it's simply unheard of!"

The chuckle forming in Elisabeth's throat retreated in shame when she heard Bernhard cough, reminding her that she was a woman of purpose in a packed opera house where the curtain was now raising on a tragedy that would fall like an anvil on the heads of German Jews.

"You do realize that he's a sodomite?" Bernhard had asked later.

Standing in attendance at yet another post-performance reception, Elisabeth had lost count of the days as she swayed on her feet from fatigue. "I know that he prefers the company of men." She sighed heavily. "As do I. Women can be quite trying. What is your objection?"

"It is not a question of my objection but the absence of your outrage." His tone was oddly familiar in its command. *Choose carefully. For if you are wrong, the fires of Hell await you with a vengeance.* "Can't you see? The devil's reach is far and wide. Like the kings of Sodom and Gomorrah, unnatural men align themselves with unnatural faiths. The Sodomite and the Jew will burn together for their crimes against Christ. And the Germans," he added.

"And do you equate the German with Christ?"

"Certainly not! But Christ's messenger on earth? Most definitely."

° ° °

The festival was nothing short of miraculous! I will simply never forgive you your absence! Was it not enough for you to forsake Richard in his finest moment? Was it necessary to send such bitter aphorisms to tear at his heart in these days that should have shown him nothing but joy? How many have you sent these meanderings of mind to? Was it you who instigated the cruel headlines in the French press?

In the way of more public embarrassment, Ludwig stands publicly accused of cowering, but I have since been informed that it is you who has secreted yourself away. Really, Friedrich! Louise Ott is a married woman. Did it not occur to you to ferret out this simple intelligence before asking her to marry you?

Your loving, if disappointed, Lizzie

° ° °

Dearest Lizzie:

If you believe that my humble opinion would find outlet in foreign press, you give me far too much credit. I simply called our musical friend an amateur, a far cry from the "lunatic" the French have taken to styling him.

Has it not occurred to you that one who cannot ferret you out of his bed is indeed low in intelligence?

It is as I have proclaimed all along: God is dead.

Your bereft brother.

"Bereft of mind is more like," Elisabeth muttered as she refolded this latest missive. She had no sooner put it away than Ludwig entered the parlor with Bernhard hot on his heels.

"*Guten Tag meine Schone, Elisabeth.*" It was so like Ludwig to play to his new audience by adding an extra flourish to his afternoon greeting. "Look who I found at your doorstep," he said with a slight, yet perceptible sniff, indicating that he thought he smelled refuse. Another unladylike snort escaped

Elisabeth. The boy-king had her behaving like a child, once again.

She advanced toward Bernhard with both hands extended in greeting. "Do forgive His Majesty, Dr. Forster. I sometimes wonder he was not raised by wolves."

"Or Bavarians," Bernhard quipped with a wide smile cloaked in an innocence that dared anyone to suggest his insult was meant as anything but a joke.

Elisabeth looked nervously between the two. "Gentlemen, you do try my patience. Before you arrived I was just reading a letter from another who sorely tests me."

"And how does Friedrich fair?"

"The same as ever, Your Majesty. Sickly, licking his wounds, and denying reality."

Bernhard leapt into the intimate ring of a conversation that had been meant for two. "I can hardly agree that your brother denies reality, Miss Nietzsche."

"Oh, but he does, indeed, Dr. Forster. My brother denies everything and disavows Truth just to be difficult."

"But this cannot be! I have read his *Meditations* with much fascination. Such insight into the duty of man, the duty of the German! We must embrace what History has handed us and forge our paths anew. Victors through and through, God has deigned to task the German with cleansing the slate of every soul—"

Ludwig could stand no more. "If I may, Dr. Forster, I fear you have made the mistake that so many make when reading Nietzsche. He is not promoting an embracing of the history of old, but rather eschewing it to make history anew . . . to discover and develop self-agency, to seek Truth, a purpose for our existence, and then to deny it all again so that we may continue searching. Jews, included, by the by. 'Cleansing souls.'" Ludwig swirled the brandy he had poured himself to better endure Forster's presence. "Those words serve as a cloak for what you really mean, do they not? If you intend to feed your ambitions, Forster, say what you mean. A leader a prevaricator will never be."

And now Bernhard *felt* like refuse. It was all he could do to hold himself in check with the reminder that he was in the presence of a king, no matter how reprehensible. He stood and bowed his departure to Elisabeth, turning his back on Ludwig as if he did not exist, for the Aryan still held some of his manhood intact.

Once alone, Elisabeth graced Ludwig with a wobbly smile. "Did they teach you such shameful behavior at court? To make a well-meaning man feel small?"

"My dear lady, I believe we long ago established that I am not fit for society, and if you hang on that man's words, then neither are you. *Mazeltov.*" He saluted before downing a final swallow.

Having forgotten that she was an independent-minded Woman of Purpose, Elisabeth squirmed uneasily in her chair. She so hated having to choose sides.

∘ ∘ ∘

CHAPTER XXXV

∞

Is it possible that a Jew holds the key to The Question for the Ages? I dreamed of Christ last night. Clad in nothing more than a bloodstained purple cloth across his loins, he quoted Sir Walter Raleigh who, upon testing the blade that would sever his head from his neck, jested: "Now this is a sharp medicine, but it is a physician for all diseases and miseries."

∞

Naumburg, 1878

More than two years had passed since the debut festival in Bayreuth and, while the Wagners had put on another production the August past, Elisabeth had been unable to attend, forced instead to while away in Naumburg with her mother. She realized that the remainder of her days would play out just so, if she did not take her future in hand. Possessing long years of experience, she suspected she knew just how to accomplish such a feat. Her relationship with Richard having run its course—as all of her relationships inevitably did—Elisabeth had arranged to spend the Christmas holidays in constant company with Bernhard Forster. He was a man just like any other man. Yes, she mused, circumstances in Naumburg were positively looking up.

"Will you be needing anything else, Miss Elisabeth?"

Unused to having a personal servant, Elisabeth had completely forgotten the new maid's presence in the parlor. Undeniably pretty, Alwine Freytag was a proud young woman, and, as Elisabeth looked at her now, she was surprised to find the maid's wistful gaze glued to the floor as her own had just been. It could use a bit of polish.

"No, thank you, Alwine. You have been more than helpful today. Please take the afternoon for yourself."

Alwine bungled a curtsey. "Thank you, miss. You are too kind."

If embarrassment had a sound, it would have been heard in Elisabeth's sigh. She would never get used to having a servant, no matter how her younger self might protest. "Do stop bobbing gratitude. We are friends, and I do wish you would look at me and not the floor." She smiled inwardly as pride resurfaced in Alwine's expression. "There now, that's more like it. Now off with you! I'm sure you have Christmas shopping to do."

With no small amount of gaiety Alwine took her exit, nearly bumping into Bernhard on her way out. He, in turn, tipped his hat and bowed his apologies, and then turned a speaking stare on Elisabeth. "Miss Nietzsche, you really must stop treating servants as if they are your equals."

"I know that I must. It's just that I have never felt quite comfortable giving others orders, particularly when I prefer to handle matters for myself. Who better to satisfy my wants than me? Besides, it's not like she's a Jew!"

Bernhard proffered an approving nod and made himself comfortable without invitation as was his habit of late. There was something proprietary about him that didn't quite sit well with her.

"What you should *want*, madam, is to restore the natural order of things to our society. As the works of Aristotle remind us, we all have a role to play. Alwine's is that of servant, and yours is . . . I have not quite determined yet."

"You need not trouble yourself, Dr. Forster. I gave up role-playing long ago. There is only one who will determine my fate."

"So true, so true." He nodded approvingly. "You are a handmaiden of God, and no woman was ever more worthy of such a calling as you."

The sudden memory of hiding her face in a chair just as quickly turned to an image of herself lying facedown in vomit. *Friedrich! How did you find me?* The man before her at once sickened and charmed her in a way that she nearly abandoned the resolution she had made just moments ago. "Yes, it is just as you say, Dr. Forster. A woman of purpose must have industry."

Bernhard cleared his throat. "Speaking of industry, I fear I am unable to remain for the holidays. As we have spoken of on a number of occasions, I, too, must fulfill my calling. I have just received word from a group of investors that they are willing to finance my expedition to South America."

Bernhard had long had his eye on the nation of Paraguay. War-savaged, it was now sparsely populated and primed for rebuilding; an opportunity Bernhard was all too eager to turn to his advantage, convinced that there the Lord would provide for the salvation of German-kind. An Aryan nation was his vision, his life's mission. A "wild-eyed pogromist," Friedrich had called him, and while Elisabeth thought it might be true, she could not help but admire a man made of more than just talk. She had long stopped denying her natural impulse to stand in awe of the grotesque.

"Of course, Dr. Forster. Your business is pressing and must be attended to right away. If I were a man, I should join you," she said with a laugh. "You'll be missed, but I can't say it's not for the best. Having recovered from his latest health setback, Friedrich will be joining us in the next day or so."

"What is your brother's objection to me? We have never even crossed paths."

"His objections have nothing to do with you and everything to do with me."

Bernhard waited for her to elaborate on this cryptic assertion. When she did not, he seized on another of his jealousies. "And will you have an opportunity to see the Bavarian?"

Elisabeth fiddled pensively with the fringe on her day dress. "I have no plans to visit the Wagners this season, and, therefore, no expectations of seeing anyone outside of Naumburg."

"And your friend Mr. Gast?"

Elisabeth hesitated before speaking. "I'm sure you understand that the Köselitzes cannot be expected to celebrate Christmas."

A sudden dawning, in the form of scarlet red, lit upon Bernhard's face, leaving Elisabeth to wonder — if he had not known that Peter Gast was a Jew, how then did he expect to identify those of his pure creed? Perhaps it was best that he could not, for — though she wasn't willing to admit it to herself — there was always the possibility that she would never be completely pure. No, she would not accept that. Friedrich was not the only one who held the power to will.

"I retract my earlier statement, Dr. Forster. Even I have a role to play."

o o o

He had done it. Though she had not yet read the book herself — she would not have a copy until Friedrich arrived with it — Cosima clearly had gotten her hands on an advanced copy. The letter Elisabeth now read left no doubt as to the response *Human, all too Human* had garnered at *Wahnfried*. Cosima's outraged voice could be deciphered from the angry handwriting that covered every page, margins and corners included.

By her own admission, Cosima had only read a few pages before condemning the book to the waste bin. She did not know this Nietzsche and would be surprised if Elisabeth professed to recognize him. The hand of Paul Rée was behind this mad rant, Cosima was convinced. Sneaky, slimy, and slippery as ever a Jew there was, Rée's influence was most assuredly behind Friedrich's aphoristic attacks on Christianity, ennoblement, higher culture, patriotism — indeed, every facet of the Wagnerian dream. He had even gone so far as to propose the Jew as a necessary ingredient for a strong Europe! Worse still, in a not-so-veiled allusion, the Antichrist had likened Richard's utopia to a community of half-wits that would serve only to breed stupidity that would *follow all stability like a shadow.*

Elisabeth paused here. How she could just hear her brother's voice in all of this. How clearly she could see the specter in her mind's eye. No, this was not the work of Rée, but the ruminations of a man who had befriended a fiend and feared he would never again know peace. Never would she succumb to such weakness! Forgotten in this moment were her youthful admonishments when her mother openly speculated about the cause of her father's death. Her duplicitous hand simply could not be stayed as it dashed off a response to Cosima, declaring that she suspicioned her brother might be going mad.

One look into Friedrich's eyes when he arrived several days later told her that his head ached insufferably. Pain swam within his squinting orbs as he leaned forward to kiss her cheek, his aim off by several inches. Elisabeth cradled his jaw and directed his lips to hers. Pliant and compliant, he relaxed into her embrace as she stroked the nape of his neck, attempting to soothe away his discomfort.

"You're looking well, Lizzie," he mumbled against her shoulder.

"A sight for sore eyes, am I? Can you even see me?"

"I have always made you out, even in the duskiest of rooms." His whisper sounded as painful as his eyes looked.

Elisabeth set him aside, intent on gathering up his luggage, Alwine beating her to it.

"I have it, Miss Elisabeth."

"*Vortreffliche Alwine*, lovely as always, I see." Right on target, Friedrich proffered a kiss to the maid's cheek. "What are you about, treating me like an old bugger incapable of carrying his own luggage?"

"I've done no such thing, Master Friedrich!" she chided fondly. "Anyone can see that you are in pain. I only meant to help."

"Thank you, my lady." He bowed in the maid's direction. "But I will manage."

Vortreffliche Alwine (the Excellent One). If she did not love Alwine so, the High Priestess may have been jealous. "Thank you, Alwine. I will assist my brother from here."

As she unpacked his things, Elisabeth came across a ledger of barely legible, scribbled notations clearly intended for a book. "Friedrich, darling, is your eyesight so bad that your aphorisms make little sense? Shall I help you organize them?"

"But, Elisabeth, my work is perfectly organized and makes a great deal of sense. Don't tell me that your brain has gone soft. Did my book *For Free Spirits* traumatize you that badly, then?"

"It traumatized the nation, Friedrich! How could you embarrass the Wagners? And so publicly, to boot?"

"I was unaware that Richard and Cosima counted themselves among the restricted in spirit. Think for yourself, dear girl, for only the insipid follow a lost cause."

"I hardly know you anymore. You once loved Richard so dearly."

"Yes, well, even God has his fools."

Elisabeth hung his final suit in the closet. "And who is the fool in this scenario?"

"Ah, now *that* is the question for the ages."

° ° °

Apparently, it was Peter who would sit by Friedrich's side as he attempted to formulate an equation for The Question for the Ages. Leave it to a Jew to stand before God with a forged invitation in hand and a proclamation of Truth on his tongue.

"What possessed you to invite him?" Elisabeth demanded of her brother.

"He has agreed to travel to Florence with me after the holidays to assist me with my writing. And, truth be told, I expected your fanatic to be here, and thought it would be great fun to watch him make a jackass of himself."

His calm arrogance chafed Elisabeth's nerves. "You've not met him, and still you abhor him."

Stroking his chin in that pompous way of his, Friedrich spared two fingers to signal a dismissal of Bernhard from serious consideration. "I don't need to meet him. I've read the papers, and I see how he has changed you. Do you know what I think? He's a shyster, who dreams of building his own empire because he'll never receive recognition among civilized society. You follow a false god, Lizzie, at the cost of your very being. Careful with that one; he bites. Was it not God who turned on himself when he impregnated Mary and gave birth to the ultimate Jew?"

Elisabeth lurched from his bedside. "My God, you are mad!"

Her proclamation was met with his self-deprecating chuckle. "Quite possibly."

° ° °

CHAPTER XXXVI

∞

Fidelity's bride once wandered in his wake. But alas! Rome calls and all quacks do quake.

∞

Not long after the holidays, Friedrich sent a letter from Florence informing Elisabeth that he had finally and permanently resigned his professorship at Basel. His health was progressively worsening, rendering ludicrous any pretense that he would be capable of fulfilling a full semester's duties. His maxim, *the best students are self-educated,* had grown iconic in its popularity. Many laughed it off as the greatest of jokes, while a select few found it to be quite true.

Elisabeth sighed as she entered his abandoned rooms at Basel. She was there to wrap up Friedrich's unfinished business and collect his belongings. Sell it all, he had instructed her. She would have to, she thought despairingly, for she couldn't fathom how they would manage without her brother's income. She dropped her head in her hands. *Why had she given such a large portion of her life savings to Richard?* Probably for the very same reason that a sizeable picture of the maestro fluttered from Friedrich's bedside table. Elisabeth's eyes widened at the intimate secrets that shone in the immortalized eyes staring back at her. They were simultaneously accusatory and mocking as she recalled once wondering if Friedrich had lain in Richard's iniquitous bed.

At thirty-three years of age, she still blushed to think of the act and the number of men with whom she had shared such shameful intimacy. Her first impulse was to rip the picture into pieces, but then thought better of it. Like herself, Friedrich had his Hell and clearly enjoyed self-loathing, as evidenced by the poem she found written on the back of the portrait in her hand.

Is this still German?
Out of a German heart, this torrid screeching?
a German body, this self-laceration?
German, this priestly affectation,
this incense-smelling, lurid preaching?
German, this plunging, halting, reeling,
this sugar-sweetish, bim-bam pealing?
This nunnish ogling, Ave leavening,

This whole falsely ecstatic heaven over-heavening?
Is this still German?
Consider! Stay! You are perplexed?
That which you hear is Rome — Rome's faith without the text.

Suddenly unsettled, Elisabeth looked about in near desperation. She had touched Friedrich's heart and patched his wounds in this very bedroom. Where was her ode? Where was her picture? Well, he must have one! As she deposited Richard's picture into a keepsake box, she slipped a photograph of herself and Bernhard in Naumburg from her reticule and placed it atop the maestro's disapproving physiognomy.

o o o

"I know you'll not take my money, but we believe we have found a way to obtain a measure of financial security for you and your mother."

As Elisabeth took in the sight of Gersdorff and Dr. Forster seated across from one another in her mother's parlor, she experienced a sort of *déja vu*, only it was Friedrich, and not Forster, that her mind conjured from a past tableau. As her heart told her to cast herself at the mercy of Fidelity, her passion for purpose perversely pointed her in the direction of Fanaticism.

"A private collection of your brother's works could be quite profitable," offered Fanaticism.

Angered by the blatant greed that filled Fanaticism's eyes, Fidelity threw down the gauntlet. "Like myself, there are a number of investors who would be happy to set up a trust." His mien silently, yet boldly challenged Fanaticism. ". . . with a trustee, of course, to monitor expenditures and to ascertain that you, your mother, and Friedrich are properly cared for."

"Have you anyone in mind?" Elisabeth queried of the baron.

Without pause, Fidelity offered up his nomination of the boy-king.

Fanaticism jumped to his feet, rage written all over his face. *"Blutig Hölle!* You would place a child in charge of a collection that may well prove to be a manifesto for German grandiosity?"

Elisabeth turned a mollifying smile upon him. "Do sit down, Dr. Forster. At thirty-four, Ludwig is hardly a child, and he is, after all, the ruler of a nation." She returned her attention to Fidelity. "I trust him, Baron. And thank you for your thoughtful consideration."

"You well know that you will always have my greatest concern, Elisabeth."

"Miss Nietzsche," Fanaticism stressed as he addressed Fidelity, "has a great many supporters." He tugged on the flaps of his military jacket. "Myself included."

A firm nod in the baron's direction was intended as a display of authority, but served only to deflate Fanaticism, as Fidelity's only reaction was a dismissive perusal of the wearer of a uniform that had borne no witness to battle.

"Speaking of supporters, did you perchance miss your ship to Paraguay?"

Elisabeth felt indignant at Gersdorff's less-than-subtle jab at Bernhard, despite the fact that she herself had every intention of inquiring as to his reason for remaining.

"I'm sorry to say that my expedition has met with a bit of a delay, but you may rest assured that my crew will prepare the way for a greater Germany."

"Yes, well, I'm sure we will all sleep better for it," Gersdorff concurred sarcastically. "However, unless you are carrying official orders from Bismarck, I would suggest you take off that uniform before spreading your quackery abroad."

○ ○ ○

As he proved to be harder and harder to locate, Friedrich was not available to offer any opinion on instituting a private collection. In fact, Elisabeth speculated, the idea would probably offend him, as it added a certain finality to a life's work that he was only truly just beginning. Peter had indeed accompanied Friedrich to Florence and then to Geneva where *The Wanderer and His Shadow* came to life. Another collection of aphorisms, a number of these ruminations Elisabeth recognized from days gone by – long, lazy days spent in her brother's arms, dreaming the awesome dream of the irrevocably awed. In truth, forever accompanied by the Silent Specter, they had never truly been alone. And from what Elisabeth read now, it was clear to her that, depending on the angle of the sun, their fiendish friend either guided or trailed Friedrich as he wandered the wilderness.

Several days later, a letter from Cosima impressed upon Elisabeth how imperative it was for Friedrich to return from the wilds. In his manuscript, The Wanderer had satirically addressed his feeling in regards to inconveniences of posts:

A letter is an unannounced visit; the mailman, the mediator of impolite incursions. One ought to have one hour in every eight days for receiving letters, and then take a bath.

Elisabeth felt that she could certainly use a good wash now. By confiding in Cosima that she thought Friedrich might be losing his mind, Elisabeth had sullied not only Friedrich's but her own reputation as well. Her brother's resignation from Basel and subsequent disappearance had fanned false rumors of his death.

With her endless connections, Cosima knew very well that Friedrich was alive and wandering. Her inquiry was not a serious one, but a warning to Elisabeth that many within the Bayreuth circle were beginning to float about their own speculations. She would follow Cosima's advice and return to Bayreuth for what had now become an annual festival, and hopefully put all rumors to rest.

° ° °

CHAPTER XXXVII

∞

*The Loathly Lady can make many a pilgrimage, but
NEVER to Asuncion!*

∞

1882

Bernhard and Elisabeth had kept up quite the letter campaign over the past several years. Though he had originally planned to return after a short venture to South America, The Friedrich School had sent word through his brother, Paul, that his teaching post was no longer available to him. The school had attempted to turn a blind eye to Dr. Forster's extreme views, but could no longer withstand the negative publicity brought on by Forster's formation of the German People's Party and his petition to Bismarck to have Jews banned from civil service and barred from holding property.

Chin up, Elisabeth had encouraged. One could not expect the unenlightened to understand the insight of a true prophet. "Over all obstacles, stand your ground." Had not these words of Goethe's been adopted as Bernhard's own motto? From what he had described to her, it did indeed sound as if the terrain presented quite an obstacle, but nothing that one so valiant as he couldn't overcome. She would think of him at the debut of *Parsifal*—he, like Parsifal, went in search of the Holy Grail and would surely receive heavenly benediction for such valiancy.

What she did not tell him was that she had been spending a great deal of time with Ludwig, as of late. As was the case with the Festival of 1876, Elisabeth had spent months in Bayreuth helping the Wagners to prepare. Part of that preparation required additional financing that could only be procured through Ludwig's special fondness for Elisabeth.

"Are you sure these letters are from Friedrich?" Ludwig asked of her as he held a missive up to the light as if to detect a forgery.

"I can assure you, I know my brother's handwriting. Besides, there are other witnesses to his living and breathing form. Malwida, for one, and then there's Peter and Gersdorff. And—" She paused, smacking her palm to her forehead. "Good Lord! Who could forget about that Paul Rée and some

Russian Jewess named Lou? He speaks a bit too fondly of her, but that's another problem for another day."

Ludwig glanced at the letter again before turning a look of something akin to wary sympathy on this woman that he loved. "I know little of male-female affairs, my dear Elisabeth, but I can read in this all that your brother is not saying. She is more to him than a passing fancy, this Lou. See here." He moved his finger across the letter, pointing out several lines that only Elisabeth would require a code-breaker to make sense of. "From Marienbad to Recoaro, from Sils Maria to Rome . . . he has experienced them all through her eyes."

Elisabeth angrily snatched the letter from his hand, shooting the messenger with the icy daggers that darted from her pupils, piercing his heart as surely as would a knife. He moved beyond the pain and reached his steady hand out to cover her shaking one. "You need not grow angry with me, Elisabeth. I feel your aching heart all too well. To love one that can never be had is God's way of reminding us that, kings and commoners alike, we are but his mortal subjects."

Elisabeth squeezed Ludwig's hand in a show of solidarity and a search for support. "Read the postscript, dear heart. God is crueler still. A broken heart not being enough, Friedrich asks me—in the wake of his banishment from Bayreuth—to receive and accompany his Jewess for the production of *Parsifal*." With an abrupt turn she added over her shoulder, "I shall have to write for Bernhard's opinion on the matter."

Rolling his eyes in exasperation, Ludwig stayed Elisabeth by the elbow. "What would possess you to seek advice from such a one as this Dr. Forster?"

"Aside from you, he is my only friend. Unlike you, he knows a great deal about affairs between a man and a woman."

Bernhard's letters were long in coming. Elisabeth had very little knowledge of Paraguay. Who knew what jungle, swampland, or desert he may be in? When she imagined him there, insects, disease, and savages came to mind. He had written to her of an insect, dubbed the sand-fly, which burrowed beneath the skin and had to be excised before infectious disease set in. A group of darkies he called Guarani had demonstrated how to knife out the parasites. But, while they would have to traverse the discomforts of the Gran Chaco River to Asuncion, he assured her that the German settlers would be taken to a colony immune to such barbarity. Indeed, the Hungarians had already demonstrated the promise that the land held; it was, after all, the Hungarian Colonel Heinrich von Morgenstern de Wisner, in his role as the Paraguayan Immigration Minister, who had served as Bernhard's guide.

Smug in her eagerness to prove Gersdorff wrong with this news, Elisabeth's spirit quickly deflated when the baron informed her that he had heard of the Hungarian aristocrat, Morgenstern, and was shocked to hear that Fanaticism had not yet sniffed out his Jewish blood and penchant for pederasty. Such jabs only served to encourage Elisabeth to redouble her efforts on Bernhard's behalf. Therefore her proposal to draft and distribute informational pamphlets, to include Morgenstern's map of Paraguay and Bernhard's proposal for an Aryan colony, was met by her fiancé with great enthusiasm in the home that he had come to call Nueva Germania.

It was the sight of these instruments of hate—ridiculed in Berlin, yet hailed in rural Saxony—that greeted Lou Salomé when she exited the train from Leipzig. As Friedrich had requested, Elisabeth was at the station to "welcome" her as best she could. After taking one look at Lou, Elisabeth was glad she had given in to Friedrich's request. Ludwig had been wrong, for this woman, so masculine in her manner, appeared to be the one who would know little of male-female relationships.

"Forgive me, dear, but Friedrich made no mention of you being in mourning."

With a quizzical expression, Lou followed Elisabeth's gaze, suddenly realizing that it was her black apparel that gave such an impression. "Oh! Pay no heed to my wardrobe." Her chuckle was as deep as Friedrich's. "I simply find that I am taken more seriously when dressed plainly and simply. We philosophers are rather sedate, you know."

Elisabeth held her tongue for a moment, afraid that either condescension or jealousy would lash forth from it. Uncouthness materialized in their stead. "Surely you need not flaunt about like a shadow," she declared as she brusquely teased at Lou's short hair and then shook her head. "Well, there's nothing to be done for it. You'll have to wear a veil in Bayreuth."

Lou, too, raised her hand to her hair, as if to smooth down locks that didn't exist, wondering how a veil would make her appear any less the shadow. "I should think I would prefer to be myself. Friedrich and Paul won't join us until we reach Bayreuth. Besides, they are quite used to me by now."

"Nonsense," Elisabeth chided, as she took her new charge's hand and directed her toward home.

It was doubtful, Lou thought, that Elisabeth would believe it *nonsense* if she knew that both men had proposed to her.

∘ ∘ ∘

Elisabeth could barely take her eyes off that dark veil as Lou turned about the dance floor in Gersdorff's arms. She envisioned herself as she must have looked to others on the night she had met Gersdorff so many years and tears ago, floating about gaily in the lilac dress befitting of a debutante. On this night, it was Lou who clung to Fidelity as would a buzzard to picked-over prey. Her partner was clearly enjoying himself. They all were on this occasion at Bayreuth, for *Parsifal* had been quite a success, well attended.

"And where is your partner, my lovely girl?" Elisabeth's shoulders slumped. Where once Richard's voice had made her blood sing, it now made her feel somewhat drained. If she had learned anything from Bernhard, it was that she did not have to dance to another's tune. *Be true to thine self*, he had instructed her, having ascertained that loyalty to others would amount to nothing more than self-abnegation. She had heard these same words on both Friedrich's and Richard's lips, but somehow they did not carry quite the same strength of purpose.

"So this is your wayward brother's heralded friend?" Richard pressed on.

"Hmm," was all Elisabeth had to offer as Lou spun around like a black cloud that had stolen the sun's bliss. "I would never have placed her in Friedrich's esteem, a reminder of how little I know my brother." Richard patiently waited out her sudden pause. "I used to draw ever so many pictures of Friedrich when I was little. Always framed in the bright halo of the sun, I sometimes think now that there was too little shadow in my depictions."

"Well, his Jewess is certainly casting a pall over my celebration."

Elisabeth followed the direction of Richard's thoughts. The cloud had parted, moving about considerably in the arms of another and then another. Elisabeth saw red and would be damned if she would put on Franziska's mask!

At the first opportunity Elisabeth marched up to Lou, who was standing by a refreshment table caught up in jovial conversation with a number of gentlemen over what appeared to be a picture in her hand. Elisabeth's temper flashed furiously when she saw, upon closer observation, that the object of the group's attention was a photograph of Friedrich and Paul Rée hooked to a cart like mules beneath a whip held by none other than Lou Salomé.

"The pose, don't you see, is symbolic of woman's rise in a patriarchal society. A spoof of who really holds the reins of destiny." Lou would have gone on to share Friedrich's assertion that existence hung in thrall to a woman's womb had Elisabeth not suddenly snatched the photograph from her hand.

"The only portrayal in this . . ." Elisabeth waved the picture angrily at Lou. ". . . is the extent of shame a harlot will stoop to in order to trap an honorable man into marriage. He would never have such a creature as you!"

"Honorable?" If Elisabeth's voice had been overexcited, Lou's was shriller still more. "It was your darling Friedrich who soiled his breeches, begging on his knees not two days after we met." Hands clasped behind her back, she slowly circled around Elisabeth, leaning in with each taunting jab. "You may rest easy, I assure you, for I'd not have him. I could spend an entire night alone with him in one room and not get excited."

Elisabeth's hand flew out, the crack of her palm leaving a red mark on her nemesis's cheek.

Lou shrugged her shoulders nonchalantly in response. "But who knows? That may all change. He has asked me to accompany him to Paris. At first I thought to decline." She studied her prey menacingly. "But now I believe I shall accept."

By now, both Ludwig and Richard were by Elisabeth's side. It was Richard who took the catastrophe in hand. "Ms. Salomé, I believe it would be better for everyone if you were to take your leave now. I cannot see any good in your remaining." He took the photograph from Elisabeth's hand and returned it to Lou, ignoring his injured friend's protest. Lou accepted the photograph, steeled her spine and waltzed out of the room, not a single sign of shame about her.

It wasn't until she stepped out into the night air that Lou realized she, like so many Jews, had nowhere to go.

Standing just outside of Elisabeth's bedchamber Richard heard Elisabeth in soft conversation with Ludwig. Given his weary mind and body, it was probably best that the boy had gotten to her first, he mused. Nonetheless, there was something about Ludwig's gentle voice that discomposed him. Was he jealous, and if so, of which one? Disgusted with himself, Richard returned to his own room and the ritual of prayer exercised by those who find themselves separated from God.

Ludwig gently wiped away Elisabeth's tears with the pad of his thumb. "Your eyes will be red and puffy if you do not cease crying."

Elisabeth laughed as her sobs subsided.

"That's my girl," her rescuer soothed, as he leaned back on the bed pillows and gathered her close to him.

As she eased into his embrace, it struck Elisabeth as odd that there was no shadow in the room. As it had been with Paul Deussen, Ludwig asked nothing more of her than what she could gladly give with her heart.

° ° °

CHAPTER XXXVIII

∞

Dear God,
Hallowed be thy name, whatever it may be. And forgive the one who,
so ruthlessly and thoroughly raped, no longer cares.

∞

When next Friedrich visited Naumburg, Elisabeth could hardly believe the changes in him. For someone who had been so ill, he looked nearly a decade younger. As buoyant as a born-again crusader, he spoke as if he could singlehandedly take on the world. *More like command it,* Gersdorff had warned in an ominous tone. He did seem off somehow, but Elisabeth was unconvinced that there was anything *unhealthy* about his sudden turn of health.

"And how did you find Lou?" Friedrich asked of Elisabeth as soon as he unpacked and settled into his room.

"Oh, let us not speak of others now," his sister suggested airily, and perhaps a bit warily. "Tell me all about you. I am pleased to find you looking so rejuvenated and full of life."

"Happy to oblige, Lizzie. I find myself all too eager to discuss the subject of myself these days. This could take a while," he teased, waggling his eyebrows up and down. He extended his hand, leading her to take a seat with him. "Here, let us sit upon . . . *Eros.* Yes, that's it! We shall call him Eros in recognition of his tale of love."

She looked at him incredulously. "You have named your bed?"

"And why not? I infuse all things with a secret essence known only to the Wanderer and his Shadow." He pointed to the corner, prodding her in a low whisper to will what he willed. "They lurk there in the darkness, you see?"

Elisabeth flinched. Yes, she did see, but was shocked beyond words to find an apparition of her brother standing next to the fiended friend who had observed impotently as life led her astray.

"I have had the most wonderful dreams, Lizzie. They have revealed to me the unreality of all that surrounds me, for, you see, I am not *in* my vision, but above it all, parting a burnished mist to uncover Truth. Just beyond Truth, I see you as a young girl, Lizzie, wearing your best dress, so beautiful, so innocent. And then a voice rings out . . . *God wishes he were Nietzsche!*"

He blinked his eyes at her as if he had indeed just awoken.

Fever, of course it had been fever, Elisabeth sighed in relief as she dabbed Friedrich's forehead with a cool cloth. "For shame!" she whispered an admonishment to herself. "Your brother lies abed in a miserable state and you can think only to be glad that he is not mad of mind."

"How is he faring?"

Elisabeth's heart jumped at the baron's voice, prayerful that he had not overheard her. "Much better, I believe. His fever seems to be subsiding."

Gersdorff took up vigil by her side. "I know you well enough to guess what you're thinking. I did hear what you said, but I would never judge you for it. Unfortunately, there may be some merit to your fears." He pulled a letter from his pocket and offered it to her. "I received a letter from Paul Rée. I'm sure he intended it to reach us before Friedrich's arrival. Your brother has been speaking madness for quite some time it seems."

Elisabeth unfolded the letter and read Rée's plea for assistance in convincing Friedrich to return to Naumburg and the care of his family. Her interest piqued when she saw Lou's name ahead of what was supposedly a direct quote from Friedrich: *Greet this Russian from me if you think it does any good. I am greedy for her kind of souls. In the future I am going to rape one.*

In vain Elisabeth attempted to swallow back the bile that had risen in her throat. She didn't even have time to reach for the small wastebasket in the corner. Vomit surged forth from her mouth, her throat a slave to bile's bidding as the sounds of the wretched and the wild preceded the flow that forever soiled the hated words written by the Jew's hand. She recognized this humiliation all too well. How often her gut had been scraped raw from the inside out!

Gersdorff was beside her in a flash, wiping her mouth with his handkerchief, wholly expecting her to fall into a fugue. Instead, she turned and placed her cares upon the shoulders of Fidelity, as if her life depended on it. "It's a lie," she cried out. "My brother would never say such a thing!"

"I don't believe his words were intended to be taken to mean physical violence. You know Friedrich, always testing the boundaries of what's acceptable. I suspect he was alluding to *reaping*, for lack of a better word, the experience of a soul that has seen the world through very different eyes"

God wishes he were Nietzsche!

"No matter how you consider them, the words are revolting and would never be spoken by one so honorable as Friedrich."

"Certainly not by the Friedrich that we know," he offered softly.

As the hour grew late, Elisabeth remained at Friedrich's bedside. His nonsensical mutterings had ceased as his fever's release soaked his sheets in sweat. She gently peeled the wet sheets from his body and replaced them with fresh ones. Tucking them in tightly, she was surprised to find that Eros was not the only essence within as her fingers fell upon a manuscript beneath the mattress. *Also sprach Zarathustra. Ein Buch für Alle und Keinen (Thus Spake Zarathustra. A Book for All and None)* was written across the opening page. Just like old times, Elisabeth sat down to read, fully prepared to praise her brother's truths.

Except, for once, she could not. She had wanted him to prove himself alive, but never had she imagined that he would emerge from the wilderness and take to the mount with a sermon the likes of which could have been preached from Christ's own tongue. This was blasphemy that she held in her hand.

Accusing man of killing "the old god," Zarathustra preaches against the state, the marketplace, and the church, exhorting mortals to vanquish themselves unto nothing, so that they may rise anew and cross the bridge to Truth. Immediately came to mind the image she had once painted of herself: a troll trapped beneath the bridge to Tribschen and what she thought would be a better life. Her brother's words from youthful days rung in her ears: *Consume yourself in your own flame so that you may rise anew.* And here in this manuscript were those very same words under the heading *ON THE WAY OF THE CREATOR.*

Elisabeth shivered as she flipped through the pages filled with the teachings of this Zarathustra to his disciples, instructing them that "some souls one will never discover, unless one invents them first." *I shall always know where my soul lay* — she knew it was within her, because he had fashioned her present being. Still perusing, her attention fell upon a passage in which evil was described as being *decked out with purple honors.* Did he know? Heart dropping, eyes filling with tears, she closed the manuscript, and her shoulders drooped at the notation written alongside the heading at the top of the page: *Part I.* She dropped her head in her hands. Still more madness was yet to come.

As she leaned forward to return the manuscript back to its resting place, Friedrich's hand shot out to wrap around her wrist. "Please don't put it away, Eli. I would have you read it. Since a boy, I have sought to identify the one who shadows me. He is Zarathustra, the millennial Persian, the ordained disciple of History's Truth." With a weak finger he tapped the manuscript cover. "It's all in here, you see. God despises himself so much that he wanted to look away, and so he created man — everything and nothing."

Elisabeth rose to retrieve a cool cloth, turning back to shush him as she gently dabbed his forehead once again. He fell into a light sleep, mumbling curiously. In His Afterlife, she hoped he would be lucid enough to shed light on his ramblings:

I love those who do not know how to live, except by going under . . .

I love the great despisers because they are the great reverers . . .

I love him who lives to know, and who wants to know so that the overman may live someday . . .

268

I love him who works and invents to build a house for the overman and to prepare earth, animal, and plant for him . . .

Elisabeth awoke suddenly, surprised the weight of her body had not disturbed Friedrich's sleep. It had not been her intention to allow herself sleep; she only wanted to warm his shivering body and soothe his nightmares away. She fell back at ease and began to stroke his hair. He had done this for her so many times.

"Why did Lou not accompany you back to Naumburg?"

Elisabeth's eyes flew open once again at his question. She squirmed about uncomfortably. Now was not the time to tell him of her falling out with that most unsuitable tart. "I suspect she was eager to return to Rome," she hedged.

"She would not return to Rome without me and Paul. Together we are the Holy Trinity; alone they are nothing."

His body was weak, but his voice was vehement enough to silence the falsehood on Elisabeth's tongue. He would never forgive her if he knew she had run the woman off. "I have no idea where she went, but will ask the baron to make inquiries."

Mercifully, he slept now, for awake, he held the power to divine Truth and condemn her to nothingness.

° ° °

CHAPTER XXXIX

∞

Beware you leaders of fanatics, flocks, and followers:
Pride doth goeth before the fall!

∞

"Friedrich's sudden decline is entirely that dreadful woman's doing. For all that your public histrionics bring great embarrassment on this family, Elisabeth, I *am* thankful that your high temperament got the better of you where this new love of his is concerned. Have you actually seen the disgraceful photograph that's on the lips of every gossip in Naumburg?"

Elisabeth cast aside a freshly delivered letter from Bernhard and raised a perturbed brow at her mother. "What makes you think he's in love with Lou?" she questioned defiantly.

"Well, of course he's in love with the doxy! And that's not the point. What of the photograph?"

"I can only tell you it's as wicked as it is said to be." Elisabeth reached to the side table, retrieving her letter, a signal to Franziska that she had better things to spend her time on.

"What is that you have there?"

"It is a private correspondence from Dr. Forster, Mother."

"Surely you have not written to him? That would be highly inappropriate for a single . . ." Upon second look at her daughter, Franziska altered track. "Well, at your advanced state of spinsterhood, perhaps there is no real impropriety in it." She took a seat next to her daughter. So near was she in her attempt to read the letter for herself, she may as well have been seated on Elisabeth's lap. "Oh, my, he misses your company. Now that *is* promising. Bring him up to scratch quickly before your opportunity is lost."

"And what would you have me do, Mother? Just a moment ago, corresponding with him was on the border of impropriety, and now you would have me throw myself at him, in writing, no less?"

"Well, you hardly have many options."

"Lizzie's options in life are unlimited, and I'll not allow her to marry that madman."

Mother and daughter looked up in surprise to find Friedrich pouring himself a stiff drink at the sideboard.

"Friedrich! You should not have strong drink in your state." Elisabeth had practically sprinted across the room to seize the glass from his hand.

Just as quickly as she had taken his drink, Friedrich wrested the spirits from her grasp. "There's not a drink strong enough to console my state of health and mind. You know what I received this morning on the very same tray that delivered your news from Forster? No? Well, do allow me to enlighten you. I received a letter from Paul Rée, who, having just returned to Rome, had a message from Ms. Salomé informing him that she was on her way to join him. Apparently, there was some type of kerfuffle in Bayreuth?"

Elisabeth bit her lip in agitated thought. Friedrich could see the cogs of deception whirring about behind her eyes. Finally, she stiffened her spine and decided to go for broke. "She is a trollop, Friedrich! She embarrassed our good name, and that of the Wagners', by flouncing about with that disgraceful picture in her hand. She made us all the laughingstocks of the gala with what was clearly an attempt to trap you into matrimony. You may have played the mule in that photo, but you came off as the ass that had compromised that opportunist's reputation!"

Friedrich's response was carried on that low whisper of a voice that preluded the storm destined to come. "That *opportunist*, as you call her, has no need of a trap. Indeed, she had every *opportunity* to marry me upon the countless occasions I proposed and was denied flat out. I am at my wits' end with you, Lizzie." He captured and held her gaze with a promise of malice in his brown eyes.

She met his challenge with equal disdain. "Do preserve what's left of your wits, dear brother, for I have had done with you, and you will need a steady mind in your solitude. You, with your arrogance and disregard for your friends and all that's proper, can just waste away in your own filth."

"Elisabeth!" Franziska rushed to her son's side. "How cruel of you to speak to your brother so, particularly now in his ill state!"

"When is he not ill, Mother?"

"I am not ill, Lizzie, when I am among those who still possess the capability to participate in some level of intellectual discourse."

"Then, please, by all means, return to your flock."

"By all means," Friedrich mocked, "you may return to your fanatics."

o o o

Dear Bernhard,

It feels so strange to address you so intimately, but I will honor your request to go forward on a first-name basis. Of course, I know better than to misinterpret such a request and must remind you that to address each other so in public might create false impressions in the minds of others. (Yes, he needed to be brought up to scratch.)

I received a packet of pictures earlier this week from one who can hardly be called your friend. His intention was to taunt me with what appears to be a dilapidated cabin, or a barn of some sort, that he claims is the home that you built for yourself in Asuncion. Surely this cannot be! You are practically the monarch of a nation of your own making. You must build a grand mansion. Otherwise, what ever will people think of you? You could have the natives do most of the work. I have enclosed 800 marks so that you may at least hire servants, as is befitting your station. And don't refuse me, for it will comfort me to know that all is as it should be at "Forsterhof"; I hope you don't think me presumptuous, but I believe you should name the estate Forsterhof. We shall put a sign in place to mark the year of its erection so that there will be no confusion for future generations as to who should receive recognition for the thriving German colony that is taking shape.

Speaking of conquering, do be careful, my dear friend. There are those in the Reichstag who would have you condemned a traitor. (I do believe these were the sources of the photos that make it appear as if only a shack awaits any who may be willing to invest in our colony.)

But please do not worry overly much. There are so many who are starved for a society established on morality, that they are willing to give their entire life savings to make a reality of what once seemed like an impossible dream. You have restored hope to so many, not the least of whom is me.

Do write often. I long to hear of every detail of your progress.

In Friendship,

Elisabeth

Elisabeth would have been surprised, Bernhard suspected, if she knew just how important her letters were to him. Once jilted, he had become skeptical of women in general, deeming them all to be manipulative and grossly calculating in their simpering wiles. He was no fool. Elisabeth was trying to force him to declare his intentions, and so she was right to. The idea of having her by his side appealed to him strongly, but looking around at his bleak surroundings, he knew that he could not ask her to join him in the miserable state in which he lived. He just needed a little more time to get the affairs of Nueva Germania in working order. He could hardly bring a wife to a hinterland of chaos. Of course, as she had reminded him, most expeditionists were taking to Africa. Paraguay, in comparison, was nothing so barbarous. Still, she was no hothouse flower.

But then, again, there was the issue of money. He would die of shame before he told her that he could barely afford to build the cabin he now lived in. The pressing worry of finances — he was having difficulty securing further loans, much less paying back those he already held — was an ever-present weight on his very being. Elisabeth's company and money would help ease that burden. He would take her companionship freely, but could never accept her money . . . unless she was to become his wife.

Dearest Elisabeth,

I have every hope of returning to Naumburg for Christmas and hope that you will grant me an audience. I do so regret that I was unable to spend last year's festivities in your company and do hope you'll allow me to make good on your open invitation.

o o o

On his month-long journey back to Naumburg, Bernhard thought of all of the reasons why he should not propose to Elisabeth. Her mother was rather aloof to him, though that would prove no discomfort in the end, given that the 10,000 kilometers that would span between his bride and her mother. No, what concerned him most was certain interference from the brother who Elisabeth was unnaturally attached to. He was godlike in her eyes and had too much sway over her for Bernhard's peace of mind. And then there was the fact that, to his countrymen, Bernhard was a villain and a hero in equal measure. He was reasonably sure that Elisabeth could bear up to the scorn they would endure even among their own, and he counted on her growing disdain for that money-grubbing, hedonistic sector of their "countrymen" that sought dominion over those of pure Aryan blood.

Nonetheless, he must have her money and, quite frankly, it surprised him to realize that he must have *her*.

Her acceptance of the proposal he made practically upon arrival was short in coming and, disconcertingly, short in tone. She rambled on and on about her plans for the colony in such detail that Bernhard feared he may be losing command of the situation. He would not stand for it, of course, but now was not the time to rein her in. There would be plenty of time for that after the holidays. For now, he planned to use their time together to shape and mold her into his ideal of a quiet-natured wife who would adhere to his every wish.

As the holiday season progressed, it became clear to Elisabeth that the man she had agreed to marry did not know her at all. Never mind that, he would figure her out soon enough and be grateful that she had accepted him. Like Friedrich, he needed an invisible hand to guide him to the highest heights of triumph. Her experience with Friedrich had taught her much — best to break Bernhard in now.

Much to his indignation, Bernhard had been summoned to discuss *strategy* with Elisabeth and a number of faithful volunteers crowded around in Franziska's small parlor

"I have 20,000 marks at your disposal and am filled with ideas as to how I want my funds to be spent," Elisabeth informed them all with a regal nod. "First of all, we need to change advertising tactics. We have been selling this venture short by *recruiting* volunteers rather than *selecting* a 'fortunate few,' if you will. I have long felt uncomfortable drafting and postings solicitous fliers — Nietzsches do not beg, you see; we bend others to our will. You'll catch on," she assured Bernhard with a pat to his knee. Blood ran red to his face as he flinched beneath her condescension.

"People are more likely to contribute to our cause when they feel it is an honor to even be allowed to participate. We will go forward with a campaign of natural selection. The Haves will write checks simply to keep up with those of their circles. True to their nature, the Have-Nots will part with every last pfennig they have to procure the slightest pretense that they are among the Haves, even more so for the opportunity to actually *be* the Haves. With little to live on here in Germany where the Jews have corrupted the markets, many patrons of meager means seek only an opportunity to prosper in a country that offers affordable land, food aplenty, and, most importantly, a healthy atmosphere, to breathe air that doesn't reek of degenerating morality and soiled currency."

It seemed as if Bernhard might speak, so Elisabeth hurried forward. "And where do we begin, you may ask? A boarding school for boys, I say. There are so many who cannot afford such a luxury here in Germany and would sacrifice life and limb to procure a better future for their children. You, Bernhard, could be its head master. It will be the Pforta of Nueva Germania, where young boys will not only learn to read, write and decipher, but will also procure a true understanding of history, their place in it, and their role in the revival of Teutonic distinction. At least that's how I would like to see my investment spent. What of you gentlemen?"

The volunteers being tongue-tied, Bernhard drew in a deep breath and then exhaled silently, finding that he was currently at a loss for words upon which to expend his wind. After all that he had achieved, she would have him be nothing more than a schoolmaster who must provide account for his expenditure of *her* funds. Hurt and jealousy boiled in his gullet as he recalled the Baron von Gersdorff's insulting remarks about the handling of funds for the Nietzsche archives.

"I believe, Elisabeth, that these are all fine suggestions, and I appreciate your initiative," he patronized as he patted the hand that had but moments ago chastened his pride. "But I think such matters are quite beyond your experience. I know that you and Friedrich spoke of starting a school in Rome, but it never came to fruition, for reasons I suspect I understand. And while your plans for a new recruitment schema seem sound, you must remember that a great deal of money has been spent on the fliers we already have on hand."

"As you say," she interrupted him, "the pamphlets are *on hand*. No one is interested. Merchants refuse to post them because the money of others would be better spent in their shops. Socialites refuse to distribute them in their circles, because people of means do not panhandle. The landed have no need of a new Germany because they believe, quite rightly, that they are immune to the threat posed by the Jews."

"That cannot be!" Bernhard rose angrily. "Many of them signed my petition to restrict Jewish-held property, much of which they obtained through usury."

"Be that as it may, it pains me to tell you that some among the gentry accuse you of the same practice." Elisabeth averted her face from him, not wanting him to see just how affected she was by the mortification written upon his mien. After a moment's pause, she stood and reached to take his hands in hers. "I believe in you, Bernhard," she said, with a nod in the direction of the heretofore forgotten in the room. "We do," she amended. "Now let's get busy." She clapped her hands cheerily. "We have much ahead of us to accomplish."

As Elisabeth exited the room with the others in tow, Bernhard realized that the accomplishments she spoke of would be her own.

o o o

CHAPTER XL

∞

I was denied illumination, and then it occurred to me that there was nothing one could forbid the Queen of the Quintessential!

∞

February 1883

Dead . . . of a bad heart. Elisabeth could hardly countenance it. And the news had come from Friedrich of all people! *I thought it only right that the Master's mistress should know that the one she loved so — the one she truly believes made her — has reached his zenith.*

Elisabeth crumpled his letter and cast it into the wastebasket as if to forever silence his words. Filled with rage, she marched over to her treasure desk and accosted her keepsakes as if to banish them to the past where memories belong. She stared at her life then, as crumpled in her hands as her heart had been in the hands of the one who created this shrine. Her eyes darted from the desk to the wastebasket, then back again to the desk. Like a tortured soul dangling at the precipice of Hell, she returned Friedrich's letters to her desk, snatched up the one just seconds ago banished to the trash, and frantically smoothed it out as if to resuscitate it back to life, though it would never be as pristine as it had once been in her brother's care.

Tears filled her eyes as she took up a piece of stationery, her pen poised to write her condolences to Cosima. How she wanted to be at Cosima's aid in these darkest of hours, but Richard had passed in Venice. She offered instead to be on hand to take charge of the children if the widow wished it of her.

This was exactly the type of reaction in Elisabeth that Bernhard most feared. He was to set sail for Paraguay again, and would have taken Elisabeth with him, had progress for the colony been further along. He should wed her immediately, he knew, but then she would demand to accompany him on his voyage. He seethed at both the idea of her discovering just how slowly things were moving and her taking flight to her brother's side in this time of grief. But no, surely his fears were unfounded. Her brother was off sulking in Rapallo, his relationship with Elisabeth marred irrevocably over the Russian Jewess, it seemed. There was nothing for it.

He would take his departure alone and trust in his fiancée to stay true to him.

As it turned out, Cosima found Elisabeth's offer to be most gracious, prompting Elisabeth to make her way to Bayreuth posthaste, where she was overjoyed to find Ludwig already in residence. They removed the knocker from the door, covered the windows in black and then mourned in each other's arms.

"He commanded the world around him as if it were one large operetta of his making. It's difficult to believe that one so god-like could depart this earth so suddenly without preamble." Lost in his ruminations, Ludwig laughed with soft remorse.

"There was *Parsifal*." Like her friend, Elisabeth sounded as if she were in a melancholic trance. "He took the conductor's baton at the end and brought the music to an earth-shattering crescendo, as only the maestro could muster. I thought it strange at the time, but perhaps he knew . . ."

Ludwig pressed soft lips to her forehead, a brotherly kiss she had not experienced outside of the monarch's embrace. She closed her eyes and rested quietly against his shoulder, her mind searching the room. The pain of her grieving heart was nothing in comparison to the bereft void that washed through her soul upon the realization that her constant companion was nowhere to be found. Had he skulked away into the twilight with Richard, or had he taken up residence in Friedrich's shadow?

"My uncle and my brother would have me locked away for lunacy," Ludwig said, breaking the silence between them. "If you are to marry a madman, Elisabeth, choose me." He slightly shifted her face toward him, and she read in his eyes the earnestness of his proposal. "A marriage to your Dr. Forster would be beyond perilous. His is not hunger for a just cause. It is, rather, unharnessed hate. Only an unhinged mind would fail to master the passions that would have us all behave like animals."

In response, she ducked her head into the crook of his neck. For a brief second, she believed herself to be back in Friedrich's arms, so profound was Ludwig's protestation and provocation. "You know you only push me closer to him?"

He cast his eyes heavenward as if to give thanks for the reminder. "Ah, yes. How remiss of me. If it is your will to thwart me at every turn, then perhaps it is better that I champion Friedrich. Better in the keeping of the devil you are related to than the devil you may set loose upon us all."

She swatted his chest as she shrugged from his embrace. "Oh, for Heaven's sake, Ludwig! I have no intention of setting Bernhard loose." She held her hands up in observation of their strength. "He requires a firm hand, and I believe I'll let him serve at my right."

Ludwig's bark of laughter bounced from the walls. "Indeed, you are a force to be reckoned with! Just, please, when you become Queen of the Quintessential, do not invade my country. Unless, of course," he carried on *sotto voce*, "I am locked away and you intend to set *me* loose."

With a firm nod to accentuate her amusement, Elisabeth solemnly promised on her brother's life to free her friend at any cost.

° ° °

Had he known that Elisabeth had agreed to marry that harebrained school teacher, he never would have sent her such a prodding letter. A Lizzie provoked was a lethal thing. Friedrich cursed himself aloud. Why had his mother not contacted him sooner? Of course, he was furious over his sister's treatment of Lou, and it was true that he had planned never to speak to her again, but that was with the view that their relationship would somehow be suspended in time until Friedrich willed it otherwise. He had intended to go to her eventually and offer his full forgiveness. She would take it graciously, of course, and then they would be as they always had: two conjoined souls beyond all understanding, their union a conundrum even unto the Cosmos. Chaos and

Fortune. Among them, he and Lizzie represented one state or the other, though he wasn't certain of the exact assignment.

He looked down at his hands, shocked to find them rising up and down in alternation like a scale seeking balance. He thought back to a day when his hands had fallen and risen in just this way before his innocent sister's eyes. Did she know then that, though unseen to her, indeterminate Good and Evil resided upon his palms? She had not chosen that eve because, like a warlock casting a spell, he had denied her free will. *Ah, but did God grant you this will? If so, then it is not free, but instead comes with an arbitrary price . . . what will become of this Maker of Man and his gifted will, when his subjects decree a definition of justice?* Friedrich flinched. He could not have known then that it would be his Lizzie who would ultimately decree the definition of justice. For though he preferred to blame it on the Frenzied One, Friedrich knew his sister was of his own doing.

Assuming the prose of equanimity, intent on mending the breach between himself and Elisabeth, Friedrich produced from his desk a fresh piece of stationary. Pen poised and ready, it hovered just above the margin, as its commander struggled for just the right words for his writing utensil to ink. Of a sudden, Friedrich shoved the stationery back into his desk drawer, taking up instead the unfinished Zarathustra manuscript. Where it had paused before, his pen sang with feverish strokes, covering one page, then another, and another.

When Peter Gast visited nearly a week later, he found an ink-smudged Friedrich in a darkened room, futilely leaning over his work with a magnifying glass. It was doubtful that he had taken food or drink for quite some time, just as it was plain that he neither bathed nor slept for a week or perhaps more, judging by the stench of the room. Without exchanging a proper greeting, Peter made haste to pull back the curtains and open the windows.

"Cease!" Friedrich bellowed as he lurched from his chair and grabbed Peter by his lapels. "Don't you understand?" he shouted as he frantically shook his friend. "You signal my shadow's return. I have bid him to stay in the darkness until Zarathustra brings forth the light!" Friedrich released his hold on Peter and hurried back to his desk chair. "That which we call Free Will ushers in a tarp of darkness on a crashing wave."

For a moment Peter had a disturbing vision of Nietzsche himself hurtling upon the rocks.

"He stands between man and Truth," Friedrich continued in a voice of quiet wonder. His face startled as if he had just seen something unspeakable. And then, "What news have you of Lizzie?" His speech had grown agitated once more.

Peter glanced away from his friend, feeling that he had no right to look upon the philosopher in so profound a state. "I couldn't say, as I have little reason or right to stay in regular contact with her. The baron informs me that she spent some time in Bayreuth in the company of Ludwig. He always lifts her spirits, you know?"

"The forbidden usually does." Friedrich's face tightened as he spoke and then melted into a wince just as he recalled Peter's forbidden love for his sister. His shoulders slumped as he admitted to himself that it was he, wielding the forbidding finger of a god, who had banished all feeling from Lizzie's heart.

∘ ∘ ∘

My Dearest Miss Nietzsche,

I write to you from Genoa where I have spent considerable time in the company of your brother, editing the final manuscript for "Also sprach Zarathustra. Ein Buch für Alle und Keinen." He tells me that you are familiar with the work, though I believe I can state with certainty that you are not aware of the dangerous turn of mind revealed within the depths of the pages. It is impossible to tell: Is he mad or brilliant? Is he mighty or benign? He writes with agitated alacrity, and has fallen to high fever on several occasions, though he refuses to see a physician. The result of his suffering is a book of biblical magnitude. I speak blasphemy, I know, but it is a minor charge compared to that which could be launched against the writer.

Please know that I would not trouble you if it were not absolutely necessary. I must return to my family, but hesitate under my strong concern for Friedrich's safety in solitude. I'm aware that the two of you have not been on the closest of terms as of late, but if there is anything that I can do to bridge the breach, I am . . .

At Your Service,

Peter Gast

The collaborative effort of Gast and Gersdorff saw Friedrich returned to Naumburg not a month after Elisabeth received Peter's letter. Friedrich had resisted, of course, intent on receiving an apology from Elisabeth before a reconciliation could even be entertained. It was only when Gersdorff pointed out that his presence would keep her far too occupied to focus her full attention on Forster's rabble-rousing that Friedrich agreed to return to her care, though he would have her repentance on one scale or another.

"I will not allow you to marry that lunatic!"

Elisabeth looked on, half amused and half amazed, as her brother paced before her like a general in attitude, but certainly not attire. It was hard to take such a one seriously — his hair was furiously mussed, his mustache was shaggy (and perhaps graying?), his trousers were wrinkled, and his shirt was tucked half in and half out. "Friedrich, have you not any idea why Bernhard appeals to me? He reminds me of Richard to some extent. Full of bravado, yes. Yet unafraid to channel his energy into action."

"At what cost?" Friedrich halted sharply and turned on her. She thought he might intend to strike her but he instead gently touched awe-filled fingers to her forehead, tracing a downward trail to her eyebrows, smoothing them out before lightly pressing her lids closed as if he had just discovered her dead. She reveled in the soft feel of those fingers that commanded so effortlessly, as she considered that her soul might, in fact, be dead. "What do you see there, in your darkness?" he whispered in wonder.

Why she answered she could not say. Her tongue spoke without leave, giving sound to a voice she did not recognize as her own. "I see purple and gold, the colors of majesty. Vultures and shadows. A widow crying over the lifeless babe in her arms. You, lifting me toward a once blue sky. And now . . . nothing."

Friedrich lifted his fingers from her eyes, yet she dared not open them. She could feel his breath on her face indicating that he was now at eye level with her. "In time, I shall will a new image for you to carry always."

When she finally opened her eyes, Elisabeth found her brother towering over her, his hand extended in invitation. "Eli, I have lost my closest friend. The hour has come."

"I feared as much," came a voice from the darkness of her soul.

And she had every right to fear, for the evening ahead brought forth the image of innocence lost. In his love-making Friedrich had conjured not only a vision, but an aura of sound. The tinkling notes of *Phantasie* haunted her senses.

She awoke some time later to the feel of Friedrich's fingers carefully tucking her curls behind her ears. He had been watching her sleep. "You and I suffer the same affliction that claimed our father," he susurrated without breaking his gaze from his task. There was no need to ask what he meant. Her heart dropped in mortification. What had happened? What had she done? Elisabeth assumed it was he who had seduced her, but knew all too well that it could have been her actions that brought on this current circumstance. She recalled Richard's declaration that he was *naught but an old whore*, and wondered now if he had meant to put her on her guard.

How lost was she that she had no recollection of her actions? How dark was her soul that her state of unconsciousness inevitably led her here? The more she tried to redeem herself, the greater she despised her beating heart.

In her deepest depths, she scraped and clawed to escape an ever-growing pit. Blood, streaking from beneath her torn fingernails, stained the barricades of her hell. She was reaching for a cruel, mocking glint of light that peeked, as if to wink, through a slight crack in the edifice she clung to.

Elisabeth tore from the bed. She would have that light! And Bernhard Forster was the key to conquering it.

° ° °

CHAPTER XLI

∞

*Why should not God aspire to death? Do we believe
it to be beyond his power?*

∞

Naumburg 1885

With much work still to be accomplished in Paraguay, communications from Bernhard were scant, and Elisabeth thought it rather unfeeling of him that he should stay so long from her. She half wondered if he was having second thoughts about their coming nuptials, half feared that he may be keeping the truth of his colony's progress from her. All the more reason to call to her! She practically fumed with exasperation. If he would but reach out, she would put it all to rights for him, just as she had always done for Friedrich.

Friedrich . . . the standard by which she measured all factors in life. He, too, was now out of reach, having spent the better part of the year in Nice. The manner of his departure was as crisp in her memory, as the moment when she had freed herself from the shrouds of Eros. "He will never have your heart!" he had bellowed at her fleeing form. And, God help her, she knew his words to be damnably true.

Elisabeth's frame shook. Here she had just been lamenting her fiancé's rare correspondence when, in truth, it was word from her brother that she was most eager to receive. Why must she be so bent on stripping herself of any shred of self-respect that she may still lay claim to? Perhaps there was some credence to this idea of a *death drive* postulated by a young neurologist from Austria that Friedrich had met in Nice.

She pulled from her drawer a collection of letters and smoothed them out side by side atop her desk, perusing them for mention of the gentleman and his theory. Ah, yes. There it was. *Freud.* She underscored the name with her finger as if to hold the man down whilst she examined others of Friedrich's letters, finally setting eyes upon a theory — *the death drive* — which expanded on Schopenhauer's *The World as Will and Representation*. Where life offered only pain and suffering, in death lay Truth, the agent that would set every soul at liberty. Therefore, it is as instinctual to die, to annihilate the self, as it is to live and procreate still more souls with the will to die another day. Discontent must reign in order for Truth to enact its *coup d'état*.

Tears made haste to cast a veil over Elisabeth's eyes, but she determinedly dashed away the moisture that threatened to spill down her cheeks. She would have none of that! No, she would far rather have her own Truth, but first she had some living to do.

o o o

May 22, 1885: As she struggled to work a brush through her tangled curls, Elisabeth wondered at the date that was her wedding day and the seventy-second year since Richard Wagner's birth. She took a long, pensive look at herself in the mirror. In a few hours she would be Mrs. Bernhard Forster. In a few weeks she would be the mistress of Forsterhoff, queen of Nueva Germania. It was everything that she had ever aspired for. Why, then, was she not happy?

Blowing out a breath of frustration, she handed her brush off to Alwine. "Can you work a miracle?" On the tail end of her words was an image of Friedrich, haphazardly piling her curls atop her head and then declaring his work a masterpiece. She could not help but laugh aloud at the memory.

"You're a gay one today, miss," Alwine teased, wrapped up in her mistress's rare joy. "But then, why shouldn't you be? He's the handsomest of men, I say."

Elisabeth stiffened and then relaxed with the realization that her companion was speaking of the man who was to be her husband in less than an hour. The girlish smile she turned on Alwine revealed both excitement and trepidation. "He is quite . . . marvelous, don't you think?"

"Oh, indeed, I do! And just think of it. Your own colony!"

Elisabeth basked in the girl's enthusiasm, not quite ready to break the spell of enchantment by admitting to herself what she already knew to be true; hers would be a difficult journey to a desolate destination. A desolate destiny? Her thoughts turned then to Friedrich, sulking in Venice, refusing to attend her wedding ceremony. Her heart sank and she knew a brief sensation of terror. In her desperation, she had not realized her sudden grip on Alwine's wrist. "Alwine, what of Friedrich? Who will care for him as I have done?"

The sudden return of allegiance for he who had always been Elisabeth's top priority took Alwine quite by surprise, evidenced by her struggle to find words. "I just assumed, miss, that you had every confidence in your brother's health and well-being in your absence. If it will ease your troubles, I promise I will care for him."

Elisabeth's eyebrows dipped in consternation. She didn't quite care for Alwine's proposed solution. "No, no," she disagreed emphatically, "he shall travel with us to Paraguay. Yes, that's it. Bernhard will see him safely removed from Venice, and I shall care for him as I always have. No other will do, for Friedrich is not like any other." She smoothed out the skirts of her off-white gown. Having never been married, and considered a virgin by most (even her bridegroom), she had every right to wear white. But somehow it wasn't quite to her taste. Hers was a clouded heart. A crowded heart. And so, perpetual light was not Bernhard's to be had. She stood tall then, her right eyebrow raising imperiously as she set a new course. "Let's have done with it, then. Shall we?"

The ceremony had been mercifully brief, and the remainder of the day cruelly so. Elisabeth knew that the marriage would have to be consummated and she knew that the ritual would inevitably bring her to this conversation. She did not, however, anticipate having to mollify Bernhard's feelings. Good God! Was there not a man on earth free of jealousy and a false sense of entitlement? Did he really think that at her age she would have no experience? His pouting was beyond trying. "Enough!" she shouted. "I owe you no explanations, for you never asked and you dared to presume."

"You owe me every explanation!" he roared. "I am your husband and I will have it out of you. It was the baron, no doubt, with his swagger and his savvy."

Elisabeth examined her nails, exhibiting no small amount of boredom. *The baron, her brother, the maestro, the Jew . . . That Man.* "Hmm, Gersdorff is savvy, I'll grant. More importantly, he is all honor and fidelity." She circled in on her husband, her voice lethal in its faintness. "But you'll not speak of him again." She looked about the room as if she had just completed a small chore. "Well, I believe we're done here."

How she despised the male form!

Once back in her own chamber Elisabeth contemplated her future. Since a small girl, she had always felt that there was nothing worse than a task unfinished. Her father had often chided her for it. *Why do you hurry so? Why do you seek the journey's end, for what is there to be found there, but life's end?*

She must see Friedrich alone before taking up a new life.

◦ ◦ ◦

"You should have considered it before you married."

Elisabeth rounded on Friedrich as he lay lazily upon his back on a chaise longue. "Contemplated what?" she questioned sharply, almost menacingly.

"He expects you to be a wife, Lizzie. In every way. Though how you can stomach lying with such a vile lunatic, I'll never understand." Friedrich spoke from a distance it seemed, his voice surreal. Not of this earth.

Elisabeth's visage was cast in uncertainty as her gaze darted to the floor, her heart dropping. Did he speak of Bernhard, of himself, or of her? She began looking about for the one who knew her best, but found each corner to be empty. She moved to sit as Friedrich made room for her at his side. "I find that I can stomach a great many things." She punctuated her words with a caress of his cheek.

He gently brought her hand to cover his mouth as he pressed reverent kisses to her palm and then lowered it to rest on his chest, taking notice of her wedding band and gently turning it about her finger as if kaleidoscopic knowledge could be revealed with each rotation. "We are no innocents, you and I, Lizzie." For a brief moment he sounded mortal again. "But if you are content in pretending it, I'll forever protect you from censure."

"Yes." She chuckled sadly. "But you cannot save me from myself."

"Ah, you forget that I can *will* it."

"And do you?"

His chest rose and fell again. "Do or die? I haven't quite decided yet."

o o o

CHAPTER XLII

∞

Der Ring . . . Fidelity's falsehood that inevitably circles back to Eros's loves, lusts, and lunacies.

∞

Elisabeth looked on inattentively as the last of the trunks were loaded onto the *Uruguay*, the Montevideo steamer that would transport twelve families, besides herself and Bernhard, to the Promised Land. She was nervous and fidgety, her right forefinger and thumb encircling her bare ring finger. "Oh, Alwine, do look again," she pleaded as she threw the lid to one of her trunks open. "It has to be here. It just has to be!"

"There, there, Mrs. I have searched every pocket, every purse, and every niche. Your wedding band is not there." Spurred on by the panic on her mistress's face, Alwine assumed a more mollifying tone. "Please don't worry yourself so. You'll make yourself sick before you even pull anchor." She patted Elisabeth's still fidgeting hand. "I'll find the ring and parcel it to you posthaste."

"Yes, that will have to do," Elisabeth concurred hesitantly. "Bernhard believes I have packed the ring away for safe keeping during our journey. I'll put off telling him the truth for as long as I can. Find — that — ring!"

"Shall I pay a visit to Mr. Friedrich myself?"

Elisabeth bit her lip as she thought on this for a minute. "No, no. Send the baron. He will be discreet."

Hearing Bernhard's voice call to her for a third time, Elisabeth threw her arms around her dear companion, holding Alwine to her like a life preserver. "This is it! I will send for you as soon as we are settled. You should hear the description Bernhard paints of our mansion! I can't wait for you all to see it." After one last hug, Elisabeth jaunted up the gangplank and onto the vessel that would test the fortitude of all aboard.

Their month at sea was most assuredly a testament to Hell's condemnation. The aged and hulking *Uruguay* swayed and creaked its way to South America, sickening gents, rats and roaches in equal measure. Everywhere Elisabeth turned, pests lay dead amidst rancid food and pools of vomit. She shook her head disgustedly. Bernhard had made no mention of the possibility of such travel conditions. He had given them all, including her, to believe that the trip entailed only minor travails. "Well I suppose we should be grateful that no human lay dead on this wreck of a vessel," she muttered to herself as she looked upon the pestilent carnage.

Any shred of gratitude soon lay cold next to the body of young Sophie Fischer. Dead at the tender age of twelve, she had been her parents' only child and would be the first to be buried in Nueva Germania. Except her body never made it to the colony. The stench of death's decay was so untenable, she was buried in an unmarked grave immediately upon their landing. *A true pioneer*, Bernhard had called her. *She and her parents would be forever remembered among those who made the greatest of sacrifices for Christ and his people.*

Where the heated stench of Sophie's body had failed to nauseate Elisabeth, she thought she would now vomit, completely and utterly owing to the way in which Bernhard's smarmy manner grated on her nerves.

She looked about the immediate area, absorbing some of the shock that they all felt. Because they still had a trying journey to Asunción ahead of them, they would have to rest until the morrow, if rest were to be had in mosquito-ridden shacks settled on scorched earth of the variety that only war can leave in its wake. "Don't worry, my love," her husband's voice carried quietly to her ear. "There is still one hotel standing. I booked ahead for our stay."

Elisabeth breathed a sigh of relief. "I'll gather the others." As she started to walk on ahead, Bernhard pulled her back by the elbow.

"I'm afraid there is not room for the others, my dear girl. They will have to camp down in these outer lodgings."

She should protest. She should prove herself to be the kind of ruler that her people would willingly put their faith in. She should stand in solidarity with them and sleep among them this night. She should, but she would not. Besides, it was a distinction in circumstance that they would have to grow used to, wasn't it? As tenant farmers they could not expect to live as lavishly as the colony's founder. It wasn't until later that she would learn that the ones she had left out in the elements were not tenants; they had purchased their land and would surely wield significantly more influence than she had calculated.

∘ ∘ ∘

When they finally arrived at Nueva Germania, Elisabeth was stunned by the reception they received. Natives formed cheering lines along the main street, bowing and applauding as her wagon passed. She waved regally, accepting their homage as her due. No, the colonists could not expect to live as she and Bernhard would. All regality forgotten, she squirmed about with anticipation when Bernhard told her they were nearing their home. *Their mansion.*

Dazzled by the gated entrance, the display of German flags, and the Spanish moss–laden trees lining the drive, Elisabeth was unprepared for the shock she received when she laid eyes on the home that all of this grandeur preceded. *Her* home, though it was certainly no mansion. It was a ranch house at most; granted, it appeared stately enough, with its stucco façade and brown shingles of the Spanish style descending from a somewhat laudable height.

"Of course, it's not finished," Bernhard rushed to appease her before she could upbraid him. "The colony will take no time in turning a profit, and then I will be able to turn my attentions back to your dream home," he finished with a tweak to her nose. Elisabeth repelled at his touch.

"You are angry," he whispered to the ground like a downcast child.

Elisabeth peeled her gloves from her sweating palms and vowed never to wear them again. "I have no time to be angry, Friedrich! I will simply have to take charge and put things to rights."

It was Bernhard's turn to flinch. "What did you just say?"

She waved her hand about in annoyance. "I said I'll have to . . ."

"That's not what I mean. You just called me Friedrich." His eyes pierced through her and she felt afraid . . . briefly.

"Well, it's no wonder!" she sputtered. "Since we set sail, you have reduced me to a child with your 'dear girl' and nose-tweaking. It's no wonder I am confused, given that you bring my condescending brother to mind at every turn."

Bernhard relaxed his pose a bit. "I did not mean to condescend. And the last thing I want to do is make an ass of myself." A twinkle replaced the anger in his eyes as he lifted his wife's fingers for a conciliatory kiss. His lips halted, hovering over the place where her wedding band should be. "Now that we are arrived, you can take up wearing your ring again. There's no reason to fear losing it now." He spread his arms wide, offering her this world he had created. "There are no Jewish capitalists to be found here."

She smiled at that and all was well again.

∘ ∘ ∘

As days turned into weeks, weeks into months, and months into years, Elisabeth had given up any hope of recovering her ring. Bernhard had incessantly questioned her as to its whereabouts, nearly causing her nerves to snap. If only he knew that Fidelity was infinite—encircled by none—her husband would realize the impotence of the symbolic piece of jewelry.

She corresponded regularly with Alwine, learning that little had changed at home. Friedrich still roamed Europe in a state of frenzy, while her mother fretted over the toll his behavior had taken on the family's good reputation. Friedrich was writing a book he entitled *The Antichrist*, the title of which Alwine always wrote in tiny hand, as if to whisper it rather than to speak it aloud. The news of this sacrilege had come from Gersdorff, Alwine wrote. No sign of the ring, but every sign of irrationality.

In return, Elisabeth wrote of her reigning role in a "flourishing" colony, the daily council meetings that she presided over, the "substantial" number of requests she and

298

Bernhard had been receiving from German citizens in want of purchasing land so that they may join the colony. What she did not divulge was that the Paraguayan government was keeping the colony afloat with a loan of 80,000 marks, lent on the condition that the Forsters would recruit 140 families to the colony within a year; nor did she reveal that for every family they recruited there was another abdicating. She said not a word about the desolate state of her husband's coffers, bled dry by his promise to refund the price of land to any purchaser who should choose to leave. Such misguided confidence he had in the colony's success!

Elisabeth threw her pen across her writing desk. She had married a fool, but she would never let on to a single soul. She turned her attention to a stack of recent letters from Friedrich, worn nearly to pieces from frequent readings. Of course, Alwine's news of Friedrich's mental state had come as no surprise to her, for she had deciphered it all in his letters. He wrote of their mutual Moorish friend, whom he insisted hovered behind his desk as he wrote, intent on holding hostage the Truth that Friedrich's hand threatened to reveal. He spoke of awaking each morning to his "Lizzie's apparition" in his bed, carrying with her the sweet scent of lilacs.

The image and illusory scent threatened Elisabeth's consciousness. She should stop reading this passage, but her perverse eyes would not obey her will. She sprang from her seat in a sudden sweat, chased by the fear of remaining in place — a place where she would surely wake up in the pools of vomit that made regular appearances in her nightmares. Of its own volition, her hand cupped over her mouth, desperate to hold back the years. *Oh dear God*, she had done this to herself — to her brother.

Elisabeth took slow, deep breaths and conjured Friedrich's comforting voice and words of yore: *Lizzie, we do nothing wrong. What transpires between us is my fault and my sin to repent. You are all innocence. I'll not let you be judged a siren.*

Coming back to herself, Elisabeth returned to her desk in hurried concentration. Scrambling for the rest of Friedrich's letters, she bound them back together and hid them deep within her trunk. These letters of love, lust, and lunacy must never be allowed to fall into another's hands.

o o o

CHAPTER XLIII

∞

Cronus castrated Uranus, and from that bleeding wound,
lunacy was born.

∞

Nueva Germania 1888

Elisabeth's writing desk, along with her stature, had grown in splendor over the years that passed at an excruciating snail's pace. She leaned on this desk now as if it were the only thing sturdy enough to endure the weight of her cares and her colony. Thoroughly exhausted and completely spent—how easy it would be to allow herself to fall into depression . . . to cut line and seek refuge and solace in the posh *Hotel del Lago* in San Bernadino, as her husband had done for the last year. But, of course, someone had to be strong, and that *someone* would have to be her. She had always tried to keep her daily missives to Bernhard as upbeat as possible, assuring him that the railway project was well in hand, making light of yet another band of Paraguayan revolutionaries taking up arms in nearby San Pedro. It was just another futile uprising that the government would soon suppress, she had assured him.

Try as she may, Elisabeth found that on this day she simply could not summon that temperance of tone that usually came so easily to her when there was an advantage to be gained. Quite frankly, Bernhard no longer had anything to offer and there was nothing that she wished from him. She could picture him now, wallowing in a self-pity antagonized by drink, while she bore the burden of his deception. She dropped her head in her hands and squeezed her eyes tight, wondering at the flashes of light she had summoned behind her lids. And then he was there in her mind's eye. *Friedrich! How did you find me?*

Truth. She must have an audience with Truth.

o o o

Having little patience for social niceties, Elisabeth barged into Bernhard's hotel room uninvited. Just as she expected, she found him draped across the edge of his bed in a drunken stupor, surrounded by all manner of trash. He made no response to her attempts to wake him, so she instead began tidying up the chaos around him. One bottle after another clinked and crashed into the waste bin with nary a stir from the ingrate. She sighed her frustration and bent down to collect the crumpled papers strewn about the room, and then froze when she recognized Gersdorff's penmanship. Her eyes scanned the letters furiously, all letters addressed to her, the majority of them quite dated. The one she concentrated her attention on now was from June of 1886:

Forgive me, Madam, the impropriety of my writing to you, but I knew that you would want to know that which was lost has been found. It being so small, he wears it on his pinky, and insists that you gave it to him as a reminder of the anguish of your love for him. He wears it as a punishment, comparing it to the discomfort of a hair shirt. His "just desserts," he claims.

You know that I am fully aware of all that has passed between you. I do not judge you for it. It would have been impossible for one so young, so innocent, with so much love to give to reject he who believes himself to be beyond good and evil . . .

Elisabeth's heart nearly leapt from her chest when Bernhard's hand shot out of nowhere, snatching the letter from her grasp and waving it before her eyes, as if it should be pinned to her frock.

"Where is the ring?" The question fell from the distorted tongue that lolled from his scarlet face. She suspected he thought he was yelling at her, but the drink had rendered his pitch no higher than a hiss.

"Where, indeed," she repeated while deftly changing the subject. "We had such hopes coming out of Bayreuth." She ambled about the room, taking in the ceiling as if she may finally have had word with Truth. "Nueva Germania was to be the realization of all that *Der Ring* had to offer." She went still for a moment, filling the air with a deafening silence before completing her thought. "And yet, here I am. The tragic ass." She rounded on him then. "Tell me, is this still German?" She neither expected nor received a reply. "But of course it is." She chuckled darkly. "For we will never admit otherwise." Just as it seemed that Bernhard would back away from her,

Elisabeth grabbed his sleeve, yanking him back to attention. "Do you understand me? Now stand straight, soldier!"

This parting order was all that Bernhard could recall of her visit.

Elisabeth breathed a sigh of relief when she reached home. She had forgotten just how much she despised her husband, and how little she could tolerate of his company. She lifted on her toes, placing her bonnet back on its hanger, her attention immediately diverting to a missive on the corner stand marked by Ludwig's seal. She dropped her bonnet to the floor and seized it, wondering just how many letters he had sent that she never received. *Choose me.* God, how she wished she had! But there was no time for such regrets now, she determined, as she tore the letter from its envelope.

My Queen of the Quintessential,

It seems that I am the only one brave enough to approach you with news of your brother. I'm sorry to say that mine is not news of the standard "Friedrich fare," and do implore you to sit down before reading further.

Elisabeth gasped on a sob as she rushed for a seat. He must be dead!

Your brother has been tucked away in Turin for some time now working on what is widely rumored to be a book filled with sin, wickedness and all manner of heresy. Reports from his colleagues provide, what I am sorry to say, is measured proof of your brother's declining mental state. He writes to them of assassinating Bismarck and all anti-Semites, decreeing that all Germans are to be lined up and executed. Unfortunately these reports did not reach those closest to Friedrich in time enough to prevent the public spectacle that soon followed.

From what the baron can make of it, your brother came upon a merchant whipping his horse on a public street. When the merchant refused to heed his command to cease harming the beast, Friedrich threw his arms about the animal's neck, apologizing to it in hushed tones for the bleeding heart that prevented him from taking mount.

Witnesses say he grew frantic and began to speak inarticulately just before he collapsed to the ground.

The doctors that examined him believe he has suffered a stroke, though they are unable to concur as to his prognosis. One believes Friedrich may yet recover while another has declared him to be insane beyond recovery. He has been removed to an institution in Jena and will remain under constant care and observation for as long as it takes for him to regain his strength.

The letter continued on with an expression of Ludwig's hope that she would find a way to return to her brother's side. *He is never as strong as he is in your presence.*

Of course, she wanted to be by Friedrich's side, but she knew the futility in exchanging one madman's cares for those of another. No, she had married Bernhard and with Bernhard she must remain. God would have to pick up his own laundry for once.

∘ ∘ ∘

CHAPTER XLIV

∞

*Then God looked over all that he had made and
saw that it was good!*

∞

Paraguay 1889

Dead by his own hand. Elisabeth had long known that she had married the most pathetic excuse for a man, but she had not thought him to be stupid enough to destroy his own legacy. If word of Bernhard's suicide were to get out, his would not be the only name mucked in infamy. Her place in history would be equally mocked. Enraged by the doctor's determination of death (a mixture of cyanide and laudanum), Elisabeth ripped the death certificate from the medic's clipboard and crumpled it in her hands.

"It cannot have been suicide," she insisted. "He had a weak heart, you know. Did you take that into consideration?"

"I have considered every possibility, Mrs. Forster, and I'm very sorry. But your husband committed suicide. I understand that you fear ridicule for your husband's sin, but I am a doctor and cannot bury the details of a man's death."

Elisabeth took a long probing look at the physician, carefully taking his measure. He knew he was damned the moment her eyes snapped and his clipboard was seized from his grip. She scribbled across the certificate frantically, and then returned it to his keeping with the cause of death officially listed as a heart attack.

"I'll expect this to be notarized and filed immediately," she warned, in a tone that defied objection.

○ ○ ○

Jena Institute for the Care and Cure of the Insane. Elisabeth read the sign in disbelief as she stood just outside, trying to work up the nerve to go on. Did she want to see her brother? Yes, of course she did. She might even admit to herself that Bernhard's passing had been somewhat of a blessing, freeing her to make this journey to the bedside of the only one who had truly ever infiltrated her heart. She could imagine Friedrich now as he was when a young boy: vivacious and filled with vital brilliance. He had welcomed every one of life's challenges, and had miraculously turned all that makes one tremble into trembling masses of insignificant matter.

Beautiful. He had been beautiful beyond words, his essence filling her every vein, every fiber of her being. He had been her breath, her beating heart.

Elisabeth startled and looked about her, wondering if she herself were mad. Her eyes darted about in communication with her thoughts. *What is wrong with me? I'm talking as if he were dead.* She blew out a breath of relief on a smile that spelled overwhelming joy. Friedrich was alive and waiting for her inside. She would breathe him back to full life. With no time to waste, little Lizzie scampered off to ferret out where her soul did truly lay.

In all his years of sickness, she had never seen him so weak. He had aged, of course. They both had. There was nothing left of the boy and girl who had shared the very essence of their beings in the shadowy hollows of Grandma Oehler's Garden of Eden. As Elisabeth reached to smooth his tangled hair from his forehead, Friedrich's right hand took control of her wrist and brought it to his heart.

"My old wound bleeds, Lizzie. Can you believe I was rash enough to attempt another smart jump?"

Elisabeth laughed falteringly even as her soothing palm caressed his wound with confident care. "Nothing so unusual about that," she teased. "You've never shied away from any opportunity to make a rather large ass of yourself." Friedrich's answering smile was weak, but she could still see the feeling it held for her even as she turned her attention to the finger beckoning her to his lips. She thought he meant to kiss her, but he was, instead, intent on sharing a secret of particular import.

"Ah, Eli. How I have loved you. I have spent my life railing against the Universe for denying me the full privilege of your love. *I would have her be mine entirely*, I demanded of Fortune. So fearful was that elusive trickster, he sent Truth to fight his battle for him. But Truth, you see, turned out to be a rather disappointing fencing partner. He calls himself 'Enlightenment' even as he secrets Knowledge in shadow. I jabbed him with Will, even as he feinted with Reality. He advanced on me, even as he cowered in the corner."

His breathing grew labored, his voice raspy. "I held him there, Lizzie. I vowed not to let him have you, for he has nowhere to take you. God is dead, Hell is empty, and Heaven is a hoax. And alas! Here lay the Antichrist, impotent in your arms, yet still strong enough to foil Truth's mystery and force its hand in revelation."

His eyes closed to the gentle sound of Elisabeth's shushing tones and the sway of her life-giving breath. She gently touched two fingers to his lips, and then raised them still higher to caress his closed lids. He knew she thought him asleep, just as he knew her hand would find its way beneath his mattress . . . *Truth*.

Elisabeth reached for the manuscript she had no doubt of finding. Expecting to see *The Antichrist* scribbled across the cover page, she was shocked and intrigued to find it entitled *My Sister and I*. With all of the love her heart had to give, she glanced upon the resting visage that would always be dearest to her.

She had never expected to be so honored! With a broad grin, she settled into the chair next to his bed and read aloud, her voice trailing off as the words of the diary in hand hit home:

Elisabeth draws me irresistibly toward her incestuous womb.

The impotence of Christian love led my sister into a desperate effort to fulfill herself in a dark and forbidden area of erotic expression. Trained by my mother to repress her natural sex-emotions, she discovered too late that her effort to dam up her erotic desires merely unleashed a torrent of dark, abnormal passions that rushed through her being in full flood till she became a destructive force of nature that broke through all barriers of morals and civilization. She began to love what she desired least, and I was flung into the treacherous undertow of her outlawed passions which sucked us into their tidal will.

Choking on her sobs, Elisabeth forced herself to continue. Truth. She had wanted Truth. And now she must face it.

I both loved and resented that wealth of warmth which Elisabeth brought to me in those unexpected hours of the night.

And what of the many, many times that he had come to her? What of the nights when, enraptured in cruel jealousy, he had used her body to banish Peter and Gersdorff from her heart and mind?

We dared to go to violent extremities because we did not dare to hope for a normal sexual relationship.

Why had he not noticed the disappearance of her favorite gown? Why had he never mentioned her dead offspring?

I used to combat Elisabeth's emotional assaults on me by trying to interest her in literature, music, philosophy, conversation in general.

Have you ever seen a girl half as pretty as an abandoned little alley-cat?

Elisabeth's tears flowed freely now. Lost and abandoned. Yes, that had been she from the day of her father's demise.

So I shrink inwardly into my despair, remembering nothing but the guilty kisses of her who blocked every exit to the life of love, dooming me to an all consummating hatred for God, for Man and for myself which gathered round me like a formless dread, trapping me in self-terror, the fear of a man who has been unshadowed by the love that he has killed . . .

Her night terrors, he had kissed them away. And yet her guilty hands were covered in his blood.

It was Lizzie who aroused the demon in me . . . spurred on by the black hooded figure on the throne.

Had not the demon been cast upon her? She had sought him. *Truth.* But she had never summoned him! It was in Friedrich's wake that it had eventually chosen to cast its shadow. A gurgle of revolting laughter emerged from her throat. Even the Antichrist's shadow had raped and abandoned her.

Yes, my sister, in the fumes of your fat piety, of greasy incest and larded lust, my holiest love was choked to death.

310

Lou. He dared to write of Lou, even as he tore his true love's soul to shreds. Were she to give in to her rebelling stomach now, the masked madman before her would be covered in scarlet. Perversely, she read on.

She will survive the mud of these notes which I splatter through a need to bathe myself clean. Truth is the decisive victory over Death.

Yes, but whose Truth? Elisabeth wondered. Was it not the deranged writer of these psalms who had declared Truth and Justice, Right and Wrong, to be indefinable? Beyond good and evil? What right had he who had put his passions first, who had promised to forever protect her, to forever shroud the siren's sin—to cast her into the fiery pits of Hell?

I am a man of genius. Therefore I can afford to smile or spit at you.

Elisabeth sucked in a breath of pure anguish, expelling it along with her own forceful spat unto his face. Her body convulsed as she turned desperate, beseeching eyes toward Heaven. Was God on his throne or did he lay before her gasping for his last breath? She could not say, but she could hazard a guess. Never the coward, she took the hand of the one who had delivered Fortune's fatal blow, watching the rise and fall of his chest.

"God is not dead," she enlightened her betrayer. "He breathes still. And if you are He, then He is naught but a bedlamite."

Elisabeth flung the hateful manuscript across the room, watching the pages randomly drift to the floor, her attention immediately grabbed by a photograph half hidden beneath the chaos of it all. She stooped to pick it up, recognizing it as the one the photographer Frith had taken of the star-crossed lovers in Lugano. There was something written on the back in Friedrich's hand:

Siamo contenti? Son dio ho fatto questa caricatura.

(Are we content? I am the god who has made this caricature.)

She turned determined eyes to the self-proclaimed deity who believed himself victorious over history. Her spine straightened with purpose; for she was the goddess who would see to it that his victory would be short lived. Steeling her spine, she marched forth, intent on unleashing bedlam upon a people guilty of nothing more than having obtained her brother's loyalty.

° ° °

God is a Bedlamite:
Channeling Elisabeth Nietzsche
Bibliography

Diethe, Carol. *Nietzsche's Sister and the Will to Power: A Biography of Elisabeth Förster-Nietzsche*. Chicago: University of Illinois Press, 2003. Print.

Kaufmann, Walter, ed. *The Portable Nietzsche*. Trans. Walter Kaufmann. New York: Penguin Books. 1954. Print.

Macintyre, Ben. *Forgotten Fatherland: The Search For Elisabeth Nietzsche*. New York: Harper Collins, 1992. Print.

Nietzsche, Friedrich. *MY SISTER AND I*. Trans. Oscar Levy. New York: Bridgehead Books, 1954. Print.

Peters, H. F., *Zarathustra's Sister: The Case of Elisabeth Nietzsche. How the High Priestess of the Nietzsche Cult Changed History Through Her Propagation of Her Brother's Message*. New York: Crown Publishers, Inc., 1977. Print.

o o o

About the Author

As an antidote to empty nest syndrome, Katie Salvo is putting her degree in political science to good use through writing. An existentialist at heart, her favorite philosophers are Friedrich Nietzsche, Georg Hegel, and Baruch Spinoza. She lives in Orangeburg, South Carolina, with her incredibly supportive husband, Jorge.

○ ○ ○

GOD IS A BEDLAMITE
is also available as an e-book
for Kindle, Amazon Fire, iPad, Nook and
Android e-readers. Visit
creatorspublishing.com to learn more.

○ ○ ○

CREATORS PUBLISHING

We publish books.
We find compelling storytellers and
help them craft their narrative,
distributing their novels and collections
worldwide.

○ ○ ○

www.ingramcontent.com/pod-product-compliance
Lightning Source LLC
Chambersburg PA
CBHW070307280626
47159CB00017B/560